To Love a Baron

COURTING *the* UNCONVENTIONAL

LAURA BEERS

1

England, 1814

Dominic Stevens, Baron Warwicke, was no hero—no matter what the newssheets printed or the whispers claimed. He had survived not through valor, but because braver men had fallen in his place. The world called it luck. He called it a curse.

The jagged scar slashing down his right cheek was a testament of what he had endured. Beneath his clothing lay other wounds, healed poorly and aching still, but even they were shallow compared to what war had carved into him on the inside. If the damage to his soul bore visible marks, no one would have been able to recognize him at all.

Even now, he could feel the weight of their stares—the curious, judgmental gazes of passersby as he walked the cobblestoned pavement of Town. He was dressed as a gentleman, but people didn't look away. They never did. Some halted mid-step, others diverted their paths entirely, crossing the street as though his very presence might soil their day. It didn't matter to him. Their discomfort couldn't reach the part of him that had died overseas.

He had returned from war with his life, modest fortune, and a title granted by the king in recognition of valor and loyalty. A grand honor, they had said. Yet to Dominic, the title felt like a cruel reminder that he had survived when so many others hadn't. That he had failed in the one thing he had been ready to do—die beside his comrades.

From the shadows of a nearby alleyway, movement caught his attention: a boy, rail-thin and unkempt, his clothes threadbare, watched him with sharp, calculating eyes. Dominic recognized the look instantly. It was desperation disguised as confidence. The boy had pegged him for an easy mark.

Dominic almost smiled. The child was in for a disappointment.

Out of the corner of his eye, he watched the dark-haired, freckle-faced boy slip from the alley, feigning nonchalance as he moved closer. The crowd didn't notice. Most wouldn't. Dominic kept walking, making no move to discourage him. He felt it then—the faintest tug at his jacket pocket. Try as he might, the boy wasn't very good at picking someone's pockets.

He stopped mid-stride and turned swiftly, grasping the small wrist. "And what exactly do you think you're doing?"

The boy's face drained of color. "I... uh..."

"You were... what? Straightening my coat?" Dominic pressed, tightening his grip just enough to remind the boy he had been caught. "No, I believe you were trying to rob me."

The boy jerked his arm back. "What's it to you?" he snapped, voice trembling with defiance. "You're flush with coins."

"That I am," Dominic said. "But I earned every one. What have you earned?"

The boy didn't run. Instead, he stared at his worn shoes, then looked up again, defiant still, but something vulnerable in his voice. "Could you spare some, Mister? Just a few coins?"

Dominic had been ready to walk away, to teach the boy a lesson about consequences. But the request wasn't snarled or slick with manipulation. It was quiet. Honest, perhaps.

"And why would I do that?" he asked.

"My mum's sick," the boy said, eyes flickering with hope. "She needs a doctor, but we've got no money."

Dominic studied him. There were always ruffians spinning lies to tug at a mark's conscience. But this one... this one didn't feel like a lie.

He found himself asking, "What's your name?"

"Tristan, sir."

"Well, Tristan," Dominic said with a flick of his wrist, "take me to your mother."

Tristan's eyes widened. "You mean it?"

Dominic gave a single nod.

The boy turned without another word and threaded his way through the throng of people with a speed and ease born of experience. Dominic followed close behind, noting the way Tristan looked back every few steps to make sure he was still there. They stopped at the edge of the alleyway, the same one where Dominic had first spotted him.

"This way," Tristan said, slipping inside.

The stench hit him immediately—sour rot, filth, and something worse beneath it all. He hesitated. It could be a trap, a lure into some ambush. He'd seen worse ploys during wartime. But something about Tristan had pierced through the armor he wore around his heart. He pressed on.

At the far end of the alley, Tristan stopped beside a worn blanket draped over a broken crate. He pulled it back, revealing a woman slumped against the brick wall, her chest rising with shallow, uneven breaths. Her hair was a dull chestnut, plastered to her forehead, and her face pale as moonlight.

Dominic knelt beside her, ignoring the pungent odor that drifted off her person. "Miss?" he asked in a gentle tone. "Are you all right?"

The woman didn't open her eyes, but her lips moved. "I will be, Tristan," she whispered. "Just need a moment."

Dominic looked up at the boy. "How long has she been like this?"

Tristan's eyes were sad. "A few days. She ain't eaten much neither."

This woman didn't need just a doctor. She needed a hospital, and quickly. Dominic didn't hesitate. He slid one arm beneath her knees and the other behind her back and lifted her with ease. She weighed next to nothing.

"I'm taking her to the hospital," he announced.

"We can't afford the hospital," Tristan said quickly, hurrying after him. "We only have a few pennies."

"You need not worry about that," Dominic replied without looking back.

"What do you want, then?"

"Nothing."

The woman mumbled a weak protest but made no real effort to stop him. In moments, they were back on the main street, weaving through pedestrians who now stared not at his scar, but at the woman cradled in his arms.

When they reached the hospital—a stout brick building with tall windows and polished brass lanterns—Tristan rushed ahead to open the door.

Dominic strode in. "This woman needs help!" he barked.

A young man with neatly combed blond hair and a sneer that could curdle cream stepped forward. "I'm afraid this is not a hospital for vagrants."

Dominic's eyes narrowed. "Did I ask for your opinion?" he demanded. "Furthermore, did I say I wouldn't pay?"

The man blanched. "Well, no, but... look at her. She clearly—"

"Prepare a bed," Dominic ordered, stepping forward. "Now."

"Sir, if I may—"

"You may not." He turned his full attention on the man, his voice commanding. "Get a doctor. Or I'll see to it your position is replaced by morning."

Another figure entered—a tall man with white hair and a long face. "Is there a problem here?"

Dominic shifted the woman's weight in his arms. "My name is Lord Warwicke. This woman needs a doctor's care."

The older man nodded his understanding. "I am Doctor Langley. This way, my lord."

Dominic followed, and Tristan remained close. The doctor pushed open a door, revealing a long hall lined on either side with narrow beds. Some were occupied, others empty, but all were curtained off in some fashion, offering only the illusion of privacy. The air was thick with the mingled scents that Dominic instantly recognized from his time on the battlefield—sickness.

Doctor Langley gestured to an unoccupied bed near the far wall. "Lay her there."

Dominic stepped forward and lowered her onto the thin mattress, cradling her fragile form until her head rested against the pillow.

The doctor moved to the bedside, already inspecting her pallid skin, taking her wrist in hand to check her pulse. "How long has she been in this condition?"

Dominic glanced at Tristan, then back to Langley. "The boy said a few days. Perhaps longer. She hasn't eaten much."

As the words left his mouth, a wave of unease surged through him. His mind betrayed him, transporting him back to makeshift field hospitals with blood-slicked floors and the constant scream of the wounded. He could smell the iron tang of blood again, hear the sharp report of distant gunfire and the ragged cries of dying men.

The doctor's voice broke through the fog. "My lord? Are you all right?"

Dominic blinked, shaken from the memory. His hands had unconsciously curled into fists. "Yes," he said stiffly, eyes refocusing on the present. "Quite."

Doctor Langley studied him for a second longer, then returned to his patient. "Does the woman have a name?"

Dominic turned to Tristan, who had quietly taken a seat beside the bed, his small hands clasped in his lap. "What's your mother's name, Lad?"

"Tabitha," Tristan replied, his voice barely above a whisper.

"Thank you," Doctor Langley said. "It's fortunate you brought her when you did. She's dangerously weak, but I believe we can still save her... assuming we bleed her immediately."

"No." The word burst from Dominic. He stepped forward instinctively, placing himself between the doctor and the bed. "There must be another way."

The doctor raised a brow. "My lord, I assure you, bloodletting is a well-established, perfectly safe practice—"

"I've seen what bloodletting does," Dominic snapped. "It leaves the strong weaker and the weak... dead. I won't have it. Not with her."

Doctor Langley exhaled through his nose, visibly restraining his irritation. "Very well. I will pursue alternative treatments, though I must warn you, without knowing exactly what's afflicting her, our options may be limited. But we shall start by giving her some food and hope some of her strength returns."

"Do what you must, but keep her alive," Dominic said firmly. "And I want to be informed of her progress. Send word to my townhouse the moment there's any change."

"As you wish, my lord," Doctor Langley replied. "Though that does leave the matter of the boy. He cannot remain here."

Dominic looked down at Tristan, who was holding his mother's limp hand with such tenderness it nearly broke him. "And where is he meant to go?"

Doctor Langley shrugged. "There's the workhouse. They'll take him in."

Dominic clenched his jaw. Working as a Bow Street Runner, he had seen what happened to children in workhouses—starvation, disease, injury... or worse. It was no place for anyone, let alone a child trying to care for his mother.

"No," Dominic said. "He'll come home with me."

Surprise flashed briefly in the doctor's eyes, but he recovered quickly. "Very good, my lord."

Dominic knelt beside Tristan, placing a hand gently on the boy's bony shoulder. "Come, Lad. Let's get you something warm to eat."

Tristan's wide eyes darted from his mother's pale face to Dominic. "But... what about my mum? I don't want to leave her."

Dominic met the boy's gaze. "The doctor's going to look after her. I promise she'll be in good hands."

Tristan's lower lip trembled. "Can't I stay?"

"I'm afraid not," Dominic said. "But you'll see her again once she's stronger."

The boy gave a small, reluctant nod. Dominic helped him to his feet, and together they walked towards the door.

As they started to walk away, Dominic glanced back one final time at the fragile woman on the bed. *Please hold on,* he thought. *For Tristan's sake.*

The hackney carriage lurched to a halt, its wheels grinding slightly against the cobblestones as it came to an abrupt stop. Dominic reached for the handle and swung open the door, stepping down onto the clean, well-swept pavement just outside his home.

Tristan scrambled after him, landing beside him with a soft thump. He froze as his gaze lifted to the towering red-brick townhouse before them. His mouth parted slightly in awe.

"Is... is this where you live?" the boy asked.

Dominic allowed himself a small smile of pride. "It is," he said. "Come along now. A gentleman does not loiter on the pavement."

Tristan hurried to match his stride. They ascended the wide stone steps and the door swung open. Standing on the threshold was Wright, his white-haired butler, dressed in his immaculate black tailcoat and white gloves, his expression calm and composed as ever.

"Welcome home, my lord," Wright greeted, stepping aside and opening the door wider.

"Thank you, Wright," Dominic replied, entering the grand foyer with measured steps. The hall beyond stretched out in quiet splendor with marble flooring gleaming beneath their feet, soft light filtering in through tall windows framed with heavy curtains, and a grand chandelier hanging overhead like a frozen cascade of crystal.

Tristan stood stiffly just inside the door, his eyes wide as they darted around the hall. He looked impossibly small in such an opulent space.

Dominic gestured towards him. "This is Tristan. He'll be staying with us for the foreseeable future. See to it that he is properly outfitted—new clothes, boots, whatever he needs."

Wright bowed his head slightly. "Of course, my lord. I shall see to the arrangements immediately."

"Good," Dominic said with a nod. "Also, inform Mrs. Dawson we're ready for our midday meal."

Without further prompting, Wright departed, his footsteps silent against the marble. Dominic turned back to Tristan, who remained rooted in place, his mouth slightly agape as he stared up at the chandelier like it might fall on him.

Dominic couldn't help but smile. "You're allowed to look. It's all real, I assure you."

Tristan blinked rapidly, then looked up at him. "You really live here?"

"I do. Though sometimes, I still find it difficult to believe." He rested a hand lightly on the boy's shoulder. "Come, let's adjourn to the dining room. You look like you haven't had a proper meal in days."

Tristan gave a vague nod and followed as Dominic led him through the corridor, past a pair of double doors, and into the dining room. The space was warm with late-day sunlight, the long table gleaming with polish. The scent of roasted meat and freshly baked bread wafted faintly through the air.

Dominic walked to the head of the table and seated himself. Before he could speak, a footman silently approached and pulled out a chair for Tristan. The boy froze, looking up at the man like he had grown a second head.

"Sit," Dominic instructed.

Tristan obeyed, lowering himself into the chair as though afraid it might collapse beneath him. "I've never sat at a table like this before," he admitted.

"It's just a table," Dominic replied with a shrug.

"But what if I dirty it?"

Dominic smirked. "Then I shall have it cleaned."

Tristan gave a nervous laugh, but his expression softened. After a pause, he glanced towards the footmen by the door and murmured, "My mum used to work in a house like this."

"Was she a maid?"

"A lady's maid," Tristan said proudly, straightening his back. "She used to help the mistress dress, do her hair... all that. But she was let go."

"Why?"

Tristan frowned. "The mistress said she stole an earring. But my mum's no thief."

Dominic raised a brow, keeping his voice even. "But you are?"

Tristan didn't flinch. He just shrugged. "Someone has to make sure there's food on the table. I'm the man of the house."

Dominic studied him for a moment. There was no guile in the boy's tone—only a kind of quiet desperation he recognized all too well. "What happened to your father?" he asked gently.

The boy's gaze dropped to the gleaming surface of the table. "He is dead."

"I'm sorry," Dominic said.

Bringing his gaze up, Tristan asked, "Do you think I could work here?"

Dominic pretended to consider it. "I do think we can arrange something, but let's not worry about that until your mother recovers."

Before Tristan could respond, the door opened and two footmen stepped inside, carrying silver trays. The lids were lifted, revealing bread, carved meats, and soft cheeses arranged beside bowls of fruit and preserves.

Tristan's eyes widened again. "Is that all for us?"

Dominic gave him a small nod. "It is. Go ahead, eat."

And for the first time since they'd met, Tristan smiled—small, uncertain, but real. He reached for the bread and took a large bite.

As Dominic reached for a slice of roasted venison, the dining room door opened with a quiet creak. Wright entered with his usual composed demeanor, but there was a slight apologetic tilt to his posture.

"Pardon the interruption, my lord," he said with a slight bow. "Mr. Wells has arrived and is requesting a moment of your time."

Dominic stilled. His solicitor. Of course. He had intended to meet with Mr. Wells that very morning, but his detour to the hospital—and everything that followed—had derailed the day entirely.

He pushed back his chair, rising. "Very well. I shall go speak with him." He turned to Tristan, who looked up with cheeks puffed, stuffed with bread and cheese.

"Chew before you swallow. I'll be back shortly," Dominic said.

Tristan gave an enthusiastic nod, clearly more interested in the feast before him than anything else.

Dominic exited the dining room and made his way down the long corridor to his study. It was a warm, book-lined room tucked into the rear of the townhouse, with long windows overlooking the gardens. The fire had been stoked, casting flickering amber light across the dark mahogany furniture.

Standing near the hearth was Mr. Wells. He was a short, barrel-chested man with thinning gray hair, wire-rimmed spectacles, and a satchel slung over his shoulder.

"Mr. Wells," Dominic greeted him as he entered. "I must apologize for missing our appointment. Something urgent came up this morning."

The solicitor waved a dismissive hand. "No harm done, my lord. I suspected as much. I thought it best to bring the documents here directly."

Dominic circled around to his desk and took his seat, gesturing for Wells to do the same. "That was very considerate of you."

Wells lowered himself into the chair and set his satchel on the floor beside him. "I've brought the documents concerning the Sidmouth estate. Everything is in order. I just need your signature in a few places."

"Very good," Dominic said. "Let's see it."

Wells withdrew a sheaf of crisp, neatly folded documents and placed them on the desk. He opened them one by one, indicating the spots for Dominic to sign with a gloved finger. Dominic took up the quill beside the inkpot and began signing with practiced ease.

When the last page had been signed and the ink allowed to dry, Wells gathered the papers and began slipping them back into his satchel.

"Well done, my lord," Wells praised. "You are now the proud owner of a profitable estate on the coast. Excellent land and healthy tenant yields. You've done quite well for yourself."

"Let's hope the numbers bear that out," Dominic remarked.

Wells hesitated as he clasped the satchel shut. His brows furrowed slightly. "There is another matter, if I may... something of a more delicate nature. It is not my place, but I feel compelled to say something."

Dominic looked up, curiosity piqued. "Go on."

The solicitor resumed his seat slowly, folding his hands atop his knee. "I've been continuing to send a stipend, as per your wartime instructions, but I must inform you that your wife appears unaware that you are still alive."

Dominic stared at him in stunned silence. For a moment, the room seemed to tilt. "*My... what?*" he asked.

"Your wife," Mr. Wells repeated calmly, though his eyes flicked to Dominic's clenched jaw.

Dominic rose from his chair so abruptly it scraped back with a screech against the floorboards. "I do not have a wife," he growled.

Wells remained seated, unflinching. "You do, my lord. The marriage is legal and was witnessed. I even verified the marriage license myself. It took place on the Continent while you were stationed abroad. The bride was a Dorothea Haverleigh."

Dominic's mind was reeling. The name struck a distant chord—*Dorothea Haverleigh*, the dutiful daughter of his commanding officer. He remembered her sitting by his bedside after he was wounded, bringing him broth, reading from her books in a soft voice. But marriage? He had no memory of proposing, of exchanging vows—nothing.

"That cannot be right," he said, his voice hollow with disbelief. "I remember her... but I do not remember marrying her. There must be a mistake."

Wells looked at him with what could only be construed as pity. "I wish it were so, my lord. But the marriage is legally recorded, and there were several credible witnesses. I'm afraid it is not in dispute."

Dominic's thoughts spun in chaotic circles. He had survived war, come home with scars both visible and not. So how could he have forgotten something as monumental as marrying someone? Had the fever clouded his memory? Or was there something more sinister at play?

"And you did not think to inform her that I had returned?" he demanded.

"I did not believe it was my place, nor did I tell her about your elevation in status," Wells replied. "I assumed you would make that decision yourself once you had... settled. Furthermore, her brother is rather protective of her and has refused to allow me to meet with her."

Dominic turned away, pacing towards the fireplace. He ran a hand through his hair, exhaling slowly. "Can the marriage be annulled?"

Wells shook his head. "As you are no doubt aware, annulments require approval from Parliament and are rarely granted, even under compelling circumstances. And if the union was consummated—"

"I wouldn't know," Dominic snapped. "I don't even remember the wedding!"

"Then perhaps it would be prudent to speak to your wife before considering such a step," Wells said carefully, rising to his feet. "She may shed light on what you cannot recall."

Dominic turned to face him, jaw tight. "Where is she?"

Wells reached into his coat and withdrew a folded sheet of paper. "She is currently residing with her brother at a town-house not far from here on a quiet street of Mayfair."

Dominic took the paper and opened it, scanning the address written in Mr. Wells's precise hand. His grip on the page tightened.

"Good day, my lord," the solicitor said with a bow before quietly exiting the study.

Dominic barely acknowledged his departure. He stared down at the address, his heart pounding and mind churning.

No. This couldn't be real.

He had not come back from war to find himself tethered to a past he couldn't even remember. To a woman he hardly knew. He wouldn't accept it. He couldn't.

He let the paper fall onto the desk and turned for the door, his long strides purposeful, his face set with grim resolve.

He needed answers—and he would get them.

Starting with his wife.

M rs. Dorothea Stevens lingered just outside the door to the study, her fingers clutching the folds of her mourning gown as though they might lend her strength. The faint murmur of quill against parchment within told her Matthew was working—likely on household accounts, as he often did at this hour. She drew in a breath, held it, and released it shakily. It had taken her the better part of the morning to gather the nerve to approach him, and still, she hesitated.

She prayed her brother was in a temperate mood. Pleasant, even. But with Matthew, one never knew. His disposition could turn with the wind, and Dorothea had learned long ago how unpredictable—and dangerous—that could be. As children, his outbursts had terrified her. As adults, they left her feeling small and powerless. Yet, despite the fear curling in her belly, she had no choice but to seek his permission today. She needed to speak with Mr. Wells, the solicitor handling her late husband's affairs.

Just as she reached out to knock, a voice sliced through the silence behind her. "Why are you loitering in the corridor like some common vagabond?"

Dorothea flinched and turned to find Arabella—her sister-in-law—standing there, arms crossed over her chest. With her striking blonde curls and perpetually arched brows, Arabella looked the epitome of what the *ton* deemed beautiful.

"I was hoping to speak with Matthew," Dorothea replied, her voice soft.

Arabella lifted her chin, her eyes raking over Dorothea with open disdain. "And you thought skulking about like a servant would accomplish that?"

"No, but—"

Arabella didn't let her finish. She never did. "Oh, do stop dithering. Just follow me. I've no patience for your mewling excuses."

Without waiting for a response, Arabella turned sharply on her heel and swept into the study. Dorothea followed, her pulse quickening with every step.

The room smelled faintly of ink and pipe tobacco. Matthew sat behind a heavy oak desk, his broad shoulders hunched as he scribbled in one of the ledgers. His red hair—so like her own—was neatly combed, but a scowl already pinched the lines of his face before he even looked up.

Arabella's tone softened to a purr. "Dear, might I steal a moment of your time?"

Matthew raised his head, his expression easing slightly. "I suppose I can spare a few minutes... for you."

Arabella waved a dainty hand. "Not for me, my love. For Dorothea."

At the mention of her name, Matthew's eyes flashed with annoyance. "Oh," he said coldly, turning his attention to his sister. "What do you want?"

His voice had lost its warmth entirely, reduced to a gruff bark that made Dorothea's knees threaten to buckle. Still, she squared her shoulders and smoothed her gown with trembling fingers.

"I was hoping," she began carefully, "to speak with Mr. Wells today. Regarding Dominic's estate."

"Why?" Matthew snapped.

Dorothea wrung her hands, feeling the familiar bloom of anxiety rise in her chest. "Dominic earned a considerable sum during the war. I have yet to receive any of it."

Matthew slammed the ledger shut. "And what did you expect?" he growled. "You married a man already at death's door. He duped you. There is no fortune. There never was. And you are owed nothing."

"I cared for him," Dorothea said, her voice barely above a whisper.

Matthew laughed, harsh and bitter. "No, you cared for what you thought he had. It was your grand scheme, wasn't it? Marry a soldier and secure a windfall. But the joke's on you. And now what do you have? Nothing."

"Dominic was entitled to compensation," she pressed, her courage flickering like a candle. "As was Father."

Matthew narrowed his eyes. "And what, pray tell, do you know about Father's earnings?"

"I know he and his men took part in the seizure of land after one of their battles. Officers were allowed to keep a share of the profit," Dorothea said.

"And?"

Dorothea lifted her chin. "Perhaps Dominic was owed something similar. I think it's worth investigating."

Matthew leaned back in his chair, studying her with contempt. "Do you truly believe you're some long-lost heiress and I've somehow missed it?"

"Well, no—"

He cut her off, rising to his feet with sudden violence. "When will you finally understand? Dominic Stevens was a poor soldier. He was a captain, yes—but barely. Father, *our* father, was a lieutenant-colonel. Had he lived, he never would've allowed you to throw yourself away on a man like that."

Dorothea's voice cracked. "He respected Dominic. He told me as much when I lived with him before his death."

"Father indulged you too much," Matthew insisted. "He should never have let you accompany him to the Continent. War is no place for a young woman."

"I wanted to go with him," Dorothea replied.

Matthew turned to Arabella, who had thus far remained silent, a smug smile playing on her lips. "What's your opinion, Wife?"

Arabella's smile widened. "Poor Dorothea is terribly naïve. No respectable woman marries a man on his deathbed. It was a scandal. And now look at you—widowed and penniless."

Dorothea bit her lip as the familiar sense of helplessness swept over her. She couldn't leave without permission—not after what happened last time. The locked bedchamber. The missed meals. The silence.

Matthew crossed the room to stand beside Arabella. "She's right. You've ruined your prospects. No one of consequence will have you now."

"I still have a dowry," Dorothea said.

Matthew sneered. "You do. But word spreads quickly. A desperate girl chasing wealth? Society will cast you out."

Arabella's gaze swept her from head to toe. "And it doesn't help that you're so... plain. That red hair does you no favors."

Dorothea reflexively tucked a loose strand behind her ear. It was the same soft copper shade as their mother's. She had always cherished that connection—until now.

Arabella turned to her husband. "At least red hair is becoming on you, my love. So very dashing on a gentleman."

Before Matthew could reply, a knock came at the door. Their elderly butler, Bennet, entered, bowing slightly.

"Forgive the interruption, sir, but a Lord Warwicke has come to call."

Matthew arched a brow. "Warwicke? I'm not familiar with the man. Show him in, by all means."

Bennet hesitated. "He has specifically requested an audience with Mrs. Stevens."

Silence fell.

Matthew slowly turned to Dorothea, suspicion etching into every line of his face. "Why," he said slowly, "would Lord Warwicke be calling on you?"

Dorothea shook her head, genuinely perplexed. "I don't know."

Stepping forward, Matthew replied, "You must know something."

But she truly didn't know. Or if, in some distant way, she did, the answer eluded her entirely. Her brows drew together, confusion warring with trepidation.

"I assure you," Dorothea said, "I have no idea why Lord Warwicke is here."

Matthew studied her for a long moment, lips pursed. "Then you won't be disappointed when I send him away."

"I... uh..." Her breath caught as she searched for the right words. "That seems unnecessary."

Apparently unmoved by her hesitation, Matthew turned towards the butler without a shred of concern. "Inform Lord Warwicke that Mrs. Stevens is unavailable to receive callers. She is still in mourning, and it would be most improper."

Bennet gave the smallest of bows. "Yes, sir." His voice was dutiful but tinged with a hint of unease as he withdrew.

Dorothea watched him go, her heart sinking with every step he took. A dull ache pulsed in her chest. She had never felt so helpless. Since Father's death, the home that once offered her comfort had become a cage. Matthew's house was no longer hers. She was merely a guest... and one barely tolerated at that.

It had been six months of this cold existence. Six months of being belittled and dismissed. If Lord Warwicke had come on Dominic's behalf, she had just lost the opportunity to learn something—anything—about her late husband's affairs.

What if he had news? What if Dominic's name had not died with him on that battlefield?

Matthew's voice yanked her from her spiraling thoughts. "I have work to attend to. I trust you ladies will find a way to occupy yourselves this afternoon?"

Arabella perked up. "Yes, I intend to call on Madame Lemoine. She's finished the first fitting of my new gowns. I've asked for embroidery in the palest lilac and dove gray. It will look so elegant for spring."

Dorothea glanced down at her own attire—a simple black gown. She had only three gowns in total now, all in mourning black. How she longed for something new, something beautiful. But Matthew would never allow such a frivolous expense. Not for her. Not when he believed she'd already squandered her worth.

Before another thought could pass between them, Bennet re-entered the room. This time, his expression was strained.

"I beg your pardon, sir," he said, directing his words to Matthew. "But Lord Warwicke has insisted he must speak with Mrs. Stevens. He says it is a matter of great urgency."

Matthew's eyes snapped to Dorothea, his gaze narrowing. "Out with it. Important men like Lord Warwicke don't make unexpected house calls without cause. What are you hiding?"

"I'm not hiding anything!" Dorothea's voice trembled with the effort to maintain composure. "I swear to you, I do not know why he's come."

Without warning, Matthew strode forward and struck her,

his hand landing across her cheek. "You dare lie to me in my own house?" he hissed.

Before Dorothea could recover from the sting, a voice thundered from the doorway.

"*How dare you strike my wife!*"

The words hung in the air like cannon fire.

Wife?

Dorothea turned towards the doorway, blinking past the burning in her eyes and throbbing in her cheek. A tall man stood in the threshold, his shoulders broad and his presence commanding. Dark hair framed a chiseled face, and across one cheek ran a jagged scar—a scar she had seen before. One she knew.

Her knees buckled.

That scar... it was the same one Dominic bore after a dagger slashed him on the battlefield. But it was his eyes that confirmed the truth to her. His steely gray eyes—so unusual, so unlike any she had seen before—locked on to hers with unmistakable intensity.

It can't be.

But it was.

"Dominic?" she whispered.

He took a step towards her, and she saw the familiar line of his jaw, the exact tilt of his brow when he was angry—or afraid. There was no mistake.

Her husband—her *dead* husband—was standing in her brother's study.

The room tilted suddenly. A ringing filled her ears. And then, the edges of her world went dark and she felt herself falling.

The instant Dominic saw Dorothea being struck, a fierce surge of protectiveness roared through him. His fists clenched at his sides, and the memory of his mother's tear-streaked face flashed before his eyes. He had been too young then, too powerless to shield her from his father's wrath—but not now. This time, he could do something. *Would* do something. He had sworn long ago that he would never stand idle in the face of cruelty again.

He watched Dorothea sway unsteadily on her feet, the color draining from her face, and he closed the distance between them. He caught her before she fell, cradling her gently in his arms. Her head lolled against his shoulder, and his heart clenched. She was far too pale, far too fragile. Gritting his teeth, he carried her to the nearby settee and eased her down with care, his eyes never leaving her face.

A scornful voice broke the silence behind him.

"And what gives you the right to be so familiar with my sister?"

Dominic didn't bother to turn around. "She is my wife," he growled. "Now send for a doctor. At once."

"You do not get to dictate terms in *my* house," the man snapped, his tone brimming with arrogance.

Dominic's patience snapped like brittle glass. He turned slowly, facing the man squarely. The resemblance between him and Dorothea was unmistakable—the same red hair, the same bone structure—but his eyes were colder, devoid of compassion.

"And you do not get to strike a woman and walk away unchallenged," Dominic shot back. "How dare you lay a hand on your sister! Have you no decency, no shame? I should challenge you to a duel for your ill treatment of my wife."

The man's lip curled. "How I discipline my sister is no concern of yours."

"It is now," Dominic responded. "She is coming with me and away from you. And don't you dare try to stop me."

The man stepped forward, his posture bristling. "And just who do you think you are?"

Dominic arched a brow. "Forgive me, you seem remarkably dim-witted," he said with biting sarcasm. "I am Lord Warwicke. Dorothea's husband."

A gasp came from the corner of the room. A blonde-haired woman, young and striking, who had until now watched the scene unfold in silence, clasped her hands together. "You must be mistaken. Dorothea's husband is dead."

Dominic's expression didn't waver. "Then I must be a ghost," he said dryly. "I am Dominic Stevens, Baron Warwicke."

The woman's mouth fell open. "That's... impossible," she whispered.

Before he could answer, a soft voice called from behind him. "Dominic? Is that really you?"

He turned instantly. Dorothea had opened her eyes. Her gaze locked with his, wide with disbelief.

"It is," he said, stepping closer.

Tears welled in her eyes. "How... how is this possible? They carted you away with the dead. I never even got to say goodbye."

"I was mistaken for dead," Dominic explained. "But I survived, and I'm here now."

Her eyes scanned him, as if trying to confirm the miracle. "You were shot... stabbed... I thought I'd lost you forever."

"I was many things," he said, brushing a lock of hair from her brow, "but not gone. I've come to take you home, Dorothea. Where you'll be safe."

She hesitated, glancing towards her brother. Fear flickered in her eyes, subtle but unmistakable. "I am safe here," she said weakly, the lie heavy in her voice.

Dominic extended his hand. "Come. Let us go."

She didn't move. "But... my things. I should pack a trunk."

"There's no need," he said. "We'll get you all new things. Whatever you are in need of."

"You're not taking her anywhere!" her brother snapped. "You show up out of nowhere, claim to be a lord, and expect us to believe this story?"

Dominic's jaw tightened. "Your sister recognizes me, and that's more than enough. But if you insist on verification"—he turned to Dorothea—"you never knew. The king honored me with a title for my service in the Royal Army. I am known as Baron Warwicke now."

Dorothea's lips parted in astonishment. "You're a lord?"

He nodded. "Which makes you a baroness. You no longer have to live under this roof, or wear mourning gowns for a man who isn't dead."

She took his hand slowly. "This... this is unbelievable."

Her brother scoffed. "And I, for one, do not believe it."

Dominic looked him squarely in the eyes. "Fortunately, I don't require your permission. Dorothea will be leaving with me."

"No!" the blonde woman suddenly burst out. "Dorothea can't leave! She's—she's family!"

Dominic's assessing gaze flicked to her. "I've seen how you treat your family. Heaven help your enemies."

Matthew stepped forward, fists clenched. "Dorothea, you don't want to leave, do you? Tell this man you don't know who he is."

Dorothea faltered, her shoulders drooping slightly under her brother's command. But then, slowly, she raised her chin. "I'm sorry, Matthew. But this is my husband. And I want to go with him."

Matthew's expression darkened. He took another step, but Dominic stepped in front of Dorothea.

"If you ever touch my wife again," he said in a low, warning tone, "it will be the last thing you ever do."

Matthew's face twisted in fury. "Then go. But know this—if you walk out that door, Dorothea, you are no longer welcome here."

A brittle laugh escaped Arabella's lips. "Matthew is being dramatic. You can always come back—"

"Stay out of this, Arabella!" Matthew barked.

Dorothea clutched Dominic's arm and leaned into him. He turned his head, his voice soft for her alone. "Shall we?"

"Yes," she said with relief in her tone.

As Dominic led Dorothea out of the study, his heart pounded with a strange, conflicting rhythm—half-disbelief, half-resolve. He hadn't planned this. He had arrived with a purpose, clear and simple: confront his wife and demand an annulment. It should have been quick, clean. Emotionless.

Instead, he was taking her home.

A thousand questions clamored in his mind, but only one truth rang clear: he couldn't walk away. Not from her. The thought of leaving her in that suffocating house with a brother who wielded cruelty like a badge of honor—it turned his stomach. No, he hated bullies. Always had. His father's voice still echoed in his nightmares and Dorothea's brother was cut from the same cloth.

He glanced down at her as they crossed into the corridor. Her hand rested lightly on his arm, and he gave it a gentle pat. She looked up at him, and what he saw in her eyes stopped him cold.

Trust. Quiet, unwavering trust.

It hit him like a punch to the chest.

Some faces carried the weight of memory so deep, so ingrained, that simply seeing them felt like coming home. That's what Dorothea was to him. *Home.* And in that instant, his mind began to unlock—rusted doors creaked open, long-forgotten moments pouring in like warm light. Hushed conversations by his bedside. Stolen glances. The way her smile had managed to anchor him during the torturous haze of recovery.

His steps faltered as the memories swelled. So much he had buried. So much he thought he'd lost.

Behind them, boots struck the floor with purposeful strides. Matthew's voice rang out across the entry hall. "*Fine!* Go, then! Do as you please. I don't care what you do—*not anymore!*"

Dorothea stopped and turned slowly to face her brother, her chin lifting just slightly. "Goodbye, Matthew," she responded. Her voice was calm, but there was an undeniable tremor in it.

Before she could move again, Arabella stepped forward quickly, her expression conflicted. She threw her arms around Dorothea, the embrace stiff despite the sentiment.

"We shall miss you, dear sister," she said. "I will see to it that your trunks are packed."

Dominic stepped between them the moment Arabella released her. "We'll send a coach to collect her things. She will not be setting foot in this house again."

Arabella nodded her understanding and took a step back. "Yes, my lord."

The butler opened the main door with a quiet creak. Cold air spilled into the marble-floored hall, and Dominic paused, letting Dorothea take her time. She turned slightly, her eyes sweeping across the familiar space. He said nothing, allowing her the moment. Some goodbyes could not be rushed.

Finally, she met his gaze. "I'm ready."

He offered his arm again and guided her down the front steps, helping her into his waiting coach with care. Once she was seated, he climbed in and settled across from her. The interior was quiet, insulated from the world outside. The thrum of tension between them was almost tangible.

Dorothea stared at him for a long moment, as if studying

every line of his face, every subtle shift in his expression. "Is this truly happening?" she whispered.

Dominic leaned back slightly. "It is," he said. "But you should know... the man you once knew... he didn't come back from the war. I did, but I am not the same."

She didn't flinch. "You saved me," she remarked softly. "Just as you promised you would."

A furrow creased Dominic's brow. "I... I don't remember making that promise."

The confession hung between them, heavy and uncomfortable. And yet, it wasn't just the words. It was the way she was looking at him now. Not with fear or hesitation, but with something far more dangerous.

Hope.

Dominic looked away. He wasn't the man she remembered. Not entirely. And he wasn't sure he could become him again. But for now, he was all she had.

3

Dorothea sat quietly in the coach, hardly able to believe that Dominic was here. *With her.* It felt surreal, as though her mind had conjured him from the fog of her longing and grief. Not even in her most desperate dreams had she dared imagine he would come back from the dead. And yet, here he was, very much alive... and pulling her from the shadow of her brother's control.

Her gaze lingered on him as he stared out the window. He looked stronger than she remembered. Healthier. The last time she'd seen him, his face had been drawn and ashen, his lips tinged with blue from blood loss. She'd been convinced he wouldn't last the night. And when word came of his death, she had wept for him.

But none of that mattered now. They were together again. *Married,* even. She didn't know everything about the man across from her, but she knew enough. He had been a respected soldier—brave, disciplined—and through all his agony, he had treated her with a gentleness few men possessed.

Now they had a lifetime to get to know one another truly, and the idea brought an unexpected warmth to her chest.

Dominic turned suddenly, catching her in the act of watching him. His brows knit together. "Stop looking at me like that," he said, his tone gruff.

"Like what?" she asked, startled.

"Like I'm your hero," he muttered, looking away again.

"But you are."

He exhaled through his nose, visibly uncomfortable. "I'm no one's hero. I just... I hate bullies. And your brother is one."

Dorothea tucked a loose strand of red hair back into the chignon she'd hastily tied earlier that morning. "That he is," she murmured. "After our father died, he changed... for the worse."

Dominic's expression sobered. "I'm sorry about your father. He was a good man."

"The best," she said, her smile touched with sorrow. "Not every father would allow their daughter to accompany them to war."

"That was reckless of him," Dominic remarked. "Foolish, even."

"Perhaps," she replied, "but if he hadn't, I never would have met you." Her voice softened as she asked, "Are you truly a baron?"

He nodded. "The title was granted for my service in the Royal Army. I returned from war with more scars than medals, but the Crown still saw fit to give me a title."

Dorothea felt an almost giddy flutter inside. *A baroness.* It sounded too grand to belong to her. "Then I owe you everything," she said, nearly breathless.

"There's no need to thank me," Dominic replied, shifting uncomfortably in his seat. "The truth is... I don't remember much of our time together. Our courtship, if there even was one."

She felt a stab of disappointment, not knowing how much he had remembered. In a steady voice, she shared, "There wasn't much. You were recovering when I met you. I used to sit by your bedside at the hospital, and I'd talk for hours—about anything, really. You seemed calmer when I was there. Less in pain."

"And that led to marriage?" he asked with a note of disbelief.

Dorothea looked down at her hands folded in her lap. "My father had just passed, and I confided in you about my brother. How I was afraid to return to live with him. You were so kind... so understanding. I think the doctors believed you had only days to live. You said you wanted to do something good before the end. That you wanted to help me."

His brow furrowed deeper. "I asked *you* to marry me?"

"You did," she said. "At first, I refused. I didn't want anyone thinking I took advantage of a dying man. But you were insistent. You even said that you hoped it would bring you peace."

Dominic sat back, stunned. "That doesn't sound like me at all."

"I disagree," she said. "You were always so gentle. I found myself looking forward to every moment we spent together."

He rubbed the bridge of his nose. "Then why can't I remember? None of this... it's like someone else lived that life."

"It could have been the fever," she offered. "You were delirious for days at a time. There were moments when you didn't even know where you were."

"Perhaps I proposed in a fever dream," he muttered.

"I assure you that you were more than lucid during our wedding. I wouldn't have married you otherwise." Dorothea tilted her head. "Are you upset... that you married me?"

He looked at her sharply, his jaw tightening. "It was a shock," he said. "To discover I was married to someone I couldn't remember... it's disorienting."

Her chest tightened painfully, and she lowered her gaze to her lap. Of course. He regretted it. All of it. And here she was, foolishly prattling on about how he had saved her—how he had been her hero.

But he had forgotten her.

The silence that followed was heavy. Neither of them spoke again until the coach rolled to a stop in front of a grand red-brick townhouse, its tall windows gleaming beneath the overcast sky.

Dominic stepped out first and turned to assist her. She placed her hand in his, the touch warm and fleeting, and quickly withdrew it the moment her feet touched the ground.

They entered the house, where a white-haired butler stood waiting with quiet dignity. His face bore the calm of a man who had seen much but judged little.

"Wright," Dominic said, gesturing towards her, "this is the mistress of the house. My wife... Lady Warwicke."

There was the briefest pause, as if he had tripped over the word *wife,* but the butler seemed to ignore it.

"My lady," Wright said with a respectful bow.

Dorothea inclined her head in response.

"Please send for the dressmaker," Dominic instructed. "Lady Warwicke will require a whole new wardrobe."

"Yes, my lord." Wright disappeared down the corridor, his footsteps echoing into the distance.

Now alone in the entry hall, Dorothea bit her lower lip to keep from nervously filling the silence. She wanted to make a good impression, to be a proper wife—even if Dominic wasn't sure he wanted her in that role.

Dominic turned to her, his expression solemn. "I have work to attend to. I trust you'll find something to occupy your time."

"Yes, of course. You needn't worry about me."

He gave a short nod. "I'll be in my study."

Before she could respond, he turned and strode away, his boots clicking against the marble floor until they faded into the quiet of the house.

Dorothea stood alone, her eyes drifting up to the grand chandelier suspended above. The house was beautiful. Elegant. But she had never felt more unsure of her place.

Just as she began to wonder what she should do next, a warm voice called out from the corridor. "What a pretty thing you are, my lady."

Dorothea turned to see a plump woman with dark hair and keen, friendly eyes approaching.

The woman offered a pleasant smile. "I'm Mrs. Cameron, the housekeeper. Where are your trunks?"

"I... I have none. At least, not yet," Dorothea said, her cheeks flushing. "This is the only dress I have at the moment."

Mrs. Cameron looked her over thoughtfully. "You're in mourning."

"I was," Dorothea replied. "But not anymore."

Understanding slowly bloomed across Mrs. Cameron's face, her eyes softening with sympathy. "Are you hungry, my lady?"

As if in response, Dorothea's stomach let out an audible growl. She gave a sheepish smile. "I could eat," she admitted.

Mrs. Cameron's lips twitched in amusement, and she gestured towards a nearby corridor with a sweep of her arm. "Then come with me. We'll have you seated in the dining room, and Cook will prepare something hot."

"That's kind of you, but I would prefer the kitchen. It's where I usually take my meals." Dorothea's voice dropped a little at the admission, her gaze flicking downward, half-expecting judgment.

If Mrs. Cameron was surprised by such a confession, she didn't show it. Not even a flicker of condescension passed over her features. "If the kitchen is where you feel most at ease, then who am I to deny such a request?" she asked with a smile. "Come along, then. It's this way."

Dorothea followed her down the narrow servants' staircase,

the scent of baked bread and roasting meat growing stronger with each step. A few passing servants paused to glance curiously at her, but no one said a word. She tried not to fidget beneath their gaze.

"How long have you been the housekeeper?" she asked, hoping to distract herself from the scrutiny.

Mrs. Cameron chuckled, her laugh full-bodied and genuine. "Oh, I suppose you could say I came with the house. When Lord Warwicke purchased the townhouse, he kept on all the staff. A rare kindness, these days. We were all quite prepared to be turned out."

"That was... very generous of him," Dorothea said, genuinely touched.

"It was," the housekeeper agreed with a proud little nod. "He surprised us all."

They stepped into the warmth of the kitchen, a spacious room with gleaming copper pots hanging above the hearth and the comforting scent of herbs wafting through the air. A tall, thin woman stood behind a broad counter, rolling dough with practiced precision. Her apron was dusted with flour, and her dark hair pulled back beneath a white cap.

She looked up and arched a brow. "And who do we have here?"

"This is Lady Warwicke," Mrs. Cameron replied, "and she prefers to take her meal here, in the kitchen."

The cook's face lit up with a smile that reached her eyes. "Well, aren't you a breath of fresh air? You're most welcome here, my lady. My friends call me Mrs. Dawson."

Dorothea offered a tentative smile. "Thank you. I hope that one day I might be honored enough to call you a friend."

"We'll see how you feel after you've tasted my cooking," Mrs. Dawson said with a wink. "Please, sit." She gestured towards a round wooden table tucked into the corner near the hearth. "I'll fix you something hearty."

Dorothea gratefully took a seat, sinking into one of the well-worn chairs.

As Mrs. Dawson began assembling a tray—thick slices of bread, an assortment of meat, and cheese—she called over her shoulder, "Is there anything you're particularly fond of, my lady?"

There was something, but she didn't want to be troublesome. "Not particularly," she said with a polite shake of her head.

"Do you have a sweet tooth? A favorite pudding? Biscuits? Or perhaps," Mrs. Dawson said with a knowing lilt in her voice, "you're fond of a warm cup of chocolate in the morning?"

Dorothea bobbed her head as the tension in her shoulders eased for the first time that day. "I do love chocolate," she admitted. It was an expense that her brother had considered frivolous, and he refused to pay for it.

Mrs. Dawson smiled, the kind of smile that made a person feel seen. "Then I'll see to it that there's always a cup waiting for you in the mornings, my lady."

"Thank you," Dorothea acknowledged.

Mrs. Cameron interjected, "You'll find that here in this house, you only need to speak your mind and it will be done. You are the mistress now."

The words stirred an old ache deep in her chest. *Mistress.* It sounded foreign, like a title meant for someone else—someone more confident, more worthy of the space she occupied.

Mrs. Dawson placed the tray on the table. "I hope this is sufficient, my lady."

"It is," Dorothea replied as she reached for a piece of bread. The familiar texture soothed her fingers, but she didn't take a bite right away. Instead, she stared down at the tray, her thoughts drifting.

To others, perhaps, it was simple to speak up, asking for what one wanted. But she had been taught otherwise. In her brother's house, silence was safer than honesty. Compliance was more valuable than opinion. Keep your head down, keep your voice soft, and no one would raise their voice in return. That had been engraved into her one bitter day at a time.

But now, she was *Lady Warwicke*. She had a place. A household to run. And a husband—however distant he may be. Maybe, just maybe... she could learn how to speak up again.

———————

Dominic stood at the tall, arched window of his study, his gaze fixed on the gardens in front of him. The sunlight filtered through the glass, warming the dark wood paneling behind him as his eyes followed a solitary figure along the winding gravel path below.

Dorothea.

She moved with an effortless grace, her mourning gown brushing the gravel path as she walked. Occasionally, she would pause at one of the rose bushes, bending slightly to inhale the scent of the blooms with a soft smile. She looked entirely too content.

Dominic felt a pang in his chest, not of longing, but of guilt.

He harbored no ill will towards Dorothea. In truth, he admired her gentleness, her resilience. But admiration did not make a marriage, and certainly not one built on foggy memories and circumstances he could barely recall. He couldn't remember proposing, much less saying his vows.

If anything, he pitied her for being tethered to a man so thoroughly changed from the one she had once known. He was no longer that man. Whatever optimism or promise had existed in him before had been stripped away, leaving behind someone bruised, bitter, and half-healed.

Perhaps, if he moved quickly enough—gathered the right

support in Parliament—he could secure an annulment. It was a slim chance, but one he would take. And he would not abandon Dorothea. No, she would be given a comfortable allowance, enough for a modest estate or townhome, somewhere quiet where she could live as she pleased, free from obligation.

In a way, he told himself, it would be a kindness.

As if sensing his gaze, Dorothea looked up. Their eyes met across the distance. She lifted a hand in greeting, a tentative smile blooming on her lips. Dominic felt his stomach twist. He forced himself to look away and crossed the room to his desk, not bothering to return the wave.

Just as he sank into his leather chair, Wright entered the room with a slight bow. "The bedchamber for Lady Warwicke has been prepared, my lord," he announced.

Dominic barely glanced up. "Good," he muttered. Why did it matter where Dorothea slept as long as it wasn't with him?

Wright hesitated. "Lord Westcott and Lord Bedford have arrived and requested an audience. Shall I show them in?"

He nodded with a resigned sigh. "Yes, let's get it over with."

Moments later, Westcott and Bedford strolled in with the smug expressions of men who were entirely too pleased with themselves. Dominic didn't even bother standing.

Westcott was the first to speak, his voice laced with amusement. "So... is it true?"

"Is what true?" Dominic asked, though he already had a sinking suspicion.

"That you're married," Westcott said, grinning broadly. "To Dorothea Haverleigh, of all people."

Dominic groaned. "Is there a blasted smoke signal I'm unaware of? How did you hear about this so quickly?"

"The *ton* wastes no time," Bedford said, taking a seat without invitation. "Is it true, then?"

"It is," Dominic admitted reluctantly. "But hopefully not for long."

Westcott leaned forward, his grin fading slightly. "You're serious?"

"Quite," Dominic said. "I was hoping to enlist your help in petitioning for an annulment."

Bedford raised a brow. "You think that's possible?"

"Do you think it's reasonable to be bound to someone you don't even remember marrying?" Dominic snapped. "I was on my deathbed, delirious. According to her own words, I offered her marriage in some fevered state."

"Were there witnesses?" Bedford asked, folding his arms.

"Apparently," Dominic said with a grimace. "Enough to make it legal."

Bedford glanced at Westcott, then leaned back in his chair. "Do you think she manipulated the situation? Married you to secure her future?"

"I don't know," Dominic said. "But I do know that Dorothea was kind to me. Before everything. That's what I remember."

"That's a foundation better than most marriages have," Westcott remarked with a shrug.

Dominic shot him a sharp look. "I was dying, Westcott. What rational man makes a lifelong commitment while teetering at the edge of the abyss?"

"But you didn't die," Bedford pointed out, lips twitching.

Dominic glared at the ceiling. "Your power of perception astounds me."

Bedford chuckled. "Well, at least I'm not the one who woke up with a wife and no memory of how it happened."

Dominic waved a hand towards the door. "You can both leave now."

Bedford ignored the gesture and settled more comfortably beside Westcott. "And miss the unfolding drama? Absolutely not."

"Why did I save you?" Dominic muttered, pinching the bridge of his nose. "I should have let you get shot."

"But you didn't," Bedford replied. "And I will be eternally grateful, my friend."

Dominic scoffed. "You and I will never be friends."

Bedford only grinned wider, his tone annoyingly smug. "Never say never."

With a roll of his eyes, Dominic turned to Westcott. "Why, exactly, did you bring him here?"

"I didn't. He followed me here," Westcott said dryly. "Now then, I must pose the question—have you consummated the marriage?"

Dominic was caught off guard by the bluntness of the question. "I... don't remember, but I doubt it," he responded honestly.

Westcott stood, the leather creaking beneath him. "Well, you must find out. That detail could prove pivotal when petitioning for annulment. If the marriage was never consummated, your case gains strength."

"I'm aware," Dominic replied with a tired nod. "I plan to broach the subject with her tonight. Over dinner, perhaps."

"Romantic," Bedford teased, rising to his feet.

"Useful," Dominic corrected.

"Well, I wish you luck," Bedford said, sweeping towards the door. "You're going to need it."

After the two men left, Dominic turned back to the desk and opened the ledger resting there. He barely skimmed the first line when a small but familiar presence made itself known.

Tristan strolled into the study with crumbs on his clothes and a sizable biscuit clutched in his hand.

"Is it true?" the boy asked between bites. "Are you really married?"

Dominic exhaled and closed the ledger. So much for getting work done. "I am," he said. "For now."

Tristan chewed thoughtfully, his brow scrunching. "I saw her in the gardens earlier. Your wife. She looked sad."

A quiet guilt stirred in Dominic's chest. He looked away, his jaw tightening. "She's an adult," he stated, as if that explained everything.

"Adults get sad, too," Tristan said matter-of-factly. "My mum cried a lot when we got word about my father. Sometimes, at night, she still cries when she thinks I'm asleep."

Dominic's voice softened. "I'm sorry, Tristan."

The boy moved to the nearest chair and clambered up, legs swinging. "Have you heard anything from the doctor about my mum?"

"Not yet," Dominic said. He glanced towards the doorway. "Wasn't a maid assigned to show you around the townhouse?"

"Yes, but I didn't feel like being followed everywhere. I can look after myself."

"How old are you again?"

"Nine."

"Well, Tristan," Dominic said, leaning forward slightly, "I trust I don't need to explain what would happen if you stole from me while your mother is recovering."

Tristan paused mid-chew. Then, after a moment, he swallowed and said solemnly, "I wouldn't do that. You're taking care of us. It wouldn't be right."

"Good. I'm glad we understand each other."

Just then, a breathless maid appeared in the doorway, her cheeks flushed and dark-haired curls escaping her cap. "My deepest apologies, my lord," she rushed out. "The boy gave me the slip."

Dominic exchanged a glance with Tristan, who gave an exaggerated shrug of innocence.

"No harm done," Dominic said. "Though it might be wise to ensure he's bathed before supper."

The maid curtsied. "At once, my lord."

At this, Tristan groaned audibly. "Do I have to?" he whined. "The water is always cold and dirty by the time it's my turn."

Dominic's lips twitched at the corners. "I think you'll find the bathing arrangements here somewhat more refined."

The maid extended her hand towards the boy. "Come now, Tristan. Let's not trouble Lord Warwicke further."

Tristan slid off the chair with a dramatic sigh. "I am not a child," he muttered, trudging towards her with the defeated air of a boy sentenced to the gallows.

Dominic watched Tristan and the maid disappear through the doorway before slowly rising from his chair. The room felt suddenly too still, the silence pressing in around him. With a low sigh, he crossed to the window once more, drawn by habit or perhaps by something else he didn't care to name.

His eyes swept over the gardens until his eyes landed on Dorothea. She was seated alone on an ornate iron bench near the fountain, and a single rose rested delicately in her hand. Her head was slightly bowed, the curl of her hair falling across her cheek, shielding her expression. But he didn't need to see her face to know the truth.

Dominic muttered a curse under his breath. Blast it all. She was sad, and whether he intended it or not, he was the cause of it.

But what could he do?

4

Dorothea sat alone on the iron bench nestled beneath the arching branches of a flowering dogwood. The air smelled of freshly turned earth and blooming roses, and birds flitted from tree to tree, singing bright, cheerful notes that only made her feel more hollow.

It was beautiful here—peaceful, even—but she felt none of that peace.

Her hands, clasped in her lap, trembled slightly as she held a single rose she'd picked during her walk, its petals soft as velvet against her thumb. She stared down at it. The gardens were everything that had been described to her—lavish, well-kept, idyllic—but they weren't hers. Nothing here felt like it belonged to her.

Least of all her husband.

Dominic was alive. That should have filled her with relief, with joy. And yet, she had never felt further from him. He barely looked at her, barely spoke, as though the affection that once blossomed between them had withered during his recovery. She missed his quick wit, their shared stories and easy silences. When had their friendship turned into this quiet, aching distance?

How did one reclaim something so lost?

Footsteps crunched on the gravel path behind her, and Dorothea glanced up, her heart giving a startled little leap. But it wasn't Dominic.

It was Mrs. Cameron, the housekeeper, her hands folded neatly in front of her, a kind smile on her face. "The dressmaker has arrived, my lady," she informed her.

My lady.

Dorothea still wasn't used to hearing that—wasn't sure she ever would be.

She stood, brushing her skirts with faintly trembling fingers. "That was quicker than I expected."

A glint of amusement danced in Mrs. Cameron's eyes. "Wait until you see the gowns she's brought with her. I daresay you'll be spoiled for choice."

Dorothea raised an eyebrow, curiosity tugging at the corners of her unease. She followed the housekeeper through the back entrance of the townhouse. They passed through a quiet corridor until they reached the parlor.

Dorothea stopped in the doorway, and her breath caught in her throat. Gowns—dozens of them—were draped over the settees and chairs, a sea of muslin and lace in every shade imaginable. Pale rose, rich greens, a daring burgundy, and a soft periwinkle blue that reminded her of twilight skies. They were beautiful. Exquisite. The kind of garments she had only seen on women of far greater means than her own.

"Ah, you must be Lady Warwicke," came a voice laced with a thick French accent.

Dorothea turned, startled, to see a woman of about forty with black hair and intelligent eyes. She wore a simple pink gown, but there was nothing simple about her presence.

"I'm Madame Duchon," she announced, stepping forward

with the air of someone entirely in control. "When I received word that you were in urgent need of a wardrobe, I knew it must be fate. A young lady commissioned these gowns, then promptly eloped to Gretna Green and left me unpaid. Tragic for her, fortunate for you."

Madame Duchon continued. "They'll need a few alterations, of course, but with your figure, I don't imagine that will be difficult."

Drawn to the nearest gown—a dark blue muslin with delicate ivory embroidery—Dorothea reached out and let her fingers glide down the fabric. "They're stunning," she whispered. "I've never worn anything so fine."

Madame Duchon's smile softened. "You will. Though you'll need more than these. A proper wardrobe requires walking dresses, morning gowns, riding habits, and, of course, ballgowns. But my team of seamstresses can handle that." She motioned to a petite girl who stood silently at the edge of the room. "Shall we begin with your measurements?"

Dorothea nodded and stepped forward, lifting her arms. Madame Duchon circled her with a professional eye, measuring tape flicking with practiced precision. Then she paused. "Did you dye this gown black?" she asked, wrinkling her nose as she examined the fabric.

"I did," Dorothea replied, lowering her arms self-consciously. "My brother wouldn't purchase mourning attire for me after my father's passing."

Madame Duchon clicked her tongue. "A lady does not dye her gowns, especially not like this. Black should be reserved for the finest silks, not—whatever this is."

Dorothea flushed slightly. "Most of my clothing was already worn thin. I accompanied my father during his service on the Continent. We moved constantly."

"Your father was a soldier?"

"With honor," Dorothea said with quiet pride. "And yes, so was my husband. They served together."

Madame Duchon gave a thoughtful nod, then returned to her task. After a few more measurements, she stepped back, clearly satisfied. "Yes. These gowns will suit you well—if you agree, of course."

"I do," Dorothea said.

"Excellent." Madame Duchon snapped her fingers. The petite seamstress stepped forward obediently. "Let's get you out of that dreadful thing. The blue gown will be perfect for dinner."

Dorothea glanced down at her dress, suddenly self-conscious. It was clean, well-mended, practical—but compared to the finery in this room, it might as well have been a rag. Still, it had served her well.

"Do you require assistance, my lady?" the young assistant asked politely.

"No, thank you," Dorothea said. "I've grown rather used to dressing myself."

Madame Duchon gasped, hand fluttering towards her chest. "You have no lady's maid?"

"I used to," Dorothea admitted. "Before I followed my father to war. My brother didn't see the need to replace her after-ward." Her voice remained calm, but bitterness tugged at the edges of her words, especially when she recalled how her brother's wife had a lady's maid.

Mrs. Cameron, who had been quietly observing from the doorway, stepped forward at last. "That will be remedied imme-diately," she said with finality. "Until a permanent maid is hired, I'll assign someone to assist you."

Dorothea hesitated. "I don't want to be any trouble—"

"Nonsense," Mrs. Cameron said briskly. "You are Lady Warwicke now. And no lady of this house will go without proper care."

Dorothea bit her lower lip. "Are you certain Lord Warwicke won't object to the additional expense?"

"I am quite certain," Mrs. Cameron replied.

Madame Duchon clapped her hands. "Then it is settled. Now, let us banish that somber gown. Just looking at it makes me sad."

As Dorothea began to undress, a flicker of something unfamiliar stirred in her chest—anticipation, maybe even a hint of joy. It had been so long since she'd worn anything new, let alone something elegant.

Once she was fully dressed, the petite assistant began the painstaking task of fastening the endless row of covered buttons along the back of the gown. Her fingers worked quickly, each button drawing the muslin snug around Dorothea's form.

Madame Duchon stood back, her hands clasped before her, eyes gleaming with satisfaction. "*Magnifique.* You look beautiful, my lady."

Dorothea turned slightly towards the nearby mirror, catching her reflection in the tall glass. For a moment, she forgot to breathe.

She looked... radiant.

And for the first time in what felt like years, she felt something close to beautiful.

She smoothed a hand over the fabric at her waist, still half-convinced she would wake from the moment. That this version of her—Lady Warwicke, adorned in muslin and lace—was just another dream she wasn't meant to keep.

The final button slipped into place, and Dorothea felt like spinning across the room, like she used to when she was a girl, barefoot and dizzy with joy. But she caught herself. That was a foolish habit—a childish impulse. And she was no longer a girl.

Madame Duchon's voice broke her out of her musings. "These gowns will serve you well until the rest of your wardrobe is complete," she said, lifting a brow. "Properly clothed, properly admired. As you deserve."

Dorothea met her eyes and replied with sincerity, "Thank you. I've never worn anything so fine in all my life."

Madame Duchon waved a hand dismissively, but her smile warmed. "Well, you'd best get used to it, my lady. You are a baroness now, and you must dress like one." She swept a hand towards her assistant. "We shall take our leave for now. But expect word soon. I have designs in mind that will leave Society breathless."

With a final nod, Madame Duchon glided from the room, her assistant scurrying behind her, arms full of folded fabric and measuring notes. The parlor door closed with a soft click.

Dorothea stood in the sudden stillness, turning slowly to gaze at the gowns draped across every available surface. These were her gowns now.

Mrs. Cameron stepped to her side. "I shall have the gowns moved to your wardrobe. But it's nearly time to dress for dinner."

"I'm ready."

"You are dressed," Mrs. Cameron agreed, then added, "but perhaps we might consider a more elaborate hairstyle, my lady. Something befitting your new station."

Dorothea reached up instinctively, smoothing her fingers along the loose twist of her hair. "Yes... perhaps you're right."

Mrs. Cameron gave a pleased nod. "Allow me to escort you to your bedchamber. We can style your hair there."

Dorothea followed her out of the parlor. They climbed the wide staircase in silence, the hush of the corridor broken only by the soft rustle of their skirts. At the far end of the hall, Mrs. Cameron opened a door and stood aside.

"I hope it is to your liking," she said.

Dorothea stepped inside—and stopped.

The room was elegant and richly appointed, awash in warm

light from the windows. A four-poster canopy bed dominated the space, its silken curtains drawn back to reveal crisp linen sheets. A carved settee sat at the foot of the bed, and a marble fireplace occupied one wall, its mantel adorned with gilded sconces. Heavy drapes in shades of ivory framed the arched windows, and beneath her feet lay a floral-patterned carpet.

"This is to be my bedchamber?" Dorothea asked in disbelief.

"It is."

Dorothea slowly stepped farther into the room, running her hand lightly along the edge of the bed's canopy post. It felt surreal, like stepping into a life that had belonged to someone else.

Then, she noticed a door tucked neatly into the side wall, its surface painted the same color as the paneling.

Her eyes lingered. "That door... where does it lead?"

"To Lord Warwicke's bedchamber," Mrs. Cameron replied matter-of-factly as she moved to the dressing table. "Now, let's see about your hair."

Dorothea crossed the room, sitting slowly, as her eyes strayed to the connecting door once more.

Would he come to her tonight?

Would she *want* him to?

She wasn't sure which question unsettled her more.

———

Dominic tugged at the folds of his cravat with growing irritation, muttering curses under his breath. The idea of enduring a formal dinner with Dorothea rankled more than he cared to admit. Before this farce of a marriage, mealtimes had been comfortably informal. Most evenings, he would request a tray be brought to his study, allowing him to eat while poring over estate ledgers or correspondence. It was solitude. It was peace. It was a far cry from the stilted pleasantries he would now be forced to exchange with a young woman he barely knew.

Behind him, his ever-efficient valet, Hale, bent to retrieve the discarded garments strewn across the floor. "Will there be anything else, my lord?"

Dominic stepped back from the mirror, adjusting the line of his coat. "Not at this time. I won't be long at dinner."

Hale gave a slight nod. "Very good, my lord."

Dominic's gaze drifted to the adjoining door that connected his chamber to Dorothea's. The thought made his jaw tighten. He gestured towards it. "See that this door remains locked at all times. I don't want Lady Warwicke entering my chambers—for any reason."

A bemused look came to Hale's expression. "If that is your wish."

"It is," Dominic said firmly, already moving towards the hallway. The request might have seemed harsh—odd, even— but he had no desire to complicate matters further. The annulment he sought depended on clear boundaries, and he meant to keep them.

As he stepped into the corridor, movement caught his eye. Dorothea emerged from her bedchamber, pausing to close the door behind her. She hadn't noticed him yet, giving him a rare, unguarded moment to observe her.

She wore a gown of deep blue, the color accentuating her fair skin and the delicate line of her shoulders. Her red hair, arranged in an elegant coif, was crowned with artful curls that framed her face. She was, undeniably, a striking young woman. But beauty alone meant nothing. They were strangers bound by circumstance, not affection, and he had no intention of pretending otherwise.

"Dorothea," he said softly, careful not to startle her.

Despite his efforts, she jumped slightly and turned with wide eyes. "Dominic," she breathed, recovering quickly.

He closed the distance between them by a step. "Seeing as we are both heading to the dining room, may I escort you?"

Relief softened her features. "That would be lovely. Truthfully, I wasn't entirely sure which way to go."

"You need only ask," he replied, offering his arm.

She took it, though her touch was tentative. "Thank you. It will be nice to dine in the dining room for a change."

"You didn't dine with your brother?"

Dorothea shook her head, her voice quiet. "A tray was always brought to my room. He preferred to eat with his wife... without me."

The pain beneath her calm words struck him unexpectedly. Dominic had no particular fondness for his new wife, but hearing the way she'd been treated by her family stirred a pang of something akin to sympathy.

"I'm sorry," he said, though he wasn't sure the words helped.

She offered a faint smile. "He wasn't entirely heartless. He did allow me to keep my horse."

"At least there was some comfort in that."

"I do love my horse," she said with a touch more warmth. "May I bring him to your stables?"

Dominic nodded. "Of course. I assume you ride, then?"

"I do," she replied quickly.

"Then continue to do so. I would ask only that you take two grooms with you when you go out."

She blinked at him, surprised. "Are you in earnest?"

"I am."

Her face lit up. "Thank you!"

Curiosity pricked at him. "Did your brother not allow you to ride?"

"No. He preferred I remain indoors. I think... I think he was embarrassed by me."

Dominic frowned. "Embarrassed? Why?"

She shrugged, a small, sad gesture. "He said that I asked too many questions. Had too many opinions."

"Is that a bad thing?"

"To my brother, yes," Dorothea replied. "He felt that women should be seen, but not heard."

"That is ridiculous."

"I thought so, as well."

He would've asked more, but they arrived at the dining room. He guided her to the chair at the far end of the long, polished table and waited for her to be seated before claiming his own place opposite her. Within moments, footmen entered and placed bowls of steaming soup before them.

The quiet clink of spoons against porcelain was the only sound for some time, until Dominic set his spoon aside and cleared his throat. "I was hoping to speak with you about... the consummation of our marriage."

Dorothea dabbed her lips with her napkin and met his gaze. "I expected as much. I know it's my duty, but I do hope you'll be patient. I have a general understanding of... of such things, from time spent on a farm."

"I assure you, the act between a man and woman is rather different than livestock."

She lifted her chin. "Regardless, I am your wife. I understand men have... urges."

He nearly laughed at the absurdity of the exchange, but her serious expression held him in check. "One would hope women have urges as well."

"I wouldn't know, my lord."

He leaned slightly to the side to allow a footman to collect his empty bowl. "As enlightening as this conversation is, I was actually inquiring whether we had already consummated the marriage."

"Oh. No, of course not. You were far too ill."

"I thought as much, but I wanted to confirm it."

She reached for her glass. "Do you wish to... tonight?"

"No."

Her brows knit. "Is there a reason?"

Dominic hesitated. He wasn't ready to reveal his pursuit of annulment, not yet. "No reason," he lied.

"Do you think you won't enjoy it?"

He chuckled softly. "That's not my concern."

"Then what is?"

The amusement left his voice. "May we not simply eat in silence?"

Dorothea lowered her eyes. "Of course."

They resumed eating, the silence between them now charged with something brittle and tense. Dominic hadn't meant to be curt, but he had no desire to encourage a deeper connection with her. Not when it would only complicate things.

After a few minutes, Dorothea looked up, her voice tentative. "Did I say something wrong?"

"No. I simply prefer quiet during meals."

"Oh." She paused. "But if I did offend you, I hope you'll tell me. We are married."

He scoffed, unable to help himself. "Only in the legal sense. This is no true marriage. We barely know each other."

"I know enough," she replied. "You were loyal to your men. My father admired you. You were brave. You even risked your life to save your comrades—"

Dominic's hand came down hard against the table, the sharp sound echoing in the room. "I do not wish to discuss this. Not with you."

"I did not mean to offend you—"

He cut her off with a hard shake of his head. "You think you understand me? You don't. You have no right to speak about what you cannot possibly comprehend."

"I'm sorry," she whispered.

He should have stopped. But the pain was too near the surface. He rose and snapped, "I think it might be best if we avoided one another for the time being."

She flinched. "But we're married."

"For now, yes," he said coldly.

"What does that mean?" she asked.

Dominic clenched his jaw. "Nothing that you need to concern yourself with."

Dorothea stood and placed her napkin neatly on the table. "Then I believe I shall retire early, my lord."

He watched her walk from the room with her head high and her back straight. A part of him wanted to call her back— to apologize, perhaps. But he remained still.

This was for the best.

So why did he feel like such an arse?

Dominic sank heavily back into his chair, the weight of his own anger and guilt pressing down on him like a leaden coat. He raked a hand through his hair and reached blindly for his glass.

How had the evening veered so wildly off course? It had begun with the simple intent of polite civility—awkward, yes, but manageable. And yet, here he sat, stewing in regret.

He knew exactly where it had all gone wrong.

The talk of war.

Blast it all! Those memories cut deeper than any blade. The wound hadn't dulled with time. It bled still, unseen but constant, tormenting him with every breath, every heartbeat. Every hour of every cursed day. It haunted him in his dreams and stalked him in his waking moments. There was no escape. No forgetting.

"Botheration," he muttered through gritted teeth, rising abruptly to his feet.

The dining room felt suffocating now—too many memories, too many words he wished he could take back. He turned and strode towards the rear of the townhouse, the sound of his boots echoing dully against the floorboards. He needed something stronger than wine. Something to quiet the noise in his head. Something to erase the look of pain on Dorothea's face.

Heaven help him, that expression had gutted him.

What had she expected of him? That he'd be gentle? Attentive? That he would somehow transform into the sort of husband young girls dreamed about in the pages of novels and poetry?

He was none of those things. And she, poor girl, hadn't realized it yet.

That was the real problem.

Dorothea had a kind heart—a tender, open thing that wore compassion like a mantle. She extended it freely, even to someone like him, who had done nothing to deserve it. People like her... they didn't belong with men like him. He would ruin her. Maybe not today. Maybe not tomorrow. But in the end, he would break her spirit, just as his own had been broken long ago.

It would not end well.

Not for her.

Not for him.

5

Dorothea sat in the corner of her bedchamber, knees drawn to her chest, her gaze fixed on the moonlight spilling through the tall windows. It was well past midnight, yet sleep eluded her as it so often did lately.

She should have been in bed. The fire in the hearth had dwindled to embers, and the house had long since gone silent. But something inside her felt unsettled—tight in her chest, like she couldn't quite breathe.

Why did she feel so desperately alone?

The townhouse was filled with people—servants, maids, footmen—all moving quietly through their appointed roles. But none of them knew her. None of them saw her. Dominic had rescued her from her brother's household, but in doing so, he had placed her in another prison. One with silk curtains and quiet hallways instead of locked doors, but a prison all the same.

She tilted her head back and rested it against the wall. At least here, she was safe from harm. Dominic could be cold and short-tempered, but he didn't frighten her—not the way her brother had. Still, there had once been something gentle between her and Dominic—hadn't there?

Or had she imagined it?

Their acquaintance during the war had been limited. He had been polite, certainly, but distant. It wasn't until after he was wounded—broken and burning with fever in that makeshift hospital—that her father had encouraged her to spend time with him.

She hadn't minded. She'd sat at Dominic's bedside, reading from whatever book she had nearby, while he listened—or sometimes just slept. He would ask her questions when he was lucid, and she had filled the silences with chatter about anything and everything. He had never told her to stop.

And when her father had died, she had confided in Dominic about the truth of her life. Her brother. Her fear. Her helplessness. It was then that he had offered to help.

So why was he so angry now?

He had wanted to help her. He had been the one to offer marriage as a shield against her brother's guardianship. And yet, he now looked at her like she was the source of all his burdens.

Am I the problem?

The thought pierced her heart. She wrapped her arms tighter around herself. She hadn't done anything wrong.

A tear rolled down her cheek and she brushed it away with the back of her hand. How she wished her father were still alive. He wouldn't have stood for this—this coldness, this rejection. He had always made her feel safe, protected. Loved.

The mantel clock chimed once, marking the hour. She should crawl into bed and at least try to sleep, but her stomach twisted with hunger. Dinner had ended in shouting—Dominic's shouting—and the ache in her chest had chased away any appetite she might've had. Now, the hunger gnawed at her with sharp persistence.

Sighing, she stood and slipped her arms into a warm wrapper, tying it around her waist. Perhaps there was something left in the kitchen—a bit of bread, some cheese. Anything.

She walked into the corridor, her bare feet cold against the polished wood, then down the staircase. The marble floor of the entryway was colder still, and she winced with each step as she made her way towards the narrower servants' stairwell.

She held her breath as she descended, careful not to lose her footing. The steps were steep, narrow, and twisted. How the maids managed to carry trays up and down these stairs without toppling over she would never know.

When she stepped into the darkened kitchen, a small wave of relief washed over her. It was still warm from the ovens, and a faint scent of herbs lingered in the air. She moved towards the counter and lifted a cloth to find a modest loaf of bread. Her stomach growled softly in approval.

She began looking for a knife and some butter when the sound of approaching footsteps made her freeze.

Someone was coming down the servants' stairs.

Panic fluttered in her chest.

Without thinking, she reached for the nearest knife—small and blunt, but it was all she had—and crouched behind the counter, her heart pounding as she stared towards the staircase.

A tall figure emerged from the shadows, broad-shouldered and silent. Moonlight filtered through the windowpanes and caught his profile.

Dominic.

Relief flooded through her, and her grip on the knife loosened. She felt foolish. Utterly foolish. Of course it was him. She'd been absurd to think otherwise.

He didn't notice her right away. He moved to the counter, tearing off a hunk of bread with one hand and chewing absently, his gaze fixed on the dark windows as though lost in thought.

Dorothea remained where she was, half-hidden, unsure what to do. The longer she stayed silent, the more awkward it became. But announcing her presence felt equally humiliating. He had made it clear he didn't want to see her, didn't want to speak to her.

She shifted slightly, and the floor creaked beneath her.

Dominic turned sharply. "Who's there?" he demanded, eyes narrowed. "Show yourself."

Her cheeks burned as she rose from her crouched position. "It's just me," she said softly. "Dorothea."

His eyes dropped to the knife still in her hand. "Why do you have a knife?"

She glanced down and winced. "I thought... I thought you might be a robber."

"A robber?" His brow rose in disbelief. "And you thought that little thing could stop me?"

She lifted the knife, wryly. "It is a scary knife."

Dominic reached for a cloth and wiped his hands. "That knife is so dull it wouldn't even cut through soft cheese."

"It was the first thing I saw. I panicked," she admitted, placing the knife back onto the counter.

His expression softened. "There's no one here who wishes you harm. You know that, don't you?"

She nodded, hesitating. "I do. But... sometimes my nerves get the better of me."

"May I ask what you're doing down here at this hour?"

Dorothea turned towards him, her fingers still resting near the loaf of bread. The moonlight slanted through the kitchen window, catching the glint of curiosity in his eyes.

"The same as you," she replied. "I couldn't sleep. I came down looking for food."

He regarded her for a moment, his expression unreadable. "I shall leave you to it, then."

A pang of disappointment surprised her, and she found

herself speaking before she could second-guess the impulse. "You don't have to leave," she said. "There's more than enough bread here for the both of us."

His brow furrowed slightly. "I don't believe it would be wise if I stayed."

"Why?" she asked, a spark of dry humor creeping into her tone. "Do you think I'll stab you with the bread knife?"

A faint grin tugged at the corner of his mouth. "No. That thought hadn't occurred to me, actually."

Dorothea turned back to the counter, searching for a suitable knife. "Then there's no reason you can't stay. We are both grown adults, perfectly capable of sharing a loaf of bread while being civil to one another."

Dominic glanced back at the narrow servants' staircase as though debating an escape. But then he gave a resigned nod. "I suppose there's no harm in that."

She sliced two generous pieces from the loaf and handed one to him. "I don't know where the butter or proper plates are kept," she admitted. "We'll have to eat like savages."

He accepted the bread with a half-laugh. "I've eaten with dirtier hands and colder meals under worse circumstances. This feels practically civilized."

He gestured towards the small wooden table in the corner of the kitchen. "Shall we?"

Dorothea rounded the counter and settled into the seat closest to the window. Dominic took the one beside her, folding his long legs under the table with an ease that belied the tension still clinging to his shoulders.

"Couldn't sleep either?" she asked after a few moments of quiet chewing.

Dominic shook his head. "No. I... had too much on my mind." He exhaled heavily, then turned to face her more fully. "I want to apologize for earlier. I had no right to speak to you the way I did."

The sincerity in his voice caught her off guard. There was no defensiveness, no veiled sarcasm. Just quiet remorse.

"It's all right."

"No, it isn't." He leaned forward, bracing his forearms on the table. "Your father would have been furious with me. He adored you."

The mention of her father made her chest tighten. She stared down at her bread, suddenly finding it difficult to swallow. "He did. He was my whole world."

"I'm sorry he's gone."

Tears prickled at the corners of her eyes, and she blinked rapidly to keep them from falling. "He was a soldier. He always knew the risks. We both did."

"That doesn't make the loss any easier," Dominic said.

"No," she agreed, her voice barely above a whisper. "No, it doesn't."

For a moment, they simply sat there, two people adrift in shared grief, finding a fragile peace in the quiet kitchen as the moonlight spilled across the stone floor.

———————— ～ ————————

Dominic was an idiot.

There was no other word for it. What had possessed him to stay and share a midnight loaf of bread with Dorothea? He should've turned and walked back up those stairs the moment he realized she was in the kitchen. Instead, here he sat—beside her, listening to her soft voice and watching the way the moonlight framed her face—and feeling his carefully constructed walls begin to splinter.

He was trying—truly trying—to harden his heart against her. But every word she spoke, every glance she offered, chipped away at his resolve.

And yet, he couldn't leave. Not now. The quiet sadness in her voice had hooked something inside of him, something he thought long buried. There were things he needed to say— truths that had lingered far too long in silence.

He cleared his throat, gaze fixed on the table. "I owe my entire military career to your father."

Dorothea glanced at him, eyebrows lifted in surprise. "I highly doubt that."

"No, I mean it," Dominic said, his voice more certain now. "After my uncle purchased a commission for me, your father took me under his wing. He didn't have to, but he did. He guided me, shaped me. Taught me what it meant to lead with honor. Without him, I would've never become the kind of soldier I could take pride in."

She studied him for a moment, then offered a soft smile. "My father may have helped guide you, but you were the one who rose to the occasion. You're the one who fought valiantly."

Dominic leaned back, his fingers tightening slightly around the edge of the table. "That's kind of you to say. But truthfully... I spent much of the war fighting myself more than the enemy. I was desperate to prove something—to anyone who would look."

He paused before he added, "Especially to my father. He always said I would fail."

Dorothea's expression dimmed. "That can't be true."

He held up a hand to stop her. "Don't defend him. Please. My father was a brute. A cold, vicious man who ruled his family with a fist instead of affection. I grew tired of the beatings. Eventually, I left."

Dominic continued. "I tried to make my own way. For a time, I worked as a Bow Street Runner."

Her eyebrows lifted again, this time in earnest surprise. "Truly?"

He gave a short nod. "Yes. Most of the work was mundane—

petty thefts, domestic squabbles—but eventually I was trusted with more serious cases. I actually... enjoyed it. Solving puzzles. Finding justice."

"That's rather impressive," she said, clearly meaning it.

He gave a dry laugh, shaking his head. "Is it? Most members of the *ton* would call it disgraceful. To work for your income? To chase criminals through back alleys?"

"Perhaps. But the *ton* also calls you a war hero. I doubt they would see you as anything less than honorable."

His eyes met hers. "And what about you? What do you think?"

Dorothea hesitated, then gave him a small, almost shy smile. "You forget, I was there. I know you're a hero."

"I'm not," he said immediately, the words bitter on his tongue.

"You can say that all you want," she replied, "but it won't change how I see you. I watched how you fought for your men. You took wounds for them. That is nothing short of heroic."

He frowned. "I wish you wouldn't say that. I only did what was expected. Nothing more."

"If it makes you uncomfortable, I won't press the matter."

"Thank you," he murmured, though the doubt still lingered in his eyes.

Dorothea tilted her head slightly. "How did you go from Bow Street Runner to a soldier in the Royal Army?"

He sighed, rubbing the back of his neck. "After my father died, my uncle came to find me. Said it was time I stepped up and behaved like a proper gentleman. Offered to buy me a commission into the Royal Army, and I—foolishly, perhaps—accepted. I thought I might actually be able to make a difference."

He stared down at the crust of bread in his hand. "But nothing prepared me for what I saw on the Continent. No training. No lecture. Nothing."

Dorothea's voice was soft. "Neither was I."

Dominic looked over at her, curious. "Why did you go with your father to war?"

She gave a faint shrug. "What choice did I have? I could stay with my brother—who resented my very presence—or go with my father, where I was wanted. Where I was loved." She smiled wistfully. "For me, it was an easy decision."

"But you were exposed to the horrors of war. That kind of life is not meant for a young woman."

"No," she said, her voice trembling just a little, "but I would do it all again if it meant more time with him." Her eyes dropped to her lap, and then, softer still, "And with you."

That final admission hung in the air like a suspended breath.

Dominic stared at her, unsure of what to say to her. The way her gaze remained fixed on her hands told him she hadn't meant to say it so plainly. And yet... it was there. Honest. Raw.

Before Dominic could form a single response to Dorothea's unexpected confession, the sound of soft footsteps echoed from the stairwell.

Instantly, he became acutely aware of just how close he and Dorothea had been sitting. He pushed back from the table and rose to his feet, creating a proper—and respectable—distance between them. The last thing he needed was for the servants to start gossiping about late-night rendezvous between their lord and his young bride.

A moment later, a small figure emerged from the shadows of the narrow staircase. Tristan padded into the kitchen, his nightshirt trailing nearly to his ankles, his tousled brown hair flattened on one side from sleep. He glanced around the room until his eyes landed on Dominic.

"Lord Warwicke?" he asked sleepily, rubbing one eye. "What are you doing up?"

Dominic raised a brow. "What am *I* doing up? You're the one who should be in bed."

Tristan's expression fell with sheepish guilt. "I was hungry, and the maid who usually brings me food fell asleep."

Dominic sighed, his tone more indulgent than stern. "Very well. A crust of bread and a glass of water. Then it's straight back to bed."

Dorothea rose smoothly from her chair. "That's hardly sufficient for a growing boy," she said. "Let me see if I can find where the butter is kept."

"There's no need—" Dominic began, but his words faltered as Dorothea was already crossing the kitchen, scanning the cupboards with determined purpose.

"Ah-ha!" she exclaimed a moment later, holding up a small crock. "I simply hadn't looked hard enough before."

Tristan moved towards the counter, his eyes lighting up as he approached the bread. "Thank you, my lady," he said with an awkward little bow.

Dominic stepped in to formally introduce them, placing a hand on the boy's narrow shoulder. "This is Tristan. He's staying here while his mother recovers in the hospital."

Dorothea's expression softened immediately. "How is your mother faring, Tristan?"

"She's still sick," he answered, "but the doctor said he'd fix her up. And I get to sleep in a real bed with feathers in it." He made a face. "I hate sleeping on the ground."

Dorothea knelt slightly so she could look him in the eye. "You slept on the ground?"

Tristan nodded. "Mum and I used to sleep in an alleyway. It's been like that since she lost her job as a lady's maid."

"I'm so sorry to hear that," she said.

"It's all right," he said with a shrug. "Before that, we shared a bed stuffed with straw, and the bits always poked through. I almost prefer the floor."

Dominic watched Dorothea as she glanced over at him, her brows slightly drawn, her eyes filled with silent questions.

He cleared his throat. "I found Tristan on the street."

The boy grinned cheekily. "I tried to pickpocket him but he caught me. Wasn't mad either. He still helped me and Mum."

Dorothea gave Dominic an approving look. "That was incredibly generous of you."

"It's probably because he was a soldier," Tristan added, popping a bite of bread into his mouth. "Like my father."

Dominic turned back to the boy. "Your father was a soldier?"

Tristan nodded solemnly. "He died a while ago. That's why I'm the man of the house now. I have to take care of Mum. I promised him I would."

Dominic squeezed his shoulder. "And you're doing a fine job, Lad."

Tristan looked up at him, his eyes full of earnest hope. "Can we go visit her tomorrow?"

Dominic paused, torn between what he should do. He had no desire to go to the hospital again, to relive those painful memories, but he couldn't deny Tristan the right to see his mother. "I have meetings all morning," he said. "But perhaps I'll have some time in the afternoon."

Dorothea interjected. "I could take him. If you have no objection, that is. It's not as though I have anything pressing."

Dominic frowned. "I'm not sure that's the best idea. The hospital isn't in the most respectable part of Town, and the doctor hasn't sent word about her condition."

Tristan clasped his hands together and looked up at him with pleading eyes. "Please, Lord Warwicke. I'm real worried about her."

Dorothea's voice took on determination. "I assure you, I've been in far worse places than a hospital in London."

"It's different now," Dominic said. "You're a baroness. You have a reputation to consider."

"I'm more concerned with Tristan seeing his mother," Dorothea replied. Her gaze held his—steady, unwavering.

He looked between them, knowing he'd been outmaneuvered. "Very well," he said at last. "You may go but I'll send two footmen with you. I'll not have either of you traveling through that part of Town unescorted."

A smile played at the corner of Dorothea's lips. "I can agree to that."

Tristan, however, had no need for subtlety. His entire face lit up, his missing teeth showing as he beamed. "Thank you, my lord!" he said with fervent gratitude. "When my mum is better, do you think she can come live here, too?"

Dominic winced slightly. "I don't know..."

But Dorothea cut in. "As it happens, I'm in need of a lady's maid. Do you think she might like to work here, Tristan?"

The boy's eyes widened. "Do you mean that?"

"I do," she replied. "But for now, you should run off to bed. You'll want to be well-rested for your visit tomorrow."

"Yes, my lady!" he exclaimed, nearly skipping as he made his way back to the stairs.

Once he'd disappeared, Dominic turned to Dorothea. "That was awfully kind of you."

She shrugged off the praise. "It was nothing. I genuinely need a maid."

"You know nothing about her."

"I know she was married to a soldier and that she's a mother doing her best to raise her child." Dorothea turned to face him fully. "That tells me she has strength and a reason to work hard."

Dominic studied her, searching for something—perhaps doubt, or hesitation—but there was none. Just quiet conviction.

He tried, unsuccessfully, to keep the admiration from his voice. "Not many women would do what you just did."

"Then I suppose I'm not like many women."

"No," he murmured, almost to himself. "You're not."

Dorothea glanced towards the darkened window, the moonlight now dimming as clouds passed across the sky. "It's late," she murmured. "I should be getting to bed."

"As should I."

She took a single step towards the staircase, then paused, her gaze flicking back to him. "Goodnight, Dominic."

He lifted a hand in a quiet farewell. "Goodnight, Dorothea."

She offered him a tentative smile—small and soft, but it lingered in her eyes. Without another word, she turned and ascended the narrow servants' stairs, her footsteps fading into silence.

As the last of her hem vanished from sight, Dominic dropped heavily into the nearest chair, elbows resting on the wooden table, and raked a hand through his hair.

What was wrong with him?

He had told himself—again and again—that he must keep his distance. That he and Dorothea were too different, too distant, too incompatible for anything resembling peace or comfort to grow between them.

So why was it that every time she spoke and looked at him with those clear, earnest eyes, something inside him softened?

6

Dressed in a pale pink muslin gown trimmed with delicate lace at the cuffs and collar, Dorothea stepped out of her bedchamber into the morning hush of the corridor. A soft breeze slipped through the tall windows at the end of the hall, rustling the curtains.

As she made her way towards the entry hall, she offered polite nods to the servants she passed. Though they bowed and curtsied respectfully, she felt the subtle weight of their curiosity, their silent observation of the new lady of the house.

When she entered the dining room, she paused, her gaze sweeping over the long table set for two. But Dominic was not there. Her steps faltered. She had hoped—perhaps foolishly—that after their conversation the night before, he might join her.

But no. She was alone.

Well, not entirely. Two footmen stood along the wall like sentinels, their gazes carefully blank. One of them stepped forward and pulled out her chair. Dorothea murmured her thanks and gracefully sat. Another placed a plate of eggs, toast, and sliced fruit before her.

She picked up her fork but found her appetite lacking. Still, she made herself eat in silence, stealing glances towards the doorway with every passing minute, hoping to see Dominic enter the room.

He had been distant, yes. Guarded. But last night... she'd seen a glimpse of something more. Of the man who had once listened to her read by candlelight in a smoky field tent. The man who had offered her kindness when no one else would.

The butler entered the room with his usual poise, a silver tray balanced in his hands. "The morning newssheets, my lady," he announced, stepping forward and offering them with a slight bow.

Dorothea accepted the newssheets, her fingers brushing the crisp edges. She hesitated. Her brother had always criticized her for reading them—said it was unseemly for a young woman to care about politics, war, or Society gossip.

As if sensing her doubt, the butler offered, "If I may, his lordship specifically requested that you read the Society pages this morning."

Her eyebrows lifted. "He did?"

"He did," the butler confirmed with a faint, reassuring smile.

With newfound curiosity, Dorothea unfolded the sheets and turned to the designated pages. Her eyes scanned the columns until one name leapt out at her.

Lady Warwicke.

"It would appear the handsome—and elusive—Lord Warwicke has at last found himself a bride. But not just any bride: a courageous young woman who reportedly followed her father to war, tending to wounded soldiers and facing danger with uncommon bravery..."

Dorothea stared at the words, rereading them once, then twice. The words didn't feel real—not exactly—but she was there in ink and rumor, laid bare for all of London to devour.

How had this Mr. Fairchild even known those details? She

had never sought out attention, and in the eyes of Society, she had been a nobody. So why this sudden fascination?

Before she could ponder it further, the butler returned to the doorway. "A Lady Sarah and her daughter, Mrs. Arabella Haverleigh, have requested an audience with you, my lady."

Dorothea's stomach gave a small lurch, but she forced a smile. "How lovely. Please show them to the drawing room."

As the butler left to escort the guests, Dorothea rose from the table, gathering her composure like a cloak around her. She had not expected to see Arabella again so soon. She had rather hoped—after being removed from her brother's household—that her sister-in-law might simply fade from her life. But Arabella had always been persistent when it served her.

Still, Dorothea reminded herself, Arabella had no power here. Not anymore.

She straightened her shoulders and made her way down the corridor to the drawing room. When she entered, Arabella was already rising from the settee, her fashionable gown pristine, and her blonde curls arranged in an elegant chignon. Lady Sarah sat beside her, silver hair immaculately coifed, her cane resting against one gloved hand.

Arabella beamed with exaggerated warmth. "Dorothea! It's *so* lovely to see you again," she gushed. "That gown is simply divine on you."

Dorothea offered a polite smile. "Is there something I can help you with?"

Arabella let out a delicate laugh, too high and too rehearsed. "You're always so amusing. No, no—this is just a visit. We were eager to see how you're adjusting to such a grand household."

"I'm settling in well, thank you." Dorothea turned to Lady Sarah with genuine warmth. "Good morning, my lady."

Lady Sarah's eyes crinkled around the edges. "Good morning, Dorothea. I understand you are now married to the most talked-about gentleman in London."

"Yes," Dorothea said with a modest smile. "It came as a surprise to me as well."

Arabella eagerly seized her hand and led her to the settee. "You must tell us everything! We're simply dying to hear the story."

"There isn't much to tell," Dorothea replied, carefully arranging her skirts as she sat. "I arrived only yesterday. Dominic and I are still becoming acquainted."

At that moment, a maid entered with a polished tea service. She set it on the low table and asked, "Shall I pour, my lady?"

Dorothea shook her head. "No, thank you. I shall see to it."

She poured the tea with steady hands, offering a cup first to Lady Sarah, then to Arabella, before preparing her own. As she took a sip, she studied Arabella discreetly over the rim of her teacup. The sudden friendliness, the unexpected call... something was not right. Arabella, who had once treated her with cool disdain, was now smiling like they'd grown up as dearest friends.

Arabella set down her teacup with a delicate clink. "I saw the article in the morning newssheets. You must be thrilled."

"I suppose it was rather flattering," Dorothea remarked, placing her own cup and saucer down.

"I imagine your new position will grant you many invitations to balls, soirées, perhaps even the duchess's house party," Arabella said. "And I was hoping—well, your brother was hoping—that you might consider inviting us to accompany you."

Dorothea raised a brow, not bothering to mask her surprise. "My brother made this request?"

Arabella nodded quickly. "It's only fair, considering how generously he cared for you after your father passed."

Dorothea sat straighter, her voice curt. "You and I seem to have different understandings of the word *care.*"

Arabella waved a hand airily. "He made mistakes. We all did. Let's not dwell on the past."

Before Dorothea could answer, Lady Sarah leaned in and said matter-of-factly, "Oh, Arabella, do stop pretending. Your husband is a cad. Let's not insult the girl's intelligence."

"He is not a cad," Arabella protested with a pout on her lips.

Lady Sarah turned to Dorothea and mouthed exaggeratedly, "*Cad.*"

Dorothea let out a surprised giggle and quickly pressed her fingers to her lips. She had always liked Lady Sarah, who had shown her kindness even when no one else in her brother's household had bothered.

Lady Sarah reached down and picked up Dorothea's teacup, extending it towards her. "Why don't we enjoy another cup of tea and speak plainly, shall we?"

Dorothea accepted the cup and took a sip. "I would prefer that."

Arabella lifted her chin. "I merely thought that since you'll be attending many important events, it would be beneficial— for me and my husband—to be seen alongside you."

Realization dawned on Dorothea. "Does my brother even know that you are here?"

Arabella shifted uncomfortably. "No... but I'm doing this for him. Truly."

"For all of us," Lady Sarah corrected. "The more we're seen in good company, the better it reflects on all of us."

Dorothea sat back, weighing her options. She could easily refuse. They had treated her poorly, dismissed her, and made her feel invisible. She owed them nothing.

And yet... there was something desperate in Arabella's voice. Not arrogant. Not scheming. *Pleading.*

"Please, Dorothea," Arabella said quietly. "Matthew won't

say it aloud, but he needs to make proper connections. Ones that will lift us up in the eyes of Society. We... we need help."

Dorothea set her cup on the tray and folded her hands in her lap. "I'm not opposed. But I'll need to speak with Dominic before I agree to anything."

Arabella's face lit up with relief. "Thank you, Dorothea."

"Don't thank me yet," she said. "He may not approve."

"I understand."

Lady Sarah gave her a knowing smile. "I hear your husband is very handsome."

A faint blush crept up Dorothea's cheeks. "He is, indeed."

"Good." Lady Sarah's smile turned warm. "I'm happy for you, my dear."

Dorothea was happy—truly, quietly, deeply happy—that Dominic had come back from the dead. That he had survived when so many others hadn't. Every breath he drew was a small miracle, one she hadn't dared pray for during those long, desperate nights in the field hospital.

But even as gratitude filled her chest, it was accompanied by something heavier. A weight she couldn't seem to shake.

Because she knew—had known from the moment she stepped foot into his townhouse—that he didn't see her as a blessing.

He saw her as a burden. And no matter how she tried to make herself small, to tread lightly and be nothing but agreeable, that truth clung to her like a shadow.

He was alive.

And she was unwanted.

Dominic sat rigidly in his coach, the wheels jostling over the uneven cobblestones as it wound its way through the bustling London streets. Outside, the city was already awake—hawkers shouting over each other, horses clattering by, the scent of smoke and fresh bread mingling in the spring air. But inside the coach, there was only the hum of his thoughts. He had risen before dawn, eaten his breakfast in a nearly empty dining room, and made sure to depart before Dorothea stirred. A coward's maneuver, to be sure, but necessary. Facing her had become... complicated.

It didn't feel like he was learning who she was. No, it felt far more dangerous—like he was *remembering*. Every smile, every look that lingered too long, pulled at something half-buried in him. A word here, a shared silence there—it was as though some part of him had always known her. That notion terrified him. He was here to seek an annulment, not to rediscover his wife.

The coach rolled to a stop before the House of Lords. Without waiting for the footman, Dominic flung open the door and stepped down, adjusting the fit of his waistcoat and straightening his cravat. The massive structure loomed ahead and he ascended the steps two at a time, tipping his head to acknowledge the guards who stood watch.

Once he was inside the long hall, he made for the benches assigned to the Whigs, nodding absently at a few familiar faces. Though he sat with them, he wouldn't call himself a staunch Whig. His years on the battlefield had taught him to distrust absolutes. Some of his leanings aligned with the Tories, whether he liked it or not.

He had just begun scanning the chamber for a quiet place to sit when a broad figure intercepted him—Lord Inglewood. He was a heavy-set man with eyes that always seemed a touch too calculating. Inglewood had been an ally of his father's, though Dominic had never determined whether that meant he was friend or foe.

"Warwicke," Inglewood drawled, voice like gravel. "A pity you've chosen the wrong side of history."

Dominic offered a thin smile. "And good morning to you."

Inglewood's gaze didn't waver. "Your father would have expected you to side with the Tories."

"I am painfully aware of what my father would have wanted," Dominic replied. "Which is precisely why I'm seated with the Whigs."

Inglewood gave a short, humorless laugh. "You were a soldier. You fought for King and Country. That should mean something."

"It does. Which is why I vote with my conscience, not with party lines."

Inglewood stepped closer, the scent of tobacco clinging to his jacket. "Then perhaps we have something to discuss."

Feigning interest, Dominic arched a brow. "Do we?"

The older man glanced around, then lowered his voice. "I hear you're seeking an annulment."

Dominic stiffened but kept his expression neutral. That kind of gossip traveled fast—and dangerously. "That is correct."

Inglewood's lips curled into something almost resembling a smirk. "I'm introducing a bill today. Higher tariffs on imported goods. It will be framed as support for British soldiers. A noble cause. If you help sway enough Whigs to vote in favor, I could convince a few influential Tories to back your petition for annulment."

Dominic's eyes narrowed. "And you think that's possible?"

"Under normal circumstances, no. But yours are exceptional," Inglewood said. "You were on your deathbed when you married, were you not? Easy to argue your bride exploited your condition."

"I was not tricked," Dominic said sharply.

Inglewood leaned in, voice just above a whisper. "Weren't

you? You were feverish, barely coherent, and somehow you found the strength to pledge yourself to her?"

Dominic's jaw tightened. "I don't want Dorothea's name dragged through the mud."

"If you pursue an annulment, scandal will follow—no matter how delicately it's handled. The stain on her reputation will be indelible."

Silence settled between them. The truth of it hit harder than Dominic wanted to admit. Dorothea would be ruined. Cast out of Society. And yet, if he stayed, if he bound her to a man like him—a man broken by war, by guilt, by obligations he never asked for—he would destroy her anyway. She might not see it now, but in time, she would. And then she would hate him for it.

Inglewood took a step back. "Think on what I've said. We could both get what we want."

Without another word, Inglewood turned and strode away, his steps echoing through the chamber.

Dominic made his way to his seat as his thoughts churned. No sooner had he sat down than he was flanked by Lord Bedford, Lord Wilton, and Lord Alcott, all looking at him with thinly veiled curiosity.

"What did Inglewood want?" Bedford asked.

Dominic barely glanced at him. "None of your business."

Bedford snorted. "He's trying to gather support for that wretched bill of his."

"I haven't read it yet," Dominic admitted.

"You should," Wilton said, his tone grave. "The tariffs could weaken the entire stock market. And between you and me, I believe Inglewood intends to use the chaos to line his own pockets."

Dominic frowned. "He said the bill would benefit the soldiers."

"It would—slightly," Alcott remarked. "But not nearly as much as it would benefit Inglewood's business interests."

Bedford tilted his head, studying Dominic. "Did he offer you something in exchange for your support?"

Dominic hesitated. "He said he'd convince the Tories to back my annulment."

A sharp whistle escaped Bedford's lips. "That's no small favor. Annulments aren't granted easily—not without causing a spectacle."

"I know," Dominic said. "But I have to try."

Bedford exchanged a wary glance with Wilton before asking, "Do you hate your wife that much?"

Dominic winced. "I don't hate Dorothea."

"Are you sure?" Bedford questioned. "I only ask because you'll ruin her. Once Society gets wind of it, she'll be cast out. No one will want her."

"I'll make sure she's provided for," Dominic replied, though the words rang hollow, as if spoken by someone else. And deep down, he feared that even the best intentions wouldn't be enough to shield her from the storm he was about to unleash.

Alcott leaned back in his seat. "I, for one, think you should get the annulment," he said with a shrug.

Dominic raised a brow. "You do?"

Alcott's eyes held amusement. "Wives are burdensome creatures. They expect things of you. Attention, affection, a presence at dull dinner parties and infernal musicales. A man can hardly breathe under the weight of their expectations."

Bedford chuckled under his breath. "Some would say there are certain benefits to having a wife."

"No one asked you," Wilton replied dryly. "You're still basking in the glow of your newlywed haze. Your opinion is hopelessly compromised."

Dominic allowed the banter to wash over him without joining in. His gaze wandered across the grand hall as more lords filtered in. He should have felt pride being here—a man with a voice, with a vote, with the power to shape the future. But instead, all he felt was the heavy press of inadequacy.

When he had worked as a Bow Street Runner, his world had been made of shadows and suffering. He had walked the alleyways no lord would ever dare enter, seen families starving in corners of crumbling buildings, and watched children claw through rubbish for scraps. Some had become criminals, shaped by desperation. But others had simply endured, surviving one day at a time with no hope it would get better.

He hadn't forgotten their faces.

Bedford's voice broke through his thoughts. "Warwicke, are you still with us?"

"No," Dominic said simply.

Bedford grinned. "He speaks! For a moment, I feared we'd lost you to your melancholy."

Dominic looked to Wilton, his tone suddenly serious. "I want to make a difference."

"In what way?" Wilton replied.

Dominic lowered his voice slightly. "We should draft a bill to raise the minimum age for children working in the workhouses. What they're expected to do—the hours, the danger—it's unconscionable."

Wilton's good humor faded. "That will never pass. And if we take the children out, what do we do with them? Leave them starving in the streets?"

"They could be taken in by the Foundling Hospital," Dominic said. "There must be a better way than condemning a six-year-old to a life of soot and sickness."

Wilton shook his head. "The hospitals aren't equipped to handle the overflow. They were never designed for that kind of volume. It's a nice sentiment but hopelessly naïve."

Frustration twisted in Dominic's chest. "Then what is the point of any of this?" he asked, voice low but intense. "What good is it to hold power in this chamber if we are powerless to do anything that actually matters?"

"I know it's unfair," Wilton said. "But we must play the game. Wait our turn. Build power slowly until we're in a position to wield it."

Dominic turned sharply towards him, the muscle in his jaw twitching. "And how long must we wait? How many speeches must we give? How many hands must we shake before we're finally allowed to matter?"

Wilton exhaled, the sound almost a sigh. "It could take years."

Dominic's hands curled into fists on his knees. "I don't have years to waste."

"You were thrust into this world when the king gave you your title," Wilton pointed out. "You didn't climb through the ranks like the rest of us. That has some advantages, but also disadvantages. You haven't yet earned the kind of influence that lets you shake the foundations."

"Then I'll shake them anyway," Dominic stated.

Wilton huffed. "If you try to do too much too soon, you'll alienate the very people whose support you'll one day need. The Whigs will turn their backs on you. The Tories will never let you in. You'll be isolated. Powerless. And all your good intentions will burn to ash."

Dominic opened his mouth to argue, but Bedford cut in. "Wilton's right. Change comes, but only to those who know how to bide their time. You must strike when the moment is ripe."

Dominic turned to look between the two of them. "And how many children must die waiting for the right moment?"

That silenced them all.

The worst part was that it wasn't a rhetorical question. Faces of soot-covered children, malnourished and hollow-eyed, flickered behind Dominic's eyes. He had walked among them. Held them as they coughed up blood.

Alcott reached out and placed a hand on Dominic's shoulder, his grip steady. "I haven't seen what you've seen. I haven't walked in your shoes. But I do understand politics. And politics, unfortunately, is not a war you win with swords. It's chess. One wrong move... and the game ends before it ever truly begins."

Dominic didn't shake off the hand, but he didn't look at Alcott either. He stared straight ahead at the chamber's great doors. His friends weren't wrong. Dominic knew that. He hated that. He was still the newcomer here—the soldier turned peer, elevated by royal favor but without the web of alliances, favors, and connections others had spent decades weaving. Every step he took was under scrutiny. One misstep, and they'd have a reason to cast him aside.

But that didn't mean he would sit idle.

He might not be able to change the game overnight.

But he could, at the very least, make the players nervous.

7

Dressed in a rich blue gown with a delicate net overlay, Dorothea sat inside the gently swaying coach. The wheels clattered rhythmically against the uneven cobblestones as they trundled through the narrow street, the scent of horses and lilacs drifting through the small window slit. She turned her attention to the boy seated across from her.

Tristan sat pressed against the window, his face lit with wonder. His breath fogged the glass as he peered out, captivated by the bustle of the Town.

As the coach turned a corner and the looming façade of the hospital came into view, she leaned forward in her seat. "Tristan," she said, drawing his attention, "before we arrive, I think it's best you prepare yourself. We don't know how ill your mother truly is. Her recovery may be slow... or uncertain."

Tristan's gaze shifted from the window to her face, his curiosity momentarily replacing his excitement. "Do you think people can see me inside the coach?"

"I do," Dorothea replied.

He sat straighter, puffing out his chest. "I wonder if they think I'm someone important."

"You are important," she responded.

His face fell. "I'm not. I'm just a ruffian from the streets. I lived in an alley with my mum."

"You must never let your circumstances dictate your worth. A person's future is not determined by where they begin. With hard work and courage, you could one day live in a fine townhouse."

His eyes widened. "Do you really think so?"

"I do. Look at Dominic—he wasn't always a baron. He began as a Bow Street Runner and later served in the Royal Army. He earned every bit of what he has."

Tristan lowered his gaze to his hands, now folded tightly in his lap. "My father joined the Royal Army to give us a better life, too, but he failed. He died."

Dorothea's heart ached for him. She reached across the carriage and took his small hand in hers. "He didn't fail, Tristan. He gave everything he had, serving with honor. That is not failure—it's bravery."

"But we're still poor," he whispered.

"Perhaps," she said gently, "but you still have your mother. I would trade everything I own to have more time with mine. She passed when I was young."

Tristan looked up, pain flickering in his expression. "But my mum's sick."

"She's not gone," Dorothea said, giving his hand a reassuring squeeze. "Treasure what you do have. Life can change in the blink of an eye."

He studied her face carefully. "Do you think she'll live?"

Dorothea hesitated, not wanting to give him false hope. "I can't say for certain but she's under a doctor's care now, and that is something."

Tristan gave a small nod. "It was awfully kind of Lord Warwicke to bring her to the hospital."

"Yes. It was."

The coach came to a gradual stop in front of the hospital's entrance. Dorothea released his hand as the footman opened the door and offered his arm. She stepped down, then turned and held out her hand to Tristan.

"Whatever we find inside, we'll face it together," she said.

He grasped her hand with surprising firmness. "Thank you, my lady."

Once they were inside, the air was cool and still. An older man with white hair approached, his eyes sharp.

"Good morning, my lady," he greeted with a small bow. "Lord Warwicke informed us of your arrival. I am Doctor Langley."

Dorothea inclined her head politely. "A pleasure, Doctor."

"Please," he said, motioning towards a door, "follow me. I'll take you to the boy's mother."

Dorothea's steps quickened. "How is she?"

Doctor Langley glanced over his shoulder with a flicker of a smile. "You can ask her yourself. She's awake."

As they entered a long hall lined with neat rows of beds, Tristan suddenly cried out, "Mum!"

He dashed ahead towards a narrow bed where a pale, chestnut-haired woman was propped up against a stack of pillows. Her eyes were sunken but alert, and they lit up the moment she saw him.

"Tristan," she rasped, holding her arms wide.

He leapt onto the bed, throwing his arms around her. "I was so scared," he said tearfully. "I thought you were going to die like Father."

She clutched him tightly. "Never, my love. I'd never leave you, not by choice."

Doctor Langley approached the bedside. "Tabitha's

recovery has been extraordinary. She was weak from starvation, but once we began nourishing her, she improved rapidly."

Dorothea stepped closer, her eyes taking in Tabitha's fragile frame and the renewed light in her expression. "That's wonderful news."

Tabitha looked past her son, her gaze tentative. "Are you Lady Warwicke?"

"I am."

Tabitha reached up to ruffle Tristan's curls. "Please tell your husband how grateful I am. Without his help, I don't know where we would be."

Tristan sat up proudly and tugged at the hem of his clean shirt. "Look at my new clothes! Lord Warwicke had them made for me."

"You look so handsome," his mother whispered.

He lifted one foot. "And new shoes! No more holes."

Tabitha's eyes welled with emotion. "What can I ever do to repay you, my lady?"

Dorothea shook her head. "There's no debt here. Just focus on getting better."

Nestling beside his mother, Tristan announced, "Lady Warwicke wants to hire you as her lady's maid."

Tabitha's mouth fell open. "Is that... true?"

"It is," Dorothea confirmed. "Tristan told me you were the best there ever was."

Tristan beamed proudly. "I did! And I told Lord Warwicke you weren't a thief."

Tears sprang to Tabitha's eyes as she pressed a trembling hand to her forehead. "This feels like a dream. I don't know what to say."

Dorothea reached out and touched Tabitha's shoulder gently. "I understand your husband was a soldier."

Tabitha's smile faded. "He died on the Continent."

"My husband and my father were both soldiers," Dorothea

shared. "We must care for one another. Your husband gave everything in service of the Crown."

Tabitha looked at her through a sheen of tears. "I miss him every day."

Dorothea offered a warm, steadying smile. "Then let us honor his memory by building something stronger—for your sake, for Tristan's. You're not alone anymore."

"Thank you, my lady," Tabitha replied, her voice thick with emotion.

Dorothea opened her mouth to reply, but a sudden tickle in her nose caught her off guard. She turned slightly away and brought a lace-edged handkerchief to her mouth, stifling a delicate sneeze.

"Excuse me," she murmured.

Doctor Langley tilted his head with concern. "Are you feeling quite well, Lady Warwicke?"

She pressed the handkerchief gently to her nose, frowning faintly. "I daresay a cold may be creeping up on me. Nothing more, I hope."

The doctor stepped forward, his brow furrowed. "Would you like me to examine you? Just to be sure?"

Dorothea waved a gloved hand in gentle dismissal. "Heavens, no, Doctor. It is merely the chill in the air or a passing tickle. I wouldn't dream of troubling you over a trifling cold."

Doctor Langley moved to a modest chest of drawers near the wall. He opened one and removed a small glass bottle filled with a white powder. "If you change your mind, this might at least help you rest more comfortably tonight." He approached her and extended the bottle. "A mild dose of laudanum. Enough for a few nights, should the symptoms worsen."

Dorothea accepted it with a grateful smile. "You are very kind, Doctor Langley. Thank you."

Tabitha let out a wide yawn and quickly raised a hand to cover her mouth, her cheeks coloring. "Pardon me."

"There's no need to apologize," Dorothea assured her. "You need rest more than anything right now. We'll come again tomorrow."

At that, Tristan jumped down from the bed with a burst of energy, nearly bouncing on the balls of his feet. "Lord Warwicke said I could ride a pony today!"

Tabitha blinked in surprise. "A pony?"

"Yes!" he beamed. "I've never even touched one before, let alone ridden! Do you think I'll be good at it?"

A smile spread across Tabitha's tired face. "I do," she replied.

Tristan flung his arms around her again in a quick, tight embrace. "I'll see you tomorrow, Mum!" Then he turned and practically skipped towards the door.

Dorothea moved to follow, but before she could step away, Tabitha reached out and caught her hand.

"You and your husband..." she began, her voice trembling, "you're a godsend, my lady. I wouldn't be alive if Lord Warwicke hadn't found me in that alleyway."

Dorothea gently wrapped her fingers over Tabitha's. "I'm grateful he did. Everyone deserves a second chance."

Tabitha's gaze shifted towards her son, who was now standing with Doctor Langley, inspecting a pair of forceps with fascination. "I haven't seen him this happy since before his father died."

"Tristan is a remarkable boy," Dorothea said, her voice warm. "There's a quiet strength in him."

Tabitha nodded, her voice barely audible. "He's all I have. I stopped eating so he would have enough."

Dorothea's heart clenched. She gave Tabitha's hand a reassuring squeeze. "You won't have to make that kind of sacrifice again. There will be plenty of food at our townhouse for both of you."

A tear slipped down Tabitha's cheek as she slowly withdrew her hand. "I promise I'll work hard. I won't let you down."

"I know you won't," Dorothea replied. "But more than that, I want you well again—for Tristan's sake. He needs his mother strong and whole."

Tabitha moved to lay her head down onto the pillow. "I would do anything for my son," she murmured.

Dorothea offered her a parting smile before she lifted her lace-edged handkerchief again and dabbed at her nose. The dull ache of congestion pressed just behind her eyes. She had little doubt that a few hours of sleep would surely chase away whatever cold threatened to take hold.

Dominic stepped down from his coach, his boots crunching against the gravel drive as he looked up at the grand façade of his townhouse. The afternoon sun caught on the windows and cast golden reflections across the red brick, and still—despite having lived there for several months—it didn't feel real.

The townhouse was his. Every polished brick and slate tile bought with coin he'd earned, not inherited.

He tightened his grip on his gloves, a flicker of disbelief still clinging to him. His father had owned estates like this. More than one. But Dominic had never expected to possess one himself. He had walked away from a fortune and a name to carve his own path. His father had called him a disgrace for becoming a Bow Street Runner, for daring to work among the common rabble. To earn a wage was, in his father's mind, a stain on the family name.

Dominic's jaw tensed. He hadn't left for pride but to save his mother. He had planned to return for her, to give her a better life. But time had stolen the chance. Illness had come swiftly and silently. By the time he received word, both his parents were gone. He hadn't even had a moment to say goodbye. At least—not to his mother. He felt no sorrow for his father's passing. The man had inflicted too many wounds, both seen and unseen. But his mother had deserved so much more.

The front door swung open as he approached, and Wright greeted him. "Good afternoon, my lord."

Dominic removed his hat and handed it over, brushing a bit of dust from his coat sleeve. "I'd like to be alone. There's work I must attend to."

"Of course, my lord. But I should inform you that Lady Warwicke's trunks have arrived, and her mare was delivered to the stables just over an hour ago."

Dominic lifted a brow. "Is she aware of this?"

Wright inclined his head. "Yes, my lord. She returned home not long ago and went directly to the stables."

Dominic said nothing more. He should go straight to his study since there were ledgers from his new estate that required review. But the thought of Dorothea, alone in the stables, tugged at him. He hesitated, torn between duty and desire. In the end, he sighed inwardly and changed course.

He crossed the rear gardens and arrived at the open stable doors. As he neared, he slowed as soft singing drifted from within. The melody floated on the air like something out of a memory.

He leaned silently against the doorframe as he watched Dorothea brush her mare's coat. Her voice was low and lovely, the same song she had sung during the darkest of nights— when pain had wracked his body and he'd teetered on the edge of death. That song had quieted the storm in his mind when nothing else could. Hearing it again now brought a strange ache to his chest.

She was good. Pure in a way the world rarely allowed. And that was why she could never be his. Not truly. Not forever.

He shouldn't be here. He should slip away and bury himself in estate matters. He had come only to see—nothing more. But as he turned to go, her song faded and her voice called out, clear and direct.

"Dominic."

He froze.

Botheration.

Slowly, he turned back to face her. "Dorothea."

She smiled, and it was full of the one thing he dreaded seeing: hope.

"How are you?" she asked.

"I'm well," he replied, his voice clipped, too formal. "I only came to inform you that your mare has arrived but I see you're already aware of that." *Idiot.* Could he have made a more redundant entrance?

Dorothea rested her hand on her mare's neck. "Thank you for allowing her to be housed here."

"They are your stables as well," he said, though he stopped himself from adding, *at least for now.*

She turned and gestured to the stall at the far end. "I see your stallion returned from the Continent with you."

That brought a smile to his lips. "He did. It took some time to arrange the transport, but I couldn't leave him behind."

"I'm glad. You asked about him often when you were recovering," she said, watching him closely.

Dominic stepped farther into the stables, the scent of hay and leather surrounding him. He moved to the stall where his horse stood and reached out, running a hand along its muzzle. "He's been with me through everything. I wouldn't have trusted another steed in battle."

"How long have you had him?" she asked, moving to stand beside him.

"My uncle gave him to me before I left for the Continent,"

he replied. "He told me to sit tall in the saddle and ride with honor."

"You smile when you speak of your uncle," Dorothea observed.

"He is a good man, unlike my father. He loved his wife fiercely and never remarried after her death."

"Where does he live?"

"Just outside London. A modest estate, nothing grand. He rarely leaves his favorite chair these days. He claims reading keeps his mind sharper than any doctor could."

Dorothea reached into a nearby bucket and drew out a shiny red apple. She held it out, and Dominic's stallion eagerly took it from her palm.

"I would like to meet your uncle," she said, brushing her fingers clean on her skirts.

Dominic looked at her. "He would like you," he replied. "Of that, I have no doubt."

"Does he know you're married?"

He gave a slow nod. "I imagine he read it in the newssheets. I should have written to him before it was made public."

Dorothea tilted her head. "Perhaps we can visit him together sometime."

Together.

The word echoed in Dominic's mind, far louder than it should have. It was an innocent suggestion—harmless, even. Together implied continuity, future, belonging. But there was no future for them. Not like that. Once the annulment was granted, they would go their separate ways.

And that was for the best. For both of them.

Dominic cleared his throat. "I have work I must attend to," he said, his tone curt.

"Yes, of course," she replied, but as the words left her mouth, she turned her head and sneezed into her handkerchief.

Instantly, his guarded expression shifted to one of concern. "Are you unwell? Shall I send for the doctor?"

She waved a hand lightly in the air. "It's only a cold," she said with a reassuring smile. "Doctor Langley gave me some laudanum to help me sleep, but truly, I feel well enough."

Still, Dominic frowned. "Perhaps you should go and rest. It's best not to let it worsen."

"I suppose you're right," she said, though her tone suggested she hadn't wanted to admit it.

They exited the stables side by side, the crunch of gravel beneath their boots and the scent of fresh hay still lingering in the air.

"How is Tristan's mother faring?" Dominic asked, breaking the silence.

That was the right question. Dorothea's entire expression brightened, her posture straightening as warmth touched her features. "Very well, actually. When we visited earlier, she was awake and lucid. Doctor Langley seemed genuinely optimistic about her recovery."

"Did he say what her illness was?" Dominic asked, though he had a suspicion.

Dorothea's smile dimmed, her gaze turning somber. "She stopped eating so that Tristan wouldn't have to go without."

Dominic winced, guilt and admiration warring within him. "That is tragic. But also noble, in its own way."

"You were wise to take her to the hospital when you did," Dorothea said.

He waved the praise away with a flick of his hand. "It was simply the right thing to do."

Dorothea's gaze lingered on him. "Tabitha wanted me to thank you for caring for Tristan so well."

Dominic clasped his hands behind his back. "No thanks is necessary. I only did what my conscience dictated."

"I think it was admirable," Dorothea said with conviction.

He stiffened at that. Praise made him uncomfortable. "You would have done the same," he said sharply. "There's nothing exceptional about it."

He saw her start to respond, her lips parting slightly, but he cut her off before she could speak. "I'd prefer we speak of something else."

A moment of silence passed before she replied, "As you wish."

He decided to ask a safe question. "How are you settling in?"

That brought back her smile, bright and genuine. "Very well. Everyone has been so kind to me. Your staff is warm and helpful, and my bedchamber is the most luxurious room I've ever stayed in. The sheets feel like silk, and I can see the gardens from the window."

"I am happy to hear that."

Dorothea clasped her hands in front of her. Her gaze dipped for a moment, and she drew in a quiet breath before biting her lower lip. Color rose to her cheeks as she spoke, her voice barely above a whisper.

"I was hoping... you might come visit me at night," she said, the words tumbling out in a rush. Her blush deepened, giving away the vulnerability she usually kept hidden behind her graceful composure.

Dominic felt his heart twist.

He hadn't wanted to have this conversation. Not yet. The thought of disappointing her made his chest tighten, but keeping her in the dark any longer would only make it worse. Perhaps now was the time to tell her the truth—that he intended to petition for an annulment. He opened his mouth, preparing to speak, but the words caught in his throat.

Just then, the sound of rapid footsteps broke the moment. Tristan came barreling across the gravel path, his face lit with pure joy. Clutched in his hands was a brightly colored kite, the long tail trailing behind like a banner of triumph.

"Look what I got!" he cried, grinning from ear to ear.

Dorothea's expression instantly softened as she turned towards him. "It's a kite," she replied.

"Do you want to fly it with me?" Tristan asked eagerly, bouncing on the balls of his feet as though the excitement couldn't be contained in his small frame.

She laughed. "I would love to." Then, turning towards Dominic with hopeful eyes, she inquired, "Would you care to join us?"

"I have work I must see to," he said firmly.

A flicker of disappointment came into Dorothea's eyes as she murmured, "I understand."

Tristan reached up and grabbed Dorothea's hand with enthusiasm. "Come on! Let's go fly the kite!"

Dorothea cast one final glance over her shoulder, her eyes meeting Dominic's for a moment—a silent question lingering there. Then, with Tristan tugging at her hand and excitement in his step, she let herself be drawn away.

Dominic remained where he stood, his boots planted firmly on the gravel path as he watched them disappear through the break in the hedge that led to the open field beyond the gardens.

It didn't surprise him how good Dorothea was to Tristan. That was who she was. Kind. Caring. And a far better person than him.

8

The low chime of the dinner bell echoed through the corridors as Dorothea stepped out of her bedchamber. She paused a moment, smoothing down the soft folds of her jonquil gown, the muslin fabric glinting under the flickering sconces. She knew Dominic might not want her company tonight—he so often didn't—but she still took care with her appearance. For herself. For him.

No matter how he tried to keep her at arm's length, she saw flickers of the man he had once been—warm, teasing, attentive. They were rare and fleeting, but she clung to them all the same.

Sniffling softly, she pulled a handkerchief from her sleeve and dabbed her nose. The cold still lingered, but her nap had done wonders for her aching limbs and heavy head. With each step towards the dining room, anticipation built inside her, lifting her spirits despite her persistent cough.

But it shattered the moment she stepped over the threshold and found the long dining table lit and laid—but empty.

Dominic wasn't there.

Before she could even form a question, Wright approached

from the far end of the room, his hands clasped behind his back and an apologetic expression shadowing his features.

"My lady," he began, "Lord Warwicke has chosen to dine at his club this evening."

Dorothea faltered. Her smile arrived late. "I see," she said, the words hollow in her throat.

Wright motioned towards the glittering display of silver and porcelain. "The cook has prepared a fine feast for you, my lady."

The thought of sitting alone at that vast table, surrounded by empty chairs and echoing silence, made her chest constrict. "I believe..." she hesitated, then straightened her spine. "I believe I shall take my dinner in the kitchen tonight."

Wright studied her for a moment, his gaze softening. "As you wish, my lady. Would you care for an escort?"

She shook her head. "No, that won't be necessary. I know the way."

Turning quickly before her composure cracked, Dorothea made her way to the servants' staircase tucked behind a tapestry. The cold iron banister was rough beneath her fingers, and the stairs creaked with age, each step uneven and narrow.

As she reached the bottom and stepped into the warmth of the kitchen, the clatter of pots, hiss of boiling broth, and hum of voices wrapped around her like a comforting shawl. Servants moved swiftly, assembling plates, washing dishes, and bustling about their duties. Near the hearth, Mrs. Dawson stirred a pot with such vigor that it sloshed dangerously near the rim.

"I need the vegetables!" she called over her shoulder, her tone brisk.

A young maid rushed forward, cradling a bowl. "I have them, ma'am."

"Well then, put them on the plate," Mrs. Dawson replied, stepping back and wiping her hands on her apron. "This meal should've already been halfway up the stairs by now."

Dorothea cleared her throat and stepped forward. "That won't be necessary."

Mrs. Dawson turned, surprise flickering across her face before softening into something more knowing. "Lord Warwicke isn't joining you, is he?"

Dorothea's lips pressed into a tight line. "I'm afraid not."

Mrs. Dawson's expression faltered, then recovered. "Well, no matter. Come, sit. You're always welcome here."

"Thank you," Dorothea murmured, moving towards the round wooden table nestled in the corner.

Mrs. Dawson followed with a steaming bowl of soup and set it in front of her. "Did he give a reason, at least?"

"He's dining at his club." Dorothea picked up her spoon and stirred the broth absentmindedly.

Mrs. Dawson gave a disbelieving snort and sat down beside her. "That's not much of a reason, if you ask me."

A sharp voice interrupted from the other side of the kitchen. "Lady Warwicke did not ask you, Mrs. Dawson. And frankly, she ought to reprimand you for such impertinence."

Dorothea looked up at the housekeeper. "It's all right, Mrs. Cameron. I prefer honesty between us."

The housekeeper raised a brow, then turned to the room. "Very well. The rest of you are dismissed."

The bustle ceased instantly. With quiet bows and curtsies, the servants slipped out, leaving the kitchen still and intimate.

Mrs. Dawson leaned forward, eyes twinkling with mischief. "I had a husband once who thought farming was more important than me. So I killed his favorite chicken and served it for supper," she said. "I told him that he would get a similar fate if he continued to ignore me."

Mrs. Cameron gasped. "You did no such thing!"

Smirking, Mrs. Dawson asked, "Or did I?"

"Henry was a good man," the housekeeper insisted.

"That he was," Mrs. Dawson admitted, "but I needed to make a point."

Mrs. Cameron rolled her eyes. "Lady Warwicke will not be killing any chickens."

Mrs. Dawson laughed. "No, but she can do other things to catch her husband's attention."

Dorothea set down her spoon, her voice tentative. "How... how does one flirt with one's husband?"

Mrs. Cameron looked bewildered. "Don't ask me. My husband has been dead for twenty years."

Mrs. Dawson perked up. "Fortunately for you, I am a master of flirtation. I have been married three times."

"Three?" Dorothea repeated, eyes wide.

Mrs. Dawson waved her hand. "Hardly my fault they kept dying. Now—flirting. It's all in the attention. Look at him when he speaks. Ask questions. Laugh at his jokes, even the bad ones. Make him feel like the only man in the room," she advised. "Here, try it on me."

Dorothea straightened in her seat and met the cook's gaze. "How are you faring?"

"I am well," Mrs. Dawson replied with a nod. "Do you come here often?"

"I do. Do you like... rocks?"

Mrs. Dawson blinked. "I do like rocks."

"Good. Because there are *boulders* of them in the gardens," Dorothea quipped with a smile.

Mrs. Dawson stared at her for a long moment, then turned to Mrs. Cameron. "Did she just make a rock joke?"

Dorothea winced. "Was it that bad?"

"Yes," Mrs. Dawson said plainly. "But worse—my dear, you haven't blinked once since you started."

Dorothea blinked rapidly. "Better?"

"Now it looks like you've got dust in your eyes." Mrs. Dawson sighed. "Oh, dear. We've got work to do."

Dorothea slumped back in her chair, her shoulders sagging. "I am hopeless, aren't I?"

Mrs. Dawson leaned forward, shaking her head emphatically. "No one is hopeless, my lady," she said. "Though—if I may be candid—while people might enjoy a well-timed rock joke, perhaps we keep those to ourselves."

Dorothea's lips twitched, but it was quickly overtaken by a sudden sneeze that she barely managed to catch in her handkerchief. "Excuse me," she murmured, dabbing her nose. "I'm still fighting off this cold. It doesn't seem eager to leave me."

Mrs. Dawson immediately pushed up from her seat, her expression turning from amused to concerned. "You need tea," she declared. "A nice strong brew with a generous spoonful of honey. Maybe even a slice of lemon."

"The doctor already gave me something," Dorothea replied. "A little laudanum, just to help me sleep. I might pour a bit into my tea and head to bed early tonight."

Mrs. Dawson paused, glancing pointedly at the barely touched bowl on the table. "You should eat something first. You'll need strength if you're feeling unwell."

"I appreciate the thought," Dorothea said, "but I'm not hungry."

With a frown creasing her brow, Mrs. Dawson stepped closer and pressed the back of her hand gently to Dorothea's forehead. "You're a little warm," she said. "Not feverish, but warm enough to worry me. Should I fetch the doctor?"

"That won't be necessary, truly. But I thank you for your concern."

Mrs. Cameron spoke up. "I'll send a servant up to your bedchamber to light a fire. The last thing you need is to catch a chill on top of that cold."

Dorothea pushed back her chair and rose. Her body felt heavier than usual, the exhaustion not just physical but emotional. "I'll be fine. I think I just need more sleep than usual."

Mrs. Dawson nodded with a sigh of acceptance. "Very well. I'll see that the tea is brought up to your room straightaway. With honey. And no rock jokes," she added with a wink.

"Thank you," Dorothea responded. She glanced around the kitchen, the warmth of the hearth and the fading clatter of earlier activity lingering like the memory of a conversation. "And I'm sorry about dinner."

Mrs. Dawson waved her hand dismissively. "Oh, pish-posh. Don't trouble yourself. The staff will be positively thrilled to enjoy such a fine spread. Nothing here will go to waste, I assure you."

Dorothea managed a genuine smile then, touched by the kindness that surrounded her. "I appreciate you," she said, looking between them. "Both of you."

Mrs. Dawson lightly touched Dorothea's sleeve. "Before you go," she started in a conspiratorial whisper, "do ask Lord Warwicke if he has a favorite chicken."

Mrs. Cameron let out an exasperated huff. "Good heavens, Mrs. Dawson. I truly doubt Lord Warwicke has even noticed the chickens."

Dorothea let out a genuine laugh, the first in what felt like days. "Goodnight," she said, then turned towards the hall, the warmth of the kitchen following her into the shadows beyond.

The sun had long since dipped below the horizon as Dominic stood before a heavy oak door, his hand suspended midair, knuckles poised to knock—but unmoving.

He stared at the door, willing himself to act, yet something held him back. Why had he come here? What was he hoping to hear?

Before he could summon the courage, the door swung open with a creak. His uncle, tall and white-haired with a few black streaks, stood on the threshold.

"Did you intend to knock at some point," he asked dryly, "or simply haunt my doorstep like a brooding ghost?"

Dominic let his hand fall to his side, offering a wry half-smile. "I was debating."

The older man's mouth lifted at one corner, deepening the creases in his wrinkled face. "Come in, then. You look like a man in desperate need of a strong drink and sturdier counsel."

Dominic stepped inside. He followed his uncle down the dim corridor, past portraits of long-gone ancestors, and into the study—warmly lit and cluttered with books and old maps.

Without a word, his uncle made his way to the drink tray, decanter in hand, and poured two generous glasses of brandy. "So..." he said, the word stretching out in the silence. "I heard you got yourself married."

There was amusement in his voice, a flicker of mischief behind his eyes, as though Dominic's marriage were some grand joke at the end of a long tale.

"I did," Dominic replied simply.

His uncle crossed the room and handed him a glass. "And here I thought you were determined to die a bachelor. A noble recluse—so tragic, so misunderstood."

Dominic took the glass and offered a half-hearted chuckle. "Things change."

"Not that much, in my experience." His uncle gestured to the two wingback chairs near the fireplace, where flames crackled softly behind a brass screen. "Come. Sit."

Dominic settled into the chair, the leather creaking beneath him. He took a sip, letting the brandy burn its way down his throat. "I married Haverleigh's daughter," he said after a pause.

His uncle's eyebrows rose with interest. "Haverleigh? As in your former commanding officer?"

"The very one."

"Well," his uncle drawled, swirling his drink, "that's bold. Even for you."

Dominic sighed, rubbing the bridge of his nose. "To be honest, I don't recall every detail of how it happened. But regardless, I now have a wife. At least until I can get it annulled."

His uncle studied him over the rim of his glass, the lines of his face shifting into something more serious. "And how does your wife feel about this... plan?"

"She doesn't know," Dominic admitted.

There was a sharp cluck of disapproval as his uncle set his glass down on the nearby table. "Do you mean to tell her? Or shall she learn about it secondhand—perhaps in one of those delightfully cruel Society columns?"

Dominic looked into his drink, shoulders hunched. "I intend to tell her. But the timing has never felt... right."

His uncle gave a snort. "Timing rarely cooperates when it comes to the truth. Do you think it ever will?"

Dominic hesitated. "Dorothea is... she's kind. Considerate. Too good for me by far. I don't deserve her."

"And so," his uncle said, "your solution is to cast her aside? As a favor to her?"

Dominic met his gaze. "You don't understand. I'm not the man I used to be. I'm broken, Uncle. I wanted to die on the battlefield. And yet here I am. Alive. While braver, better men are buried in shallow graves far from home. How is that fair?"

"You fought. You bled. You survived," his uncle replied, his voice firm. "That is not a crime."

"I was wounded while my men fought valiantly around me. I fell, and then they fell. And still I was the one given a title—as if my sacrifice was somehow greater than theirs."

His uncle leaned forward, eyes steady. "You were given a second chance at life."

Dominic's jaw clenched. "I don't want it."

"Want it or not, it's yours," his uncle said, sitting back. "And with it comes responsibility. You must move forward and let go of the past."

"That's easy for you to say," Dominic snapped, his grip tightening around the glass. "You didn't see what I saw. You didn't hear the screaming, the endless gunfire, or the pleas of the dying men."

His uncle nodded solemnly. "You're right. I didn't. And I cannot pretend to understand that pain. But I do know you. You gave everything you had to your men. To your King and Country."

"Not everything," Dominic muttered.

His uncle's gaze sharpened. "Who, pray tell, are you angry with?"

There was a long pause before Dominic answered. "Myself."

His uncle exhaled, slow and deliberate. "You've been given much, Dominic. More than most. Don't waste it by clinging to what can't be changed. Embrace what you've been given. Go home. Go to your wife."

"I can't." The confession fell from his lips like a weight. "She smiles at me... and all I feel is guilt. Crushing, suffocating guilt."

His uncle leaned in, his voice gentler now. "Would it be so terrible to smile back?"

"Yes," Dominic said without hesitation. "Because it would give her hope."

"And what," his uncle started, "is so wrong with hope?"

Dominic drained the last of his brandy, his gaze fixed on the flames. "Hope is only for the foolish."

His uncle spread his arms. "Then you must consider me a

fool, Dominic. Because I still believe hope is one of the finest things a man can possess."

"I do not. I never have."

Leaning forward, his uncle picked up his glass and took a slow sip. "Your father was a cruel man."

"I know. You don't need to remind me since I lived through every moment of it."

"And yet," his uncle replied, setting his glass down with a click, "you've learned nothing."

Dominic stiffened in his chair, the words cutting deeper than he'd expected. "That's not true. I learned that I wanted to be nothing like him."

"As you should," his uncle agreed. "But despite your good intentions, your father still managed to take something from you. And you've never gotten it back."

Dominic glanced heavenward. "Let me guess. You're going to say he stole my 'hope.'"

A knowing look softened the lines of the older man's face. "I always said you were clever."

Dominic exhaled, frustrated. "Uncle, I know what you're doing. But I've already made my decision. I cannot—*will not*—be the cause of dimming the light in Dorothea's eyes. She doesn't deserve that. She doesn't deserve me. Staying married wouldn't be fair to her or to me."

"And what if the annulment doesn't come through? What then? What happens when Dorothea finds out she was never wanted?"

Dominic shifted in his seat, uncomfortable under the weight of the question. "She'll manage. I'll see to it she's provided for. She won't want for anything material."

"That's not the same as being wanted." His uncle held up a hand and pointed to the simple gold ring on his finger. "Have you ever noticed this?"

"Yes. You've worn it every day for as long as I can remember."

"I have," his uncle said, removing it and holding it out. "Because it holds a lock of Deborah's hair. I had it made after we wed. Do you know why?"

Dominic took the ring gently, turning it over in his hand. "Because you loved her."

His uncle's voice thickened with memory. "Yes. I loved her with every beat of my heart. But more than that, I wanted to keep some part of her with me. Always. It's the little things I miss most. The way she'd toss her hair over her shoulder in the mornings. The way she'd fall asleep at the opera, no matter how grand the production. Even how she'd chide me for reading the newssheets at breakfast. Her presence filled every corner of my life, and now, those corners feel empty."

Dominic could hear the pain in his uncle's voice. It was a pain that came from a love so deep that it didn't die with the person.

His uncle gave a sad smile. "Do you know when I really started to love Deborah?"

"Wasn't it from the moment you met her?"

His uncle chuckled. "Heavens, no. I thought she was an insufferable debutante, and she thought I was a rake and a bore. We argued constantly. Then one day, I realized... I didn't want to argue with anyone else, ever again. That's when I knew."

Dominic turned the ring between his fingers. "I'm glad you found her, Uncle."

"I tell you this," his uncle said, "because I know how hard your life has been. You've seen horrors most can't even imagine. But that doesn't mean you don't deserve love. You do. You deserve someone who sees the man you are now and loves you all the more for it."

"Uncle..."

He raised his hand to stop his nephew. "No. It's time, Dominic. Time to stop hiding behind walls of grief and guilt. Let someone in."

Dominic rose slowly and placed the ring on the table between them. "I'm sorry. But I can't."

His uncle picked up the ring and stared at it for a moment before slipping it back onto his finger. "Then it is I who is sorry."

"Goodnight, Uncle." Without another word, he turned and left the room.

His uncle had meant well, of that he was certain. But pity— he didn't need that. Nor did he need a lecture on love from someone who had stumbled into a perfect, enviable marriage. His uncle hadn't lived through blood-soaked fields and the unrelenting sounds of gunfire that still echoed in Dominic's ears like a phantom chorus. He hadn't watched his comrades fall one by one.

Outside, Dominic climbed into the waiting coach and sank into the velvet cushions. He stared out the window, watching as the city passed in shadows. No wife, no child could mend what had been shattered inside him. He was terribly, painfully aware of that. The emptiness was a constant companion—familiar, and oddly comforting.

By the time the coach pulled to a stop in front of his town-house, the streets were quiet. A servant opened the door, and Dominic climbed the steps with weary precision. Inside, the air was still. Silent. Just as he liked it.

It was only in the silence that he could breathe.

He ascended the staircase. As he stepped into his chamber and removed his jacket, he noticed something strange—smoke curling under the door that separated his room from Dorothea's.

His blood turned cold.

He rushed forward, unlocked the door, and flung it open. A

thick haze billowed into the room. Dorothea's bedchamber was clouded with smoke, the fire in the hearth roaring far too high.

Covering his mouth with his sleeve, he darted to the bed. "Dorothea!" he shouted, grabbing her shoulders and shaking her. "Wake up!"

She groaned faintly but didn't rouse.

The smoke stung his eyes and throat. Coughing, he gathered her into his arms and hurried back through the door into his own chamber. He laid her gently on the bed and turned for the hallway.

Throwing the door open, he shouted into the corridor. "Help! I need help—now!"

Within moments, Wright appeared, his hair mussed, eyes alert. "What is it, my lord?"

"Lady Warwicke's chamber is filled with smoke. The damper must have been left closed."

Wright nodded without hesitation. "I shall see to it immediately."

Relieved that someone would handle the fire, Dominic returned to Dorothea's side, kneeling beside the bed. "Dorothea," he said urgently, shaking her again. "I need you to wake up. Please."

She didn't move.

"Dorothea," he said again, louder now, a note of panic creeping in. "I command you to answer me!"

A voice from the doorway interrupted. "I believe she is not responding because she took laudanum for her cold, my lord."

He turned sharply to see Mrs. Cameron. "Do you think that's all it is?" he asked, heart pounding.

"I do," she replied.

Still, uncertainty gnawed at him. "Send for the doctor. At once."

With a curt nod, Mrs. Cameron turned to obey.

Left alone, Dominic sat on the edge of the bed and looked

down at Dorothea's pale face. He reached out, his fingers trembling slightly, and brushed a few strands of her red hair away from her forehead.

"Please wake up," he whispered, his voice breaking.

Not as a command.

Not as a husband.

Just as a man who suddenly realized how terrified he was to lose her.

D orothea stirred beneath the weight of warm blankets, her mind sluggish as though emerging from a thick fog. A dull ache lingered behind her eyes, and for a moment, she couldn't tell whether it was morning or night. The room was cloaked in shadow, with only the faintest sliver of light leaking through the drawn curtains.

Somewhere in the room, the clock chimed once, a hollow, echoing tone that made her blink. What time was it? How long had she been asleep?

Her lashes fluttered open, vision blurring slightly before focusing on the carved wood of a canopy overhead—one she didn't recognize. Panic bloomed quietly in her chest. This wasn't her bed. This wasn't her room.

She turned her head slowly. Just a few feet away, in a high-backed chair pushed against the wall, sat Dominic. His head lolled to one side, chin tilted upward as he slept, arms crossed loosely across his chest. His mouth hung slightly open, a soft snore rising and falling in the quiet.

Her anxiety eased, replaced with a kind of puzzled wonder. Her eyes wandered around the room and she realized that she was in his bedchamber. She glanced down. She was tucked beneath a thick coverlet, dressed in her night-gown. Nothing seemed amiss, and yet she remembered none of it.

What had happened last night?

Then it struck her—laudanum. She'd taken it to ease the lingering cold. It always sent her into an unnaturally deep sleep, but this time it must have dulled her awareness entirely.

Still, she felt better. Her head was clearer, her limbs lighter. The congestion was gone. She was herself again. Almost.

Her gaze drifted back to Dominic, watching the gentle rise and fall of his chest. He looked so peaceful in sleep, far from the guarded, distant man he often became in her presence. For a fleeting moment, she considered letting him rest. But ques-tions burned in her mind, and he was the only one who could answer them.

"Dominic," she called out, her voice little more than a whisper.

He stirred, a slight twitch of his shoulders, before his eyes fluttered open. He blinked as though unsure of where he was, then locked eyes with her.

"You're awake," he said, the disbelief clear in his voice. He leaned forward, eyes searching hers as though needing to confirm it wasn't a dream.

"I am," she replied. "But I don't understand. What happened last night?"

Rubbing a hand through his tousled hair, Dominic looked away briefly, as if gathering the right words. "The maid... she forgot to open the damper before lighting the fire in your room. By the time I noticed the smoke, it had filled the chamber. You were sound asleep. You didn't even stir when I called your name."

"I had taken laudanum," she explained. "For my cold."

"I was told as much," he said with a nod. "But in the

moment"—his voice caught slightly—"I was terrified. You weren't responding. I thought you might never wake up."

A small smile curved her lips as she attempted to lighten the situation. "Well, you're stuck with me. I'm not so easy to get rid of."

Dominic didn't smile. His gaze was heavy with emotion—guilt, perhaps, or something even more difficult to name. "That's not the least bit funny," he murmured. "I thought I'd lost you."

He stood abruptly, as though the moment had grown too intimate. "I should fetch the doctor. He'll want to examine you."

"The doctor is here?"

"Yes. I sent for him last night. Everyone's been waiting for you to wake."

She looked towards the clock on the mantel. "What time is it?"

He followed her gaze. "Almost noon."

Her brows shot up. "I've slept half the day away. I'm so sorry —I didn't mean to worry anyone."

Dominic returned to his chair but didn't sit. Instead, he rested a hand on the bedpost and studied her. "There's nothing to apologize for. I'm just relieved you're all right."

The gentleness in his tone caught her off guard. It was the same tone he'd used the day before in the gardens—the one that made her feel seen.

"Thank you," she said softly. "For saving me... again."

A trace of a smile touched his lips. "I will always save you."

She held his gaze, her breath catching at the sincerity in his words. "I know." And she meant it. She trusted him in a way she didn't entirely understand.

Something shifted in that silence. Something unspoken but unmistakable. The air between them seemed to hum, charged with emotion neither of them dared voice.

A knock interrupted the moment, and the door creaked

open to reveal Mrs. Cameron. Her eyes immediately softened when she saw Dorothea awake.

"My lady," she breathed, stepping into the room. "Thank heavens. The entire household has been beside itself with worry."

"I'm sorry," Dorothea said, flushing with guilt. "I didn't mean to frighten everyone."

"Oh, pish-posh." Mrs. Cameron waved a hand. "You've done no such thing. Though I should tell you that Sally has been dismissed for her carelessness. She claimed she didn't realize the damper was closed."

Dorothea's brows drew together as she began to sit up. Dominic was at her side in an instant, placing a steadying hand on her back.

"Careful," he said.

She gave him a grateful glance before turning back to the housekeeper. "I don't want her dismissed. It was an accident."

Mrs. Cameron didn't look convinced. "A rather dangerous one. You could have died."

"Which is why I think reassignment is fair," Dorothea said. "She should not be punished so harshly for one mistake."

Mrs. Cameron hesitated, then sighed. "Very well. You're too kind for your own good, my lady. But I'll see to it."

Dominic reached for a pillow and placed it behind her. "You should rest a while longer."

Dorothea gave him a mock glare. "I'm not an invalid, you know."

Instead of arguing, Dominic only smiled. "I know. But even the strongest need time to recover."

She studied him for a moment, warmed by his attention. It felt nice to have someone fuss over her. Especially him.

"Very well," she relented, leaning back into the pillows. "But only because you asked so nicely."

"Mrs. Cameron," he said, turning towards the housekeeper,

"inform Doctor Taylor at once that Lady Warwicke is awake. He'll want to examine her."

Mrs. Cameron dipped her head with brisk efficiency. "Yes, my lord," she said. Without another word, she exited the chamber, her footsteps fading as the door clicked shut behind her.

Silence settled briefly over the room.

Dorothea shifted slightly beneath the blankets, her gaze drifting towards the adjoining door that led back to her own bedchamber. "Should I return to my room now?"

"That would not be wise. Your bedchamber still reeks of smoke. The windows are open, but it needs more time to be properly aired out."

"Oh," she said, then looked up at him, uncertain. "Then where am I to sleep?"

"In here."

Her eyes widened, startled by the suggestion. "With... you?"

Dominic's mouth twitched, almost—but not quite—a smile. "No," he replied. "I had one of the guest rooms prepared for me earlier this morning. I'll be sleeping there for the time being."

Dorothea hesitated, staring at him. Her heart beat a little faster, her fingers nervously curling against the blanket. Then, with a steadiness she didn't quite feel, she asked, "Would it be so terrible if we... shared a bedchamber?"

Dominic's jaw visibly clenched. His eyes dropped from hers, his face tightening with something she couldn't quite decipher.

"I..." He drew in a breath, as if bracing himself. "It would be, considering I'm seeking—"

The door opened abruptly, halting his words mid-sentence.

A short man stepped into the room, his blond hair neatly combed and spectacles perched on the bridge of his nose. He carried a well-worn leather bag in one hand.

"Lady Warwicke," he greeted, crossing the threshold with purposeful steps. "I'm Doctor Taylor. I understand you've given everyone quite a scare. How are you feeling?"

Dorothea offered him a polite smile. "Much better, thank you. I slept deeply and seem to have recovered from my cold."

Dominic took a step back from the bed. "I should go," he murmured, avoiding her gaze.

Doctor Taylor glanced at him over his spectacles. "You're more than welcome to remain, my lord. The examination will be brief."

Dominic shook his head. "I have work that requires my attention that I've put off long enough."

Doctor Taylor gave a nod of understanding and set his bag at the foot of the bed, unlatching it with the practiced ease of a man who had done so a thousand times. "As you wish. I assure you, I'll take excellent care of Lady Warwicke. You've nothing to be concerned about."

Dominic turned to her then and there was something vulnerable in his expression. The way he looked at her was raw and unguarded.

"Rest, Dorothea." He lifted his hand, almost touching her arm—then stopped. His fingers hovered for a breath, then fell silently to his side. "I will return shortly."

And just like that, he turned and strode from the room, the door closing behind him.

Dorothea stared at the place where he'd stood, her heart twisting. Despite everything he tried to hide... he did care. She just didn't know if he would ever let himself show it.

———————⌒〰⌒———————

Dominic sat alone in the shadowed corner of White's, a glass clutched tightly in his hand. Around him, the club buzzed with its usual polite murmur of conversation, the clinking of glasses, and the occasional burst of restrained laughter. But he heard none of it. His thoughts crowded out every sound, every distraction.

Dorothea had nearly died.

If he had arrived just a few minutes later... he couldn't finish the thought. It twisted in his chest like a blade.

He cared for her. Of course he did. That wasn't the question. The problem was that his feelings didn't matter. This was about keeping her safe. He had made his decision for her benefit. She deserved freedom. A life unmarred by a broken man.

So why, then, was he beginning to question everything?

No.

He shook his head and took a long sip of brandy. The annulment was the only way forward. It was what he'd decided from the start. She would understand eventually. Given time, perhaps she would remarry someone capable of giving her the future she deserved. Happiness, security, maybe even a family.

The thought of her being with another man made his stomach turn.

A voice, loud and entirely too cheerful, broke through his musings. "Isn't it a bit early in the day to be drinking, even for you?"

Dominic didn't bother to look up. "Go away, Bedford."

Bedford ignored the warning and dropped into the chair opposite him, still grinning. "And miss an opportunity to be insulted before my midday meal? I wouldn't dream of it."

A second, more apologetic voice joined the conversation. "I'm sorry, Warwicke. My wife insisted I bring him with me."

Dominic looked over and gave Lord Westcott a nod. "You're welcome here. Bedford... not so much."

Bedford placed a hand over his heart. "I didn't realize you cared so deeply."

Westcott sat down with a sigh. "You look troubled, Warwicke."

Bedford raised a brow. "Troubled? His face always looks that way. Like he's contemplating murder."

"And yet you remain seated across from me," Dominic said dryly.

"Because I'm an excellent listener," Bedford replied, unbothered. "And modest, too. One of my many virtues."

Dominic looked heavenward. "Don't you have somewhere else—*anywhere* else—you could be?"

Bedford leaned back, folding his hands behind his head. "Not a one."

Westcott cast a long-suffering look at him. "You'll have to forgive Bedford. He's my wife's cousin. I'm obligated to tolerate him."

"This is you being tolerant?" Bedford asked.

Dominic downed the remainder of his drink and stood. "Good day, gentlemen."

"No, don't go," Westcott said, leaning forward. "I'll make Bedford promise to behave. Sit. Tell us what's weighing on your mind."

Dominic hesitated. A part of him wanted nothing more than to be alone. But another part—the quieter, more uncertain part—wanted to say it aloud. To speak the thing he had been dwelling on since last night.

"I'll stay," he said, slowly returning to his seat. "Assuming Bedford doesn't say anything intolerably stupid."

"He most absolutely will," Westcott assured him. "Just by opening his mouth."

"Hurtful, but also accurate," Bedford said with a smile.

Westcott glanced at Dominic. "What happened?"

Dominic stared into his empty glass. "Dorothea nearly died last night."

That silenced them both.

Westcott straightened, concern etched onto his features. "What do you mean?"

"A maid lit a fire in her room but forgot to open the damper. I found her unconscious, the room filled with smoke," Dominic shared.

Bedford's humor vanished. "Is she all right?"

"She is now," Dominic replied. "Doctor Taylor was examining her when I left. But I couldn't stay there any longer. I felt like I couldn't breathe." He paused. "She was asleep. Peaceful. And all I could think about was what would've happened if I hadn't come home when I did."

Westcott gave a slow nod. "I am glad that you found her when you did."

Dominic's jaw tensed, the muscle near his ear twitching as he fought to contain his emotions. "I keep replaying it in my head. The what-ifs. The smoke. Her not waking up."

Westcott leaned in slightly. "Are you still planning to go through with the annulment?"

"I never said I wasn't."

"No," Westcott agreed. "But your face says otherwise."

Dominic gave a bitter laugh. "I care for her. Enough to let her go."

Bedford furrowed his brow. "That's absurd. Why is it you're allowed to say completely ridiculous things and I get scolded for it?"

Dominic shot him a look. "Because you enjoy being irritating."

"Guilty as charged," Bedford responded.

Westcott exhaled and looked at Dominic. "Have you even bothered to ask Dorothea what she wants?"

"I've tried," Dominic admitted. "But I keep getting interrupted."

"Try harder," Westcott said. "Have you considered she might want to stay married to you?"

"Please," Bedford said, raising a hand. "We all know she can't be happy. She's married to Warwicke."

Dominic turned to him, his lips pursed. "I might shoot you."

"If you do, you'll end up in Newgate," Bedford replied with a shrug.

"It's a risk I'm willing to take."

Westcott waved a hand, exasperated. "No one is shooting anyone. The point is—Dominic, you clearly care about her. Deeply."

Dominic's voice lowered. "I do care. But that doesn't mean I have feelings for her. That is a vast difference."

Westcott leaned back, studying him carefully. "You say her name like she's the only thing that matters to you."

"I do?" Dominic asked.

"Well, well, well," Bedford said. "Perhaps I am not the stupidest man in the room."

Dominic groaned. "You just insulted yourself."

"I know," Bedford replied with a smug expression. "It was worth it."

Rising, Dominic said, "I do believe I've had more than my fill of Bedford for one day."

"He's an acquired taste," Westcott remarked dryly.

As he turned towards the exit, Lord Inglewood stepped into his path. "Warwicke," he said. "Fortune must favor me, for I'd hoped to run into you."

Dominic stilled, his expression carefully neutral as he offered a stiff nod. "Inglewood."

The older man's eyes narrowed slightly, a calculating glint dancing just beneath the surface of his smile. "I wanted to speak with you regarding the upcoming vote. I trust I can count on your support for my bill?"

Dominic kept his voice carefully composed. "I haven't yet decided. I intend to read the bill in full before I come to any conclusions."

Inglewood waved a dismissive hand. "A waste of your time."

"Let me be the judge of that." Dominic went to brush past him, but Inglewood reached out and clasped his arm, halting him.

"I thought we had an understanding," Inglewood said, his voice lowering. "I assist you, and in return, you back my bill. That was the arrangement."

Dominic pulled his arm free. "I don't make promises in the dark. If I vote for your bill, it will be because I believe it serves England and the people—not because of some backroom bargain."

Inglewood adjusted the lapels of his coat, his jaw twitching with irritation. "My bill will benefit everyone. Especially the soldiers."

From behind, Westcott cleared his throat—loudly and pointedly. "Not quite," he murmured, just enough to be heard.

Inglewood turned with slow deliberation. "Something to say, Westcott?"

Westcott didn't flinch. "Raising tariffs on imported goods will do more harm than good. You know that. If those countries retaliate with their own tariffs, we'll be facing a full-blown trade war."

"They'd be fools to do so," Inglewood remarked.

"And yet, nations do foolish things all the time," Westcott countered, folding his arms. "We're already seeing price instability. Escalating the issue would only hurt the poor."

Inglewood lifted his chin. "England's economy is strong. It would recover swiftly from any such skirmish."

"Perhaps," Westcott allowed, "but what about those who can't afford to wait for the economy to bounce back?"

Bedford, who'd been watching the exchange with an unusually serious expression, finally joined in. "What about the poor, Inglewood? They are already struggling to put food on the table. They won't be able to afford the additional costs."

"They'll adjust. They always do," Inglewood said, turning

back towards Dominic. "Tell me, Warwicke—do you still want that annulment?"

"I do," he replied.

Inglewood smiled, thin and cold. "Then you'll need allies in Parliament. My backing would go a long way. But as you surely understand... support doesn't come without a cost."

Before Dominic could answer, Inglewood pivoted smoothly and strolled away, threading between the tables with the arrogance of a man certain he'd left his mark.

Bedford gave an exaggerated shudder. "Every time I speak to Inglewood, I feel like I need a bath. Possibly two."

Dominic didn't respond. Instead, his eyes remained fixed on the door through which Inglewood had vanished. Why did it feel like he had just danced with the devil?

10

Dorothea reclined against a stack of pillows, a book balanced in one hand and a half-eaten biscuit in the other. Sunlight poured through the open windows and she could hear the birds chirping a cheerful tune. It was, she decided, a perfectly pleasant way to pass the afternoon. There had certainly been worse days in her life.

A soft knock disrupted the peaceful quiet.

Her gaze lifted from the page. "Enter," she ordered.

The door opened slowly, and Dominic appeared in the doorway, hovering like a man unsure whether to flee or step forward. He looked deucedly uncomfortable, shoulders taut, his hand still resting on the doorframe.

She smiled, feeling a need to tease him. "You do not need to knock. This is your bedchamber, after all."

"Not for the time being," he replied. "Are you well?"

She nodded. "Very much so. The physician declared me the epitome of health. Even the cold has passed."

"I'm glad to hear it." He hesitated, as though unsure how to continue. "Do you need anything—anything at all?"

"I wouldn't say no to a bit of company."

For a moment, she feared he might retreat, offering some vague excuse and disappearing down the hall. But instead, to her surprise—and delight—he stepped into the room and let the door close softly behind him.

"I suppose I can spare a few moments," he said, walking towards the chair beside her bed.

"Thank you," she responded, setting her book aside. "Perhaps you can regale me with a story or two."

That earned the faintest curve of a smile. "I'm not much of a storyteller," he said, lowering himself into the chair. "But I can read to you, if you like."

"Or you could tell me one from memory. Surely you had some memorable cases when you worked for Bow Street."

His expression shifted, something flickering in his gaze. "I did."

"Well then—will you share one with me?"

He paused, as if weighing how much to say, then gave a small nod. "There was one case that stayed with me. A series of thefts in Mayfair, all occurring during lavish social events. I was asked to investigate after it became clear that the incidents were more than mere coincidence."

"Was it the butler?" she asked, her tone teasing.

He grinned. "No. It was a young maid. She'd stolen a gown from her mistress and used it to pass herself off as a lady. She blended seamlessly with the crowd—dripping in stolen jewels, no one ever questioned her presence. During the height of each ball, she'd slip away and pilfer whatever valuables she could find."

"How clever. How did you catch her?"

"I recognized a necklace she was wearing—one that had been listed among the stolen items weeks earlier. I kept my distance and followed her when she left the ballroom. I caught her red-handed in an upstairs chamber."

"And what happened to her?"

"I arrested her. She was transported for her crimes," he said, his voice sober. "Frankly, she was lucky to escape the noose. The value of the stolen items was staggering and not everything was ever recovered. I suspected she had help, but she refused to reveal who it was."

Dorothea popped the last bit of biscuit into her mouth and brushed the crumbs from her fingers. "It sounds like dangerous work. But thrilling, too."

He shrugged, eyes distant. "It had its moments."

She considered him for a moment, then ventured, "May I ask you something?"

"That depends on what it is."

Taking a deep breath, she asked, "What happened to you after... after you were carted off with the dead?"

He visibly tensed. The warmth drained from his face, replaced by a shadow that darkened his features. "It doesn't matter."

"But I want to know," she prodded. "How did you survive?"

He turned his face away. "It matters not. What matters is that I did survive."

"Dominic—"

He raised a hand, cutting her off. "I should go."

Her heart dropped. "Please don't," she said. "I didn't mean to upset you."

"You have no right to ask me such questions," he responded gruffly.

The words stung. "No right?" she repeated, her voice rising slightly. "I am your wife. Or does that mean nothing to you?"

"I don't want to dwell in the past."

"Then let me in," she pleaded. "Let me understand. Let me *see* you."

His expression softened—just barely. "I can't. I'm sorry."

"You used to trust me," she whispered. "You once told me

about your father. How he treated you... even the time he shot your dog on the hunting trip."

His head jerked slightly. "I told you that?"

"You did," she said. "Among other things. You were quite talkative when the laudanum first took effect."

He stared at her, wary. "What else did I say?"

"You showed me the scars. The ones he left behind."

Dominic inhaled sharply. "I did?"

She nodded. "But I know there are others—ones no one can see."

He lifted a hand and touched the jagged scar on his cheek. "Scars are reminders of our past."

"They are also proof that we survived," she said. "That we lived through the worst and came out the other side."

His gaze lingered on her, thoughtful now. "What scars do you bear?"

She gave him a weak smile. "More than I care to admit."

He moved to the chair beside her once more, this time lowering himself slowly. "I'm sorry. I wish I could take them from you."

"I don't," she said. "They're part of me now. They remind me that the hurt is over, and I came out the other end stronger than before."

Dominic leaned forward. "People see this," he said, motioning to his face. "But they don't see the rest."

"Do you want to know what I see when I look at you?"

He met her gaze, wary but curious. Then, he nodded.

She shifted to the edge of the bed, reached out slowly, and traced the scar on his cheek with gentle fingers. "I see a man who survived what others could not. A man who protected the helpless. A man who feels deeply, even if he tries to pretend otherwise. I see strength. I see kindness."

He looked away. "I'm no such man."

"You are," she insisted. "You are my hero."

At those words, he reared back. "I am no hero, Dorothea. I'm just a man."

She saw the anguish in his eyes, but she had to tell him what she felt. "I disagree."

He stood abruptly and began pacing. "I am not the man you think I am. You cling to some ideal, some imagined version of me. You hope for things that are not there."

Dorothea sat still on the bed, watching him. "No, Dominic," she insisted. "I see what is there. You just haven't let yourself believe it yet."

"I shouldn't even be alive," Dominic said. "If I had my wish, I would've died alongside my comrades."

The way he said it, with such raw honesty, left no doubt in her mind that he meant every word. "I'm glad you didn't," she said, rising from the bed. Her voice trembled with feeling. "My life is better because you are in it."

He halted mid-step, turning to face her, his expression twisted with disbelief. "You don't mean that."

"I do," she insisted, stepping towards him. "With my whole heart."

He looked as if her words pained him more than they soothed. "No... I can't accept that."

"You can accept it or not, but it does not change how I feel."

He shook his head. "I know you mean well, but you're wrong. You would be better off without me."

Her heart clenched at the sincerity in his tone. "How can you say such a thing?"

"Because it's true," he said, voice growing tight with emotion. "I will never be the man you want me to be. I don't even know if that man ever existed in the first place. Perhaps I was just playing a part, wearing a mask even I didn't know I had on."

Dorothea's feet moved before her thoughts could catch up. She crossed the distance between them, standing before him in her bare feet. "I know he existed. Because he's standing right here."

Dominic turned his face away. "Dorothea... you don't understand."

"I do," she whispered. "More than you think. And did you honestly believe I only married you for your wealth?" Her voice caught, her brows drawing together with hurt. "If that's what you believe, then you never truly saw me."

He closed his eyes for a moment. "Then why?" he asked, barely above a whisper. "Why would you bind yourself to someone like me?"

She took another step forward, close enough now to reach for him, but she didn't. Not yet. "Because even when you were gone, even when I believed you were lost to the war, I wanted to remain tied to your memory. I wanted to honor the man you were and the man I still see."

"You wanted to be tied to a failure?" he murmured, his voice cracking.

She waited for him to meet her gaze before saying, "You are no failure, Dominic."

He gave a hollow laugh. "Why? Because the king granted me a title and called me a hero?"

"No," she said, her voice growing fiercer. "Because I was there. I saw you. Even when you were too weak to lift your head from the pillow, you asked about your men—each one—by name. You mourned them. You grieved them as if they were your own brothers."

She continued, hoping her words gave him a semblance of peace. "You saved lives. You gave them someone to follow. You gave them a reason to hope, even in the blood-soaked chaos. That's what makes you a hero—not what the king said, not what Society thinks. But who you were when no one was watching."

Dominic stood there, breathing raggedly, studying her.

What he saw, she did not know. But she had to say one more thing. "I see you, Dominic," she whispered. "Even when you try to disappear."

―――――――――――――

Dominic stood frozen in place, unable to summon a single word. What could he possibly say to the woman standing before him, her gaze full of trust and tenderness, as though she truly believed he could be more than what he was? He could see it in her eyes—that unwavering hope—and it gutted him. He knew, with a grim certainty, that he would only disappoint her in the end.

A part of him—a quiet, desperate part—wanted to be the man she saw. But that part had been buried beneath the weight of all he had endured. What he had endured on the battlefield had taken so much from him.

They stood so close. Just one step, one motion, and she would be in his arms. Would she welcome his touch?

He couldn't chance it. Not for her sake. And not for his.

It was safer to walk away, to maintain the distance he had so carefully preserved between them. Because if he let that wall fall, he wasn't sure he'd be able to rebuild it. And once Dorothea was let in—truly in—he feared there would be no turning back.

But still... he looked at her. Held her gaze and felt himself unraveling, bit by bit. He got lost in her eyes, and he found himself wishing, irrationally, that he could remain there forever.

A small furrow formed between her brows. "Dominic," she murmured.

The sound of his name on her lips—so soft, so filled with care—cracked something open inside him. He realized, then, that his feelings for her were no longer fleeting or fragile. They had taken hold deep in his chest.

And that terrified him more than anything else.

He took a step back, severing the space between them. "I should go."

He didn't miss the flash of disappointment that passed over her face, nor the way her posture subtly wilted. "Please don't," she said, her voice scarcely more than a whisper.

"I must," he replied, struggling to keep his voice even. "Besides, you need rest. I'll have the cook send up more biscuits for you."

"Thank you."

He glanced towards the adjoining door between their chambers. "Wright mentioned your room has been thoroughly cleaned and aired out. It's safe for you to return now."

"I shall do so at once," she said, her gaze dropping to the floorboards.

He lingered for a moment longer, torn between guilt and restraint. Part of him longed to close the distance again, to apologize, to say anything that would wipe away the sadness in her voice. But what she needed from him, he wasn't ready to give.

"I'll be dining at the club again tonight," he added.

"Very well."

Her tone was polite, measured. But the sadness was unmistakable, and it hollowed him out to hear it, knowing he was the reason behind it.

"Good day, Dorothea."

He turned to leave as she said, "Goodbye, Dominic."

The word *goodbye* settled heavily on his shoulders. He didn't stop walking. It wasn't until he reached the entry hall that he saw Wright approaching from the far end.

"Mr. Wells is here to see you, my lord," the butler informed him. "He's waiting in your study."

"Thank you." Dominic moved to continue on, but paused.

"Would you see that more biscuits are delivered to Lady Warwicke's chamber? And... perhaps some flowers as well. Something bright. Cheerful."

Wright inclined his head. "At once, my lord."

With a nod of appreciation, Dominic turned and strode towards the study. The door was already ajar, and as he stepped inside, he found Mr. Wells standing at the center of the room, a well-worn satchel clutched in one hand.

"Good afternoon, Mr. Wells," Dominic said, making his way to the desk.

The solicitor gave a respectful nod. "Good afternoon, my lord. I looked into the matter we discussed."

Now, Mr. Wells had his full attention. "And what did you discover?"

Mr. Wells crossed the room and set the satchel down on the settee before removing a small stack of documents. "The stipends you arranged for Lady Warwicke were never received by her directly. They were deposited into an account controlled by her brother. There is no record of your wife ever being made aware of the source of those funds."

Dominic's jaw clenched. "As I suspected. Her own brother was stealing from her."

"It appears so," Wells confirmed. "Moreover, I attempted to speak with Mr. Haverleigh regarding his sister's dowry. He claims she was not given one."

Dominic raised a brow. "Dorothea has no dowry?"

"I'm still attempting to verify the truth of that claim," Wells said. "But Mr. Haverleigh has not been forthcoming, and complicating matters further—the late Lieutenant-Colonel Haverleigh's will is not filed with the probate court."

Dominic sat behind his desk, frowning. "That seems... unlikely. A man of his rank and discipline would not have left his affairs in disarray."

"I thought the same thing so I made some inquiries," Wells

agreed. "He did, in fact, file a will years ago, but it was with-drawn from the probate court. Most likely in preparation for a new will to be filed. Which never was."

Mr. Wells continued. "I decided to press further and contact the solicitor who once served both the lieutenant-colonel and his son, but unfortunately, Mr. Poole passed right after the late Mr. Haverleigh went off to war. Sudden illness, from what I was told."

Dominic's brow furrowed. "Was there any suspicion of foul play?"

"The coroner ruled it a natural death. A cold that progressed rapidly. The family said he worsened over the course of a week until he succumbed."

Dominic exhaled slowly. "Unfortunate timing."

"Indeed," Wells replied. "Without a will or a surviving solic-itor, it may be difficult to prove any claim or discrepancy regarding your wife's inheritance."

Dominic tapped his fingers restlessly against the desk's edge. "Someone must know something. That man would not have left his daughter's future to chance."

"Agreed," Wells said, taking a seat across from him. "Have you considered asking your wife? She may know if her father discussed the matter or left any indication."

Dominic hesitated. "I could. But I do not want her to know I am investigating her brother—not until I have proof."

"I do understand the need for discretion, my lord," Mr. Wells said. "You have my word that I'll continue looking into the matter. Rest assured, I will leave no stone unturned."

"Thank you. I know I can rely on your thoroughness."

The solicitor rose from his chair. "I'll be in touch the moment I uncover anything of significance."

With that, Mr. Wells offered a polite bow and exited the study, leaving Dominic alone. He had barely turned back to his desk when a voice carried in from the open window.

"Can I visit Lady Warwicke now?" Tristan asked.

Dominic turned towards the window. "No, she's resting at the moment."

A dramatic sigh echoed up from the boy. "Your house is boring without Lady Warwicke. She makes everything more fun."

Dominic couldn't suppress a smile. "My sincerest apologies that my household staff cannot amuse you."

Tristan boosted himself through the open window. "They try, but it's not the same. Lady Warwicke tells me jokes. Do you know any jokes?"

"I'm afraid not."

Tristan gave him a hopeful look. "Could I at least have more biscuits? The maid said I'd ruin my supper, but I think she just wanted to keep them for herself."

"I suspect the maid was exercising sound judgment."

Tristan's shoulders sagged. "I'm always hungry," he muttered, clearly displeased with the ruling. "Will you fly my kite with me, then?"

Dominic's gaze drifted to the ledger he'd just opened, the columns of numbers blurring slightly as guilt tugged at his conscience. "I have a great deal of work to finish, Tristan. Where is the maid I asked to watch over you?"

"We're playing hide and seek," the boy announced. "She's not very good at finding me."

Dominic gave him an amused look. "And are you making it easy on her?"

Tristan's grin turned sly. "Not even a little," he admitted with obvious pride. "Can we visit my mum today?"

Dominic looked at the eager little face turned up towards him, the boy's eyes so open—so full of hope. A tightness seized in his chest. "Not today," he said.

The light in Tristan's expression dimmed. "Then maybe tomorrow?"

Dominic's gaze shifted to the waiting stack of correspondence, the ledger still spread open, and the ever-growing list of responsibilities tied to his title. But none of it seemed to matter as much as the boy standing before him.

"Yes," he said at last. "Tomorrow. I promise."

Tristan's smile returned in full force, wide and triumphant.

Just then, a voice called from outside—faint, but unmistakable. "Tristan!"

Tristan's head jerked towards the sound, and he immediately dropped beneath the windowsill. Pressing a finger to his lips, he looked up at Dominic with wide eyes. "Shhh," he whispered.

A shadow passed back and forth from just outside of the window. Finally, the voice grew much more distant.

"I think she finally gave up," Tristan whispered, rising from his crouch.

Dominic leaned back in his chair and asked, "Why don't you go find something to read in the library?"

Tristan let out a dramatic groan. "Do I have to?"

"I believe it's a more productive use of your time than evading my household staff," Dominic remarked. "And if you go now, I'll see to it that you're given an extra biscuit after supper."

Tristan tilted his head, clearly intrigued. "Can you make it two extra biscuits?"

Dominic allowed the corner of his mouth to lift. "I believe I can arrange that."

A broad smile spread across Tristan's face. "Very well. I shall be in the library until supper," he declared before skipping towards the door.

Just as he reached the threshold, a flustered voice rang out from the window. "*Tristan! I see you!*"

Dominic turned just in time to glimpse a young maid's

flushed face peering through the open window, her cheeks puffed in exasperation.

Tristan glanced over his shoulder and laughed, utterly unrepentant. "Too late!" he called back, disappearing into the corridor with a gleeful whoop.

The maid sighed. "That boy will be the death of me," she muttered before withdrawing from view.

Dominic turned his attention towards his ledgers and figured it was as good a time as any to get some work done.

11

T he moon hung high in the sky, casting a pale silver glow through the curtains of Dorothea's bedchamber. She lay on her back, unmoving, eyes fixed on the canopy above. Sleep had evaded her completely.

She had been lying awake for hours now, ever since her conversation with Dominic earlier that evening. For one breathless moment, she had believed she had reached him—that the armor he wore so tightly around his heart had cracked, just a little. But true to form, he had withdrawn again, shuttering his thoughts behind those guarded eyes and carefully measured words.

Her thoughts circled back again and again, looping like a melody she couldn't silence. She clutched the blanket tighter to her chest, her senses still haunted by the faint smell of smoke lingering in the air. It was a stubborn reminder of how close to death she had come. How Dominic had risked his life to save hers.

How could she not feel something for him after that?

But it wasn't just gratitude. She knew it, deep down. She had fallen in love with Dominic long before the fire—back when they were on the Continent, side by side in that dim, makeshift hospital. In those endless hours of shared silence and whispered confidences, something in her had changed. He had become more than a wounded soldier. He had become... hers.

The mantel clock chimed once, then again, breaking the silence of the room and marking the slow approach of dawn. She turned towards the sound with a sigh, aware she would greet the morning unrested once more.

A sudden noise cut through the stillness. It was a muffled cry, harsh and fractured. Dorothea sat upright, heart pounding. The sound had come from the adjoining bedchamber. Dominic's.

Then came another: a garbled shout, and the sound of something—perhaps a pillow—thudding against the floor.

She reached for her wrapper, shrugging it over her shoulders, and walked across the room. Her bare feet made little sound on the carpet as she approached the door that separated their rooms. Her fingers hesitated on the handle. Could she go in? It felt like an intrusion. But another shout shattered her uncertainty.

"No, John! No!"

Her breath caught. *John?*

Without further thought, she turned the handle and opened the door a fraction, peering into the dim space. The faint glow of embers in the hearth illuminated the figure of Dominic, twisted in the grip of a nightmare. His sheets were thrown aside, his brow slick with sweat, his fists clenching and unclenching as he thrashed against invisible demons.

"Dominic," she called out, stepping into the room.

She crossed to the bed and reached for him, placing a gentle hand on his shoulder.

In a flash, his hand shot out and closed around her wrist,

his grip tight. "What do you think you are doing in here?" he growled.

"You were having a nightmare," she said, struggling to keep her voice calm. "I thought it best to wake you before your shouting woke the entire household."

His grip didn't ease at once, but she saw the confusion in his eyes as he slowly surfaced from the dream. At last, his fingers loosened. "Oh," he muttered, as if disoriented.

In the quiet that followed, she noticed the ragged rhythm of his breathing and the way his chest heaved beneath his linen nightshirt.

"Are you all right?" she asked.

"No," he answered, the word clipped.

She glanced down. He was still holding her hand. "Who is John?" she asked carefully.

At once, Dominic stiffened. "No one you need to concern yourself with."

His curt dismissal stung more than she wished to admit. "Can I get you something?" she offered. "Perhaps a warm glass of milk?"

"I don't need milk," he snapped, his voice edged in frustration.

"Then what do you need?" she asked, not out of obligation, but because she truly wanted to know.

He sat up in bed, dragging a hand through his damp hair. "Nothing you can give me," he muttered.

Dorothea nodded, swallowing the ache in her throat. "I see," she whispered, though it wasn't the truth at all. She turned to leave.

"I'm sorry," Dominic said suddenly, his voice quieter. "I should be thanking you for waking me."

"No thanks are necessary," she replied, pausing at the doorway.

He studied her. "Did I wake you?"

She shook her head. "No. I was already awake."

"Couldn't sleep?"

She gave him a tired smile. "Sometimes my thoughts are too loud to ignore."

He let out a soft breath. "I understand that... more than I'd like."

She hesitated. "Well, I'll let you return to bed."

But as she reached for the door, his voice stopped her. "John was the one who saved me."

Turning back, she asked, "Pardon?"

Dominic's face was shadowed by memory. "John Cooper. He was in my unit. A good man. Better than most." He swallowed. "He's the reason I'm still alive."

"I'm afraid I never met him."

"I'm not surprised. He didn't take well to attention or praise. But when it mattered most, he was there." His voice grew rough. "I was broken, bleeding... certain I would die. And John found me. Carried me across the battlefield, even as bullets tore through the air."

"What happened to him?"

Dominic's eyes closed, and a muscle twitched in his jaw. "He died the next day in battle. A rocket exploded and he died instantly. Alone."

She stepped closer, instinctively reaching out. "You were wounded. You couldn't have helped him."

He opened his eyes, pain shining in their depths. "That doesn't matter. He saved me, and I wasn't there when he needed someone most."

There was no easy answer, no comfort that would erase the guilt etched in his voice. So Dorothea simply reached for his hand again. It was not to drag answers from him, but to offer what comfort she could.

"You're still here," she whispered. "And I'm grateful for that."

Dominic looked down at their joined hands and, for once, didn't let go. "Why is it fair that I am here but John is not?"

Dorothea's brows drew together in quiet sorrow. "I cannot say why," she said. "Some questions have no answers."

His gaze darkened as it dropped once more to their entwined fingers. "I was ready to die, but I was not prepared to live," he admitted. "How does one even go on after that?"

Still holding his hand, Dorothea eased herself down beside him on the edge of the bed. The mattress dipped beneath her weight, bringing her closer to him, close enough to see the exhaustion etched in every line of his face.

"You take one day at a time," she said. "And then another. You move forward—even when you don't think you can. Especially then."

"It's not that easy."

"No," she agreed. "It's not. It's never easy. But if you keep looking behind you—if you let yourself live in the past—you'll never see what's ahead. You'll never give yourself the chance to heal."

Dominic turned his face away, jaw clenched. "How do I accept that I'm here because a braver man died?" he whispered, the confession edged with torment.

"You honor him by living. By making your life matter," she said, her voice trembling with conviction. "You carry him with you—not as a burden, but as part of your strength."

A comfortable silence descended over them. After a long moment, he looked back at her, and there was something in his eyes—something raw and searching. "Why are you here?"

Caught off guard, she began, "I heard you shouting. I thought—"

"No," he said, cutting her off. "I mean... why are you *here* with me? Still. After everything. Why haven't you walked away?"

The question struck deep, bypassing pretense and landing

squarely on truth. She could have told him everything—how she had loved him since France, how her heart twisted every time he looked away, how she ached for the version of him he didn't believe still existed.

But she knew he wasn't ready for that kind of truth. Not yet.

So she offered the piece of it he could carry for now. "Because I care about you, Dominic. I always have. And I always will."

He looked down again at their hands, his fingers tightened around hers once more. "I'm glad you're here," he said.

Her brows rose. "You are?"

A faint smile tugged at one corner of his mouth. "I don't know why you look so startled by that."

"It's just..." She gave a soft, rueful laugh. "You often seem like you're barely tolerating me."

That earned her a full, if weary, smile. "I more than tolerate you, Dorothea."

"I'm glad to hear that," she said, returning his smile.

Unexpectedly, Dominic asked, "Would you care to go riding tomorrow?"

Torn between the abrupt change in subject, she replied, "I... um... yes."

He seemed pleased by her answer. "Before breakfast?"

"I'd like that very much."

The faint crow of a rooster drifted in from the fields beyond the manor, breaking the quiet with the first herald of dawn. The sound drew her gaze to the window, where the edges of the sky were just beginning to lighten with the promise of morning.

"I should at least try to get some sleep before we go riding," she said, slipping her hand out of his and rising.

As she walked towards the door, Dominic's voice trailed behind her. "Thank you, Dorothea." The words held a sincerity that she had yet to hear from him.

She paused at the open door and turned back to look at him. "You are welcome."

Dominic smiled at her, and for the first time, it reached his eyes. "Until later."

With a small nod, Dorothea slipped quietly from the room, the door closing behind her with a gentle click.

Dominic adjusted his cravat as he stared in front of the mirror. The sun was streaming through the long windows in his bedchamber. The faintest hint of lavender lingered in the air, reminding him of Dorothea and the words she had said just hours before.

Her words comforted him in a way that nothing had before. Perhaps it was the way she had looked at him—with quiet understanding instead of pity, with no trace of judgment in her eyes. And when her fingers had entwined with his, suddenly and without explanation, life made sense.

Behind him, his valet cleared his throat. "Will there be anything else, my lord?"

Dominic released his cravat and lowered his hands. "Not at this time. I am going riding with Lady Warwicke."

"Very good, my lord."

With a nod of dismissal, Dominic crossed the room, the heels of his boots clicking on the floor. He opened the door and stepped into the corridor. Just as it shut behind him, the tapestry at the far end of the hallway lifted, and a tousle-haired Tristan emerged from behind it with a wide grin.

"Good morning, my lord," the boy said cheerfully, as if he had done nothing the least bit suspicious.

Dominic raised a brow. "May I ask what you were doing in the servants' corridors?"

"I was exploring," Tristan said, utterly unrepentant. "They're everywhere in this townhouse. Like a maze."

"That they are," Dominic said with a sigh, "but they are meant for the servants, not for young boys with a habit of mischief. And where, may I ask, is the maid assigned to keep an eye on you?"

Tristan shrugged as if it were hardly worth mentioning. "I'm not quite sure. I left while she was fetching my breakfast."

Dominic gave him a look meant to be stern, though it was softened by reluctant amusement. "I would prefer if you remained under her care."

"But Anna is so dull," Tristan complained. "She insists I sit still and eat oatmeal. I'm not used to someone trailing after me like a lost duckling."

Before Dominic could offer a rebuttal, a nearby door opened and Dorothea stepped out into the corridor. She was dressed in a blue riding habit and her red hair had been pulled neatly into a chignon at the nape of her neck.

"Good morning, my lady," Tristan chirped.

Dorothea jumped slightly. "Gracious!" she exclaimed with a hand to her chest. "I wasn't expecting anyone to be here."

"We do live here," Dominic teased.

"That you do," Dorothea replied, glancing between them. Her eyes narrowed with mock suspicion as she looked to Tristan. "Let me guess—you lost Anna again?"

Tristan beamed. "I did."

She shook her head with a soft laugh. "That poor girl. I do hope you're at least keeping up with your studies."

"I am," he said proudly. "I even read a book from the library last night."

"Oh? Which one?"

Tristan paused, frowning. "It was... a book. With words."

Dorothea laughed, the sound bright and warm in the quiet

hall. "A promising start. Perhaps next time you'll remember the title."

Dominic stepped towards her and offered his arm. "May I escort you to the stables?"

Her brows lifted slightly, but then she smiled and placed her gloved hand on his arm. "Thank you."

Tristan followed eagerly, quickening his pace to keep up. "Can I ride with you? The groom said I'm a natural."

"As tempting as that sounds," Dominic said, "I would like to spend time with Dorothea alone this morning."

Dorothea glanced over in surprise. "You would?"

He met her eyes without hesitation. "I would."

A flush bloomed on her cheeks at his quiet sincerity, and she ducked her head. "I would like that, too," she murmured.

They descended the stairs together. Tristan tagged along behind until they reached the entry hall, where Anna stood waiting with her arms crossed and one foot tapping furiously against the marble floor.

"Tristan," she scolded, "you were meant to remain in the nursery while I fetched your breakfast. Now it's gone cold."

"I don't mind cold food," he said with a shrug.

"Well, good, because you're going to eat every last bite," she retorted, pointing firmly towards the staircase. "And don't think I'll take my eyes off you today—not for a moment."

Tristan sighed with theatrical resignation and began his reluctant march back upstairs.

Dorothea giggled. "I'm sorry. I know I shouldn't laugh, but she has her hands full with that one."

"She certainly does," Dominic agreed.

Wright appeared and bowed to them. "If you would care to wait here, my lord, the horses will be brought around to the front."

Dominic shook his head. "That won't be necessary. We'll retrieve them ourselves."

"As you wish," Wright replied, stepping aside.

They exited through the side doors and walked down a gravel path bordered by clipped hedges and blooming flowers.

"Did you manage to sleep?" Dominic asked as they walked.

"A little," she said. "But not much."

He gave a quiet nod. "I dozed off and on. Still, it was far preferable to the nightmare I was having before you woke me."

She turned her head towards him, her brow faintly furrowed. "Do you... often get nightmares?"

"More often than I would like," he admitted, not quite meeting her gaze.

She didn't press him further, only nodded in understanding.

As they reached the stable yard, a liveried footman was leading out two horses. He halted in front of them and bowed slightly. "Your horses, my lord," he announced, holding out the reins.

Dorothea accepted hers and moved to the side of her mare.

"Allow me," Dominic said, stepping forward and crouching to offer his hands.

She placed her boot in his cupped palms and let him lift her into the saddle. Once she was properly seated, she glanced down at him with a soft expression. "Thank you," she said.

Now that Dorothea was securely in the saddle, Dominic turned to mount his own horse. But the moment his foot found the stirrup, a sharp, jarring whinny split the air. To his horror, Dorothea's horse reared onto its hind legs, front hooves pawing at the sky. She let out a startled gasp, her hands gripping the reins instinctively—but it was too late.

The horse bucked violently, and Dorothea was thrown.

She hit the ground with a sickening thud, her body crumpling on the gravel.

"Get these horses away from us!" Dominic bellowed,

hurling his reins towards the stunned footman. His boots scraped against the gravel as he rushed to her side.

"Dorothea!" he cried, his voice tight with panic. He dropped to his knees beside her, but hesitated, terrified that touching her might worsen an unseen injury. "Dorothea, can you hear me?"

She didn't answer.

"Dorothea!" His voice cracked with urgency.

At last, she let out a groan and shifted, eyes fluttering open. "That hurt," she mumbled, wincing as she attempted to lift her head. "What happened?"

"I don't rightly know," Dominic said, crouching closer. "One moment you were astride your horse, and the next, you were flat on your back."

His gaze swept over her, his eyes scanning for blood, bruises, anything that might hint at the severity of her fall. "Are you injured?"

"My shoulder aches, but nothing seems broken," she said, slowly pushing herself upright, though her movements were stiff and cautious.

"We should summon the doctor," he stated.

She gave him a look. "And say what? That I have a bruise and a sore shoulder? That hardly warrants his time."

Dorothea tried to stand but faltered, her balance slipping from under her.

Dominic didn't wait for permission. In one swift motion, he scooped her into his arms, ignoring her weak protests.

"I can walk, Dominic," she said, though her voice was faint.

"I know," he murmured, holding her close, "but that doesn't mean I'll let you."

By the time they reached the back of the townhouse, a footman had already opened the door. Dominic stepped inside, striding through the hall until he spotted Wright.

"Send for the doctor," Dominic commanded, not slowing.

"That's not necessary—" Dorothea began.

He cut her off, his tone firmer. "Just let the doctor examine you, Dorothea. Please."

"Very well. But I still think you're overreacting."

"Duly noted," he said as he carefully set her down onto the drawing room settee, adjusting the cushions behind her. "Can I get you anything?"

"I'm truly fine," she replied with a wan smile. "Although I do wonder what startled the horse. She's normally very calm."

Dominic moved to sit beside her but stopped. Instead, he began to pace, his agitation evident in every rigid line of his body.

Dorothea's eyes followed him. "You're making me nervous. Sit down."

He raked a hand through his hair. "Do you know what could have happened if your horse had spooked like that on the street? You could have been trampled. Or worse."

"You mustn't dwell on such possibilities," she said. "I'm right here, and I'm perfectly well."

He strode towards the drawing room door and flung it open. "Wright!"

A moment later, the butler reappeared. "Yes, my lord?"

"I want to see the head groom in my study. At once," Dominic said sharply. "Someone saddled Lady Warwicke's horse improperly, and I want to know who."

As Wright bowed and left to carry out the order, Dorothea let out a long sigh. "You're making a big ado out of nothing. Accidents happen."

"I will be the judge of that," Dominic said, his tone clipped. But a moment later, his voice softened. "Forgive me. I shouldn't have snapped."

She gave him a knowing look. "If confronting the groom brings you peace of mind, then by all means. But please, don't dismiss him over something so minor."

Dominic gave a tight nod and turned for his study.

The moment he stepped inside, he strode to the drink cart and poured a generous serving of brandy. It burned down his throat as he drank it in a single swallow. It was far too early to drink, but his hands were still shaking. Rage. Guilt. Fear. All of it twisted inside him like a noose pulling tighter.

He needed clarity.

The door creaked open and in stepped a short, broad-shouldered man with thick black hair and nervous eyes. He held his cap in both hands, wringing it with anxiety.

"You sent for me, my lord?"

Dominic turned, setting the empty glass aside. "Yes. Care to explain what happened with Lady Warwicke's horse?"

The man's throat bobbed as he swallowed. "There was... a burr under the saddle, my lord."

"A burr," Dominic repeated flatly.

"Yes," the man confirmed, his gaze now fixed firmly on the carpet.

"And who saddled her horse?"

"I did."

Dominic's jaw tensed. "And you didn't notice the burr? Did you even check the saddle properly?"

"I did, as I always do," the man said, his voice wavering. "But I—I don't know how it got there. I swear it wasn't there when I checked."

Dominic's fists clenched at his sides. "The only reason I'm not dismissing you this instant is because my wife asked me not to."

Relief flooded the man's face. "That's generous of you, my lord. Thank you."

"But understand me," Dominic said, stepping closer, his voice dropping to a growl. "If this ever happens again—if any horse under my care or hers is not checked with thorough attention—you'll be dismissed. And without a reference. Do I make myself clear?"

"Perfectly. I'll be more careful. Thank you," the man stammered before backing quickly out of the room, his cap crushed in his grip.

Dominic stood alone for a moment, the silence in the study pressing in around him. Then he exhaled through his nose and ran a hand down his face.

Dorothea was safe. That was all that mattered.

12

After a much-needed nap, Dorothea emerged from her bedchamber at the sound of the dinner bell echoing through the halls. She paused just outside the doorway to smooth the sleeves of her lavender gown. Her hair had been neatly pinned, a few tendrils falling loose about her temples, framing her face.

She made her way down the corridor, her slippers soundless against the carpet. As she approached the top of the staircase, her gaze landed on Dominic in the entry hall below. He stood tall and composed, dressed in a dark jacket, and she couldn't help but notice how devastatingly handsome he looked.

He looked up the moment she began to descend, his eyes locking on hers. With quiet purpose, he stepped forward and waited at the base of the stairs.

"Good evening, Dorothea."

"Good evening, Dominic," she returned, a smile tugging at her lips.

His gaze swept over her with a mixture of scrutiny and concern. "How are you feeling?"

"I'm well," she replied quickly, perhaps too quickly.

His expression remained grave. "Does your shoulder still pain you?"

She gave a half-hearted shrug. "Only when I move it."

The faint attempt at levity was lost on him. He frowned. "I wish you wouldn't make light of it. You could have been seriously injured. Killed, even."

"But I wasn't," she replied, trying not to let his anxiety unsettle her. "And I have no intention of dwelling on what might have been."

His brow furrowed more deeply, but after a pause, he gave a reluctant nod. "Very well. I shall concede—for now."

"Thank you," she said, offering him a grateful look.

He extended his arm towards her. "May I escort you to supper?"

As she slid her hand into the crook of his arm, a subtle spark passed between them—a jolt of awareness that made her pulse quicken. She wondered, as she had so many times before, if he felt it, too. But his expression remained as inscrutable as ever.

Dominic led her into the dining room, guiding her to her place at the far end of the long, polished table. He released her arm and pulled out her chair. She sat, unfolding her white linen napkin with deliberate ease, trying not to show how flustered his nearness had left her.

He crossed the room to take his customary place at the opposite end. The footmen moved efficiently, placing steaming bowls of soup before them.

Dorothea lifted her spoon, then called across the table in a voice meant to carry, "How was the visit to the hospital with Tristan?"

"It went well," Dominic replied in kind. "Tabitha seems to have made a full recovery. She should be released tomorrow.

She mentioned she's eager to begin work immediately. I hope that won't be a problem."

"Not at all," Dorothea said. "I'll be glad for the assistance. Mrs. Cameron has been assigning different maids each day, and while I appreciate the effort, it will be a relief to have someone consistent."

Dominic inclined his head slightly. "It was generous of you to take her on. Not many would have shown such kindness."

"I do believe Tabitha and I will get along well. And I am rather fond of Tristan."

"As am I," Dominic said, a flicker of warmth in his voice. "I've been thinking about his future. Perhaps it's time to hire a proper tutor or even send him to boarding school."

Dorothea nodded in approval. "That would be a remarkable opportunity for him. With education, he might truly make something of himself."

Without warning, Dominic stood and took his wine glass in hand. "I can barely hear you over the crackle of the fire," he said as he walked the length of the table. "Forgive me, but I'd prefer to sit nearer."

A footman hurried to arrange a new place setting beside her, and Dominic took the seat to her right.

Dorothea arched an amused brow. "Do you always cause such a stir when you dine?"

His lips twitched. "I do. Especially when I know what I want."

She leaned in slightly. "Well, I, for one, enjoy having you closer. I no longer have to shout my thoughts across the table."

Dominic's smile faded into something more contemplative. He set his glass down and looked at her with a seriousness that prickled her curiosity. "May I ask you a question?"

"You may."

"Do you have a dowry?"

The question caught her off guard. "Yes. Ten thousand pounds. It may not be a fortune, but it's respectable enough."

"A very tidy sum."

"It's yours now," she said simply. "If you like, I can contact my father's solicitor—Mr. Poole—for any documents you may need."

"I'm afraid Mr. Poole passed away."

"That is unfortunate. He was always kind to me."

Dominic shifted, his fingers tapping once on the table before stilling. "Do you know if your father left a will?"

She stared at him, puzzled. "Of course he did. Why would you ask such a thing?"

"How can you be sure?"

"Because he told me so," she said, reaching for her napkin to dab at the corners of her mouth. "He revised it just before we left for the Continent. I remember distinctly."

Dominic studied her closely, his expression unreadable once again. "Did he mention any of its provisions at all?"

"No," she said with a furrowed brow. "Dominic, why are you asking me all this?"

He smiled, but it didn't reach his eyes. "I was curious."

"Well, if you truly wish to know, you might try speaking to my brother," she said, her tone cooling slightly. "Though I don't envy you. He's not known for his charm."

Dominic fell silent, his features darkening with a quiet intensity. "Did your father know your brother abused you?"

Dorothea flinched at the question, though she didn't look away. "He knew," she said, her voice laced with old pain. "He tried to intervene, but every time I told him what he had done, Matthew would find a way to punish me."

She continued. "That's why my father allowed me to join him when he left for the Continent. He knew I was safer with him—safer on a battlefield than under Matthew's roof."

Dominic didn't speak right away. But then, without a word,

he reached across the space between them and took her hand gently in his own. His thumb brushed over her knuckles with a tenderness that caught her off guard.

"You will never be abused again," he asserted, his eyes locking with hers. "I swear it."

Something in her chest fluttered, fragile and unsteady. Not just at his words, but at the way he looked at her—as though she mattered. Truly mattered. "I know," she murmured. "I feel safe here... with you."

A flicker of emotion passed through his expression—too swift and guarded to name—but it left a trace behind. Then he released her hand and leaned back in his chair, his posture suddenly more reserved.

"I'm glad," he said, though his voice was rougher than before.

As the footmen returned to clear the soup bowls and replace them with the next course, Dorothea couldn't stop watching him. Not just watching—studying. Searching. There was something behind his calm exterior, a weight he carried in silence. Would he ever let her see all of it? Would he ever let her in?

Dominic cleared his throat, breaking the silence between them. "May I ask about your mother?"

The question startled her, but it also brought a soft smile to her lips. "My mother was extraordinary. Gentle, curious, and entirely unlike anyone else I've ever met. She had a rather eccentric habit of collecting bones."

"Bones?"

She laughed. "Animal bones. She fancied herself an amateur naturalist. One time, when we were in Bath, she found several large ones near the edge of a quarry and insisted we bring them home. They were strapped to the top of our coach like prized relics."

His mouth tugged upward in amusement. "That must have been quite the sight."

"It was," Dorothea agreed. "She died when I was eleven."

The mood shifted instantly, and Dominic's expression grew solemn. "That's much too young."

"It was. But truly, is there ever a good age to lose your mother?"

"No. I suppose there isn't."

"My mother always dreamed of a large family," Dorothea shared. "But she lost one baby after another. Miscarriage after miscarriage, until she gave up hope." Her gaze dropped to her plate, though she wasn't looking at the food. "When she fell pregnant again, my father was overjoyed. He thought it was a miracle. But she bled to death not long after childbirth. They both died."

"I'm sorry," he said, and the words, simple as they were, carried a weight that told her he meant them.

Dorothea waved her hand faintly, attempting to brush the moment aside. "I shouldn't have brought it up. It's far too gloomy for dinner conversation."

"I don't care about that," he said. "I want you to speak your mind, regardless of the occasion."

"You may come to regret saying that," she teased. "I can be quite opinionated."

"I'm already well aware of that," he said, lifting his glass with a half-smile of his own.

The moment felt lighter now, steadied by mutual understanding. And yet something still lingered between them—unspoken, unfinished.

So Dorothea took a chance. "Do you want a large family?" she asked.

Dominic had just taken a sip of wine and nearly choked. He coughed into his napkin, then looked at her with raised brows. "Pardon?"

"I don't believe the question could have been any simpler."

Setting his glass down carefully, he wiped his mouth before replying. "No," he said, a touch too quickly. "I don't want children."

His admission stunned her. "At all?"

He leaned back in his chair, arms resting loosely on the armrests. "My father was a cruel man," he shared. "He belittled, berated, and broke everything he touched. Including me. I wouldn't even know where to begin raising a child without becoming what he was."

"You are not your father," she said firmly.

Dominic looked away. "It's not that simple."

"But maybe it is," Dorothea countered. "I see how you are with Tristan. Kind. Protective. And in return, that boy adores you."

His gaze returned to hers, something raw flickering there— part disbelief, part longing. But he said nothing.

Dorothea reached for her glass, her fingers brushing the stem. "You may not want children now. But I think, in time, you might surprise yourself."

Dominic didn't answer. But he didn't look away either.

And for now, that was enough.

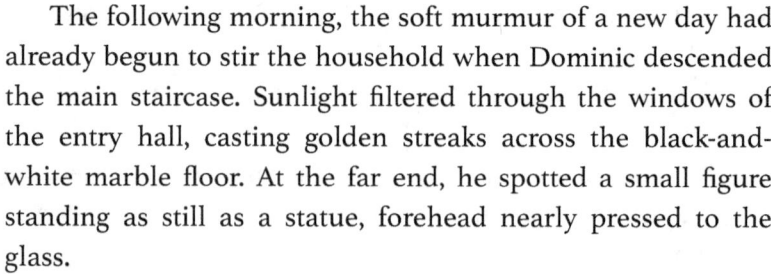

The following morning, the soft murmur of a new day had already begun to stir the household when Dominic descended the main staircase. Sunlight filtered through the windows of the entry hall, casting golden streaks across the black-and-white marble floor. At the far end, he spotted a small figure standing as still as a statue, forehead nearly pressed to the glass.

Tristan.

Dominic came to a stop beside the boy. "What are you doing?"

Tristan barely spared him a glance, his eyes trained on the road just beyond the gates. "My mum should be arriving soon," he said, his voice bubbling with anticipation.

"Ah, yes," Dominic murmured. "This is the day."

Before he could say more, a soft rustle on the staircase caught his attention. He turned his head and saw Dorothea descending. She wore a pale yellow morning gown that clung to her slender frame before flowing gently to the floor. The color made her hair seem more golden than red, and the faint smile playing at her lips gave her the air of quiet contentment.

There was something radiant about her that morning. She was truly a beautiful young woman, on the inside and out. And the more time he spent with her, the more Dominic started to question if he wanted an annulment.

"Dominic," she said, her eyes meeting his as she reached the final step.

He moved to greet her. "Dorothea," he said with a small bow.

She gave him a look edged in teasing. "You're being rather formal this morning. Should I be concerned?"

"Not at all. I trust you slept well?"

"I did. And you?"

"For once, yes," he admitted. "It was... unusual, but welcome."

Her gaze shifted towards Tristan. "He looks as though he's been standing there for hours."

"He might've been," Dominic replied.

Just then, Tristan gave a cry of delight. "She's here!" he shouted and, without a second's hesitation, flung the front door open and darted outside.

Dorothea watched him with a smile. "It's good to see him so happy."

"That it is," Dominic agreed, though his voice turned thoughtful. "I only hope you aren't making a mistake by hiring Tabitha."

"I'm not," she said with certainty.

A moment later, Tristan returned, hand tightly clasped in his mother's. His face was flushed with excitement. "She's here," he announced proudly.

Tabitha stepped into the entry hall, her eyes wide with wonder and her smile tentative but sincere. She wore a dark blue gown and her hair had been neatly braided back. She looked both grateful and slightly overwhelmed.

"My lady," she said, dipping a quick curtsy. "Thank you for sending the gown. That was more kindness than I expected."

Dorothea stepped forward. "You are more than welcome here, Tabitha. We've thoroughly enjoyed having Tristan with us."

Tabitha glanced down at her son, then back up. "I hope he hasn't caused too much mischief."

"Not in the least," Dorothea assured her.

"Well then," Tabitha said, straightening slightly. "Shall I begin work at once?"

Dominic interjected before she could move. "Have you already eaten this morning?"

"I haven't broken my fast yet, no, but—"

"You must have breakfast," Tristan interrupted, tugging at her hand. "Mrs. Dawson makes the best scones with clotted cream. You'll love them. Come on—I'll show you where the kitchen is."

"Tristan, slow down!" Tabitha said with a laugh, trying to keep pace as he dragged her along the corridor.

Dorothea laughed. "I would just go with him. He has a certain determination about him."

Tabitha smiled. "That sounds wonderful," she said, allowing herself to be led towards the servants' entrance.

As they disappeared, Dominic turned to Dorothea. "It was thoughtful of you to send her a dress."

She shrugged off the praise with a wave of her hand. "I saw the condition of the one she had and couldn't imagine how uncomfortable she must feel in it."

Dominic studied her. "How is it you always notice those little things?"

"I don't know," she said, as though the answer were simple. "I saw a need, and I did what I could. Nothing more."

"It's more than that," Dominic said. "You continue to impress me, Thea."

She blinked. "What did you call me?"

With a slight wince, he replied, "Thea. I hope that wasn't too forward."

"No," she said, shaking her head. "My mother used to call me that. Hearing it again... it brings back such fond memories."

"Then Thea it is," he said, offering his arm. "May I escort you to breakfast?"

"I would like that very much," she replied, taking his arm.

As they walked down the hall together, Dominic turned slightly towards her. "I was wondering if you'd like to take a carriage ride through Hyde Park later today."

Her smile widened. "That sounds delightful."

He found himself smiling back before he could stop it. "Wonderful."

They stepped into the dining room where the table had already been set. He led her to her chair and helped her settle before taking the seat beside her.

A moment later, Wright appeared, carrying a silver tray stacked with envelopes. "These have been arriving all morning, my lady."

Dorothea reached for the bundle and gave an excited squeal. "Invitations! These are invitations to social events."

Dominic made a face. "That sounds... dreadful."

Her excitement was palpable. "I never imagined I'd receive an invitation from a duchess," she said, holding up a cream-colored envelope adorned with an elaborate seal.

"One of the many curses of being part of the *ton*," Dominic muttered as he reached for his coffee.

She looked at him curiously. "You don't wish to attend?"

He took a sip before replying, "I have no great desire to mingle with preening aristocrats and dull dinner companions. But..." He glanced at her. "If you would like to attend one or two, I suppose I could endure it."

She beamed at him. "I'd like that very much."

And strangely, Dominic realized, he didn't entirely dread the idea either.

The footmen stepped forward, placing freshly prepared plates before them. Dominic reached for his fork while Dorothea sat back and began opening the pile of envelopes in front of her.

"Ten," she announced after a moment, her voice tinged with pride.

Dominic glanced at her. "Ten what?"

She grinned as she laid the final envelope on the stack. "We've received ten invitations. Balls, soirées, and a garden party hosted by Lady Melgrave. We've become quite the fashionable couple, apparently."

He raised a brow. "Is that so? Well, you choose. Pick one or two that sound tolerable."

"Just one or two?" she teased. "What if I wish to attend them all?"

"Then I shall wish you well and remain at home," he said with mirth in his voice.

Before she could reply, Wright reappeared in the doorway carrying a silver tray with the day's newssheets neatly arranged atop it.

"*The Morning Post* has just arrived, my lord," he said, offering the tray.

Dominic took the newssheets with a nod of thanks, immediately removing the Society section and extending it across the table to Dorothea.

"Thank you," she said, unfolding the newssheets with eager fingers. As he turned his attention to the front page, scanning headlines of political shifts and parliamentary squabbles, he heard her draw in a quick breath.

"We're mentioned again," Dorothea said. "In the Society pages."

He didn't look up. "Are we scandalous or merely fashionable this time?"

"It's another article by Mr. Fairchild," she replied, eyes scanning the column. "And this time... it's about an annulment."

He froze.

Dorothea lowered the newssheets, her gaze lifting to meet his. Her expression was unreadable at first—curious, yes, but shadowed by something darker beneath the surface.

"The article says that you're petitioning for an annulment," she said. "Is it true?"

A cold weight settled in his stomach. He swallowed, his voice low. "It is."

Her lips parted slightly, but no sound emerged at first. "You don't want to be married to me?" The words were quiet, almost tentative—hopeful, perhaps, that he would deny them.

Dominic shifted uncomfortably. "It's not that simple."

"But it is," she said, setting the newssheets down with trembling fingers. "You've made a decision. Without telling me. After everything we've been through—everything we've shared —you were planning to cast me aside?"

"Dorothea," he began, "please, just listen—"

"No," she said firmly, pushing her chair back with enough force to make it scrape loudly against the floor. She stood, her hands clenched at her sides. "How could you do this to me? To *us*?"

He let out a dry laugh. "There is no us. There never was. I married you under the assumption that I was going to die. It was a formality. A kindness. I never intended to stay married."

The words landed like a blow. She staggered back a step, as if his admission had physically struck her. Her face crumpled with disbelief and hurt.

"You made me believe..." Her voice cracked. "You made me believe we could be something more."

"That we could have a happy marriage?" he asked. "That was never the plan. I thought it better to be honest now than let you believe in a future that doesn't exist."

"Better for whom, Dominic?" she demanded, her voice rising, eyes shining with unshed tears. "For me? Or for you?"

Dominic stood slowly. "If you would just let me explain, you would understand."

"I can't even look at you right now," she said, her voice rising. She turned away, her breath uneven as she moved to the door.

He took a step forward. "Dorothea—"

She paused in the doorway, her head high. "You were right about one thing," she said without turning. "You are not the man I thought you were."

"I told you that man died on the battlefield. You just refused to believe it," Dominic asserted.

She walked out without another word, leaving him alone.

Dominic returned to his seat, but he was in no mood to eat. This was what he had wanted. What he had planned for. An annulment—clean, final, logical. He had convinced himself it was the best course of action. Safer. Simpler.

So why did he feel like he had just made the worst mistake of his life?

13

Dorothea stood motionless at the window of her bedchamber, her forehead nearly resting against the cool glass. Tears streaked down her cheeks and she made no effort to wipe them away. There was no one here to see her—no reason to pretend.

She was grieving.

Not for a man who had died, but for one who had never truly existed.

Dominic had never intended to stay with her. All this time, as she slowly began to believe that perhaps he could come to care for her, he had been planning to set her aside. The betrayal stung more than she could bear.

She had been foolish. Naïve. She had fallen in love with a shadow—a man who had shown her glimpses of tenderness, only to retreat behind walls she could not scale. How was she to go on, knowing he didn't want her? That he never had?

A soft knock at the door broke through her thoughts.

She stiffened, her breath catching. For a moment, panic flared—what if it was *him*? She didn't think she could bear to see him. Not yet. Not like this.

"Enter," she called out, schooling her voice into something resembling calm.

The door opened with a quiet creak, and to her great relief, it was Tabitha who stepped into the room. Her eyes filled with a compassion that Dorothea hadn't known how much she needed until now.

"My lady," Tabitha said, "Lady Sarah and Mrs. Haverleigh are in the drawing room. They're rather insistent about seeing you."

Dorothea turned her head away, brushing a stray tear from her cheek at last. "I do not feel like entertaining guests," she admitted.

"I understand. But they refuse to leave until you speak with them."

A long sigh escaped Dorothea's lips as she turned from the window. Her voice was weary but resigned. "Then I suppose I should face them."

Tabitha hesitated, then stepped farther into the room. "Forgive me, my lady, and please chide me if I overstep, but... I do not believe all hope is lost."

"And why would you say that?"

"I saw the way Lord Warwicke looks at you. That is not a man who is indifferent towards you."

Dorothea's throat tightened. "You're mistaken," she said briskly. "Whatever you saw, it was not affection. He doesn't want me."

Tabitha opened her mouth, but closed it again just as quickly. She gave a small nod instead. "Of course, my lady. Perhaps I misspoke."

Dorothea walked towards the door. "Would you send regrets to all of the invitations we received?"

"All of them?" Tabitha asked. "You don't intend to go to any?"

"If I do, I will only invite gossip and stares. Best to remain out of sight... for now."

Tabitha frowned. "You did nothing wrong."

Dorothea paused in the doorway. "Didn't I?" she asked. "I trusted the wrong man."

And with that, she stepped into the corridor, her heart heavy as lead, and made her way to the drawing room.

Inside, she found Lady Sarah and Arabella seated together on the settee, deep in conversation.

Dorothea cleared her throat. "Good morning."

Arabella's head whipped up, and she sprang to her feet. "Oh, my poor dear!" she cried, rushing across the room and enveloping Dorothea in a tight, dramatic embrace. "Are you quite all right?"

Perhaps it was the need for comfort—or perhaps just sheer exhaustion—but Dorothea allowed herself to be held.

"I'm fine," she murmured.

Arabella leaned back, holding her at arm's length to inspect her tear-streaked face. "You are not fine. You're humiliated."

Lady Sarah spoke up. "Arabella, really. That is not the least bit helpful."

"I meant nothing by it," Arabella insisted. "It's simply the truth. The article was in the Society pages, plain as day. The entire *ton* knows about the annulment now."

Dorothea groaned softly. "Thank you for the reminder."

Arabella grabbed her hand and tugged her towards the settee. "You must tell us everything. Did you know Lord Warwicke was seeking an annulment?"

She shook her head. "No. I found out with the rest of the world."

Arabella gasped and clutched at her chest as though Dorothea had just confessed to murder. "He didn't tell you? You found out by reading the newssheets?"

Dorothea's cheeks flushed. "I would rather not talk about it."

Lady Sarah leaned forward and placed a comforting hand on Dorothea's knee. "Of course. And you don't have to. We're not here to interrogate you. We're here because we're your family, and we are worried about you."

Dorothea managed a nod. "Thank you, but truly, I'll be all right."

"This is the most scandalous thing to happen all Season," Arabella announced.

Lady Sarah shot her daughter a warning look. "Do stop. You're upsetting her."

Dorothea raised a hand. "It's all right. Arabella's only saying what everyone else is thinking."

"Exactly," Arabella replied. "But you needn't fret. Parliament almost never grants annulments. He'll likely be stuck with you."

Dorothea flinched. "Does it even matter? He's made his feelings perfectly clear. He doesn't want me."

Arabella's mouth opened to reply, but Lady Sarah cut her off. "You are strong, Dorothea. And I promise, you will get through this. One day, all of this pain will feel distant. It may not seem like it now, but you do not know what blessings the future may hold."

Dorothea's shoulders slumped. "It feels impossible."

Lady Sarah offered her a warm smile. "Sometimes the greatest trials come just before something beautiful."

Arabella leaned closer, her voice dropping to a whisper. "Are you quite certain you didn't do something to offend him?"

Lady Sarah rolled her eyes. "Perhaps you should wait in the entry hall until you've remembered how to behave like a friend."

At that moment, a footman stepped into the room carrying a gleaming tea service. Dorothea recognized him—he had been present the morning of the riding accident. He moved with practiced grace and placed the tray down on the table.

"Will there be anything else, my lady?" he asked, straightening.

"No, thank you," Dorothea acknowledged.

Lady Sarah gave Arabella a meaningful nudge. "Do pour the tea, dear."

"But I'm the guest," Arabella argued.

"Yes, and we are here to comfort Dorothea, not you," Lady Sarah replied firmly.

With a dramatic sigh, Arabella lifted the teapot and poured three cups. Lady Sarah took one and handed it to Dorothea with great care.

"There you are," she said. "This will help calm your nerves."

Dorothea accepted the teacup and lowered her gaze, unsure if she wanted to sip or weep. She didn't want tea. She wanted to not feel so utterly unwanted.

But then Lady Sarah offered, "Don't give up hope yet."

And for one fragile, flickering moment... Dorothea almost believed her.

Dorothea brought the teacup to her lips. The warmth seeped into her hands first, then spread through her chest as she swallowed. It was soothing, but it did little to temper the storm within her. Her heart still ached, raw and sore, as if bruised from the inside. The tea couldn't reach that place.

Lady Sarah watched her over the rim of her own cup, her expression kind. "So... do you intend to move back home?"

Home.

The word landed with unexpected weight. Dorothea's gaze drifted across the drawing room. This place had begun to feel familiar, but it wasn't truly hers. And yet... the alternative made her stomach twist.

She could not return to her brother's house. The very thought of it filled her with dread.

Setting the teacup back into its saucer with careful delibera-tion, she said, "I have not yet decided what I shall do."

"You have time to make that decision," Lady Sarah said. "But know that you are always welcome with us."

Arabella interjected, "But our townhouse is already rather crowded, is it not? I don't believe there's any proper room left for Dorothea."

Lady Sarah's smile thinned. "We will make the room."

Arabella pursed her lips. "Her room is being used as storage for my gowns. I've nowhere else to keep them."

"We must all make sacrifices for the sake of family, dear," Lady Sarah replied, her voice edged with a quiet sharpness.

Arabella crossed her arms with a huff. "Why must I make all the sacrifices?" she muttered.

Lady Sarah slowly rose from the settee, steadying herself with her cane. "And on that note, I believe it's time we took our leave."

Dorothea stood as well, though as she pushed herself to her feet, a strange wave of dizziness swept over her. Her vision blurred at the edges, and the room seemed to tip slightly beneath her. She raised a hand to her forehead and closed her eyes, willing the sensation to pass.

"Dorothea?" Lady Sarah asked, her voice ripe with concern. "Are you all right?"

"I just..." She pressed her fingertips to her temple, her other hand gripping the back of the chair. "I just need a moment."

The aching in her limbs had worsened—deep, pulsing aches that settled in her shoulders and lower back. And her stomach had begun to churn, the nausea rising with discon-certing swiftness.

She sank back into her chair as the room slowly righted itself. Her hands trembled slightly in her lap.

"I feel... unwell," she admitted. "Like I've taken ill."

Lady Sarah moved closer and touched her shoulder. "You're pale as a sheet. Arabella, go fetch someone—now."

As Arabella rushed towards the door, Dorothea leaned back into the settee and let her body sink into the cushions. Her limbs ached, her head throbbed, and her stomach twisted in protest. But it was none of those things that truly unsettled her.

It was the thought of *him*.

If Dominic came...

She closed her eyes.

She did not want his pity. Not his sudden, hollow attempts at comfort when he had already made it so devastatingly clear that he wanted nothing to do with her.

Let it be anyone but him, she pleaded silently. A maid. Or even the footman who had witnessed her fall from the horse.

But not Dominic.

Dominic sat at his desk, a quill poised above an open ledger, when a sharp, panicked cry pierced the stillness of the study.

"Help! Someone—please!"

The voice was female—urgent, unmistakably distressed.

He was on his feet in an instant, the chair scraping loudly against the wood floor as he bolted into the corridor. As he reached the entry hall, he spotted Mrs. Haverleigh standing with Wright, her gloved hands fluttering as she gestured wildly towards the drawing room.

His chest tightened. "What's wrong?" he demanded.

Mrs. Haverleigh turned to him. "It's Dorothea," she said breathlessly. "She's taken ill rather suddenly."

He didn't wait to hear more.

Dominic pushed past them and strode into the drawing

room, his heart pounding. The sight that met him made him falter.

Dorothea was slumped back on the settee, her eyes closed, and her skin flushed unnaturally beneath the morning light. Her hands lay limp in her lap, and her breathing seemed shallow. A white-haired woman stood nearby, her face taut with concern.

"Dorothea," he said as he crossed the room in swift strides. He crouched down in front of her. "What happened? What's wrong?"

Her eyes fluttered open, and the moment she saw him, her eyes flashed with annoyance. "Go away," she said flatly.

"No," he replied, unperturbed. "I'm afraid I can't do that."

"I told you—"

"I heard you. But I'm not leaving."

From behind him, the woman answered his earlier question. "She nearly fainted when she stood. Said she felt light-headed and ill."

"It's nothing," Dorothea insisted, attempting to sit up straighter. "I just need a moment."

Dominic turned towards the door and ordered, "Send for the doctor. Immediately."

"That isn't necessary—" Dorothea began, but her protest was cut off by a sharp gasp as Dominic leaned forward and swept her into his arms.

"What do you think you're doing?" she snapped, squirming against him as he carried her towards the entry hall.

"I should think it's rather obvious," he said, not breaking stride. "I'm taking you to your bedchamber."

"I do not need—nor want—your help."

"And yet," he said, adjusting his hold on her, "you have it."

"Put me down this instant!"

"No."

"Dominic—"

"You need to be examined by a doctor."

"This is absurd," she muttered, wriggling again.

"What's absurd is that you're fighting me while clearly unwell," he retorted.

"I merely stood too fast. You're making a fuss over nothing. You needn't concern yourself with me."

Behind them, Mrs. Haverleigh's voice rang with thinly veiled exasperation. "Stop being so stubborn, Dorothea. Let the man help you."

Dorothea scowled, folding her arms as best she could while being carried. "I am not an invalid."

"I never said you were," Dominic replied.

At the top of the stairs, Tabitha appeared, eyes wide with worry. She hurried to open the door to Dorothea's bedchamber and stepped aside to let them pass.

Dominic carried Dorothea inside and gently laid her down on the bed, brushing a few stray curls from her flushed cheek. "How are you feeling now?"

She turned her face away and crossed her arms again. "I am still very angry at you."

"That's reassuring. But I meant physically. What ills you?"

Dorothea shifted her gaze to Tabitha. "Will you kindly inform Lord Warwicke that I merely have the symptoms of influenza?"

Tabitha blinked. "Do you want me to tell him that when he's standing two feet away from you?"

Dominic studied Dorothea's complexion. "You're flushed. And you were perfectly fine earlier. Why do you think it's influenza?"

She huffed in frustration. "Because my stomach is churning, my body aches, and I got lightheaded. Influenza symptoms, every one of them."

"So, how were you eating breakfast without complaint just an hour ago?"

With a groan, Dorothea reached for a pillow and placed it over her face. "Go away, Dominic."

But something gnawed at him. The sudden onset. The odd timing. The symptoms came too swiftly.

What if it wasn't illness at all?

What if it was poison?

He grabbed a chair and dragged it closer to the bed, sitting down without invitation. "Did you eat or drink anything during your visit with your guests?"

Her voice came muffled beneath the pillow. "Why do you care?"

"Just humor me."

The pillow shifted slightly as she peeked out at him, clearly annoyed. "I had a sip of tea. That's all."

"Only one sip?"

"Yes," she said with a sigh. "And now, do you mind leaving me so I can continue loathing you in private?"

He ignored the jab. "Who brought the tea in?"

"What does that matter?"

"Please."

She relented. "It was the footman. The same one who witnessed my fall from the horse."

Dominic stiffened. "Isn't tea usually delivered by one of the maids?"

"Yes, normally," Dorothea said. "But today, it was him."

A cold sensation began to curl in Dominic's gut as he pressed, "Has that footman ever brought tea to you before?"

"No," she replied, clearly puzzled now. "Never. Why?"

Dominic rose from the chair with slow, deliberate movements, every instinct sharpened. "Because I believe I may need to have a word with him."

"Good," Dorothea said dryly. "Does that mean you're finally leaving my bedchamber? I only ask because you are not welcome in here."

"I shall take my leave... for now."

Before stepping away, he turned to Tabitha, who stood dutifully near the hearth, her expression tight with worry.

"Do not give Lady Warwicke anything to eat or drink unless you fetch it yourself. No one else. Do you understand me?" he asked.

"Yes, my lord," Tabitha replied.

Dorothea huffed. "If I weren't feeling so wretched, I'd be throwing my pillows at your head to drive you out."

A faint smirk tugged at Dominic's lips, but it was fleeting. He turned towards the door. "Do try to feel better, Dorothea."

She lifted her chin defiantly. "Don't pretend you care."

He paused on the threshold, one hand resting on the doorframe. His voice was quieter this time, almost gruff. "I do care."

Then, without another word, he stepped out and closed the door gently behind him.

Dominic descended the stairs two at a time, his mind racing. Something was wrong—*deeply* wrong—and he could no longer ignore the unease that had been gnawing at the edge of his thoughts since the moment Dorothea had grown ill.

He found Wright in the entry hall, conversing with another servant.

"Wright," Dominic said sharply.

The butler turned immediately. "Yes, my lord?"

"I need to speak with the footman who delivered tea to Lady Warwicke's drawing room this morning. At once."

Wright offered him a bemused look. "My lord... footmen don't deliver tea. That task belongs to the maids."

"Well, one did today. Lady Warwicke told me as much."

A flicker of unease crossed Wright's face. "I see. I'll make inquiries right away."

Dominic stopped him with a raised hand. "That's not the only thing. That same footman brought our horses around front yesterday morning."

Wright's brows drew together in confusion. "That's highly irregular, my lord. The grooms are responsible for the horses. I assigned no footman to do such a task."

Dominic's back stiffened. "Then who the blazes was that man?"

Wright looked deeply troubled now. "I... I don't know, my lord. But I'll get to the bottom of it."

"Start by rounding up every footman in the household. I want them all accounted for. Now."

Wright gave a crisp bow and turned on his heel, calling for one of the under-butlers as he disappeared down the corridor.

As Dominic stood in the entry hall, the pieces began to fall into place—one troubling detail after another. Dorothea's sudden illness. The footman no one seemed to recognize. The wrong person delivering tea. And now, a memory returned with a jolt: the fireplace damper being closed, filling Dorothea's bedchamber with smoke.

At the time, he'd dismissed it as an oversight—a careless mistake by one of the servants. But now? Now he wasn't so certain.

What if it hadn't been a mistake at all?

What if someone had wanted to harm Dorothea?

The thought struck him like a blow to the chest, and without another moment's hesitation, he turned on his heel and ran up the stairs, taking them two at a time. His boots pounded against the polished wood, his breath tight in his throat.

He didn't knock.

He threw the door open and burst into her bedchamber.

Tabitha, seated in the corner with a basin of cool water and a cloth, let out a startled gasp. "My lord—what is it? Is everything all right?"

"It will be," Dominic said, though the words rang hollow to his own ears. He forced his voice steady, willing himself to remain calm. "I'm only here to ensure Lady Warwicke remains undisturbed."

Dorothea, propped against her pillows with a blanket tucked around her, narrowed her eyes with displeasure. "Do you truly intend to make a nuisance of yourself?"

"I do," he replied as he went to sit down in the chair beside the bed.

She gave him a withering look. "I don't want you here."

He leaned forward slightly, lowering his voice. "I know. But I'm not here for conversation or forgiveness. I'm here to keep you safe. That's all."

"Safe from what?"

"I am not sure yet, but I will know soon enough."

Not looking the least bit impressed, she turned her body pointedly away from him, her back to his gaze.

He didn't flinch from her anger. He deserved it. Every ounce of it.

Still, no matter how furious she was with him—no matter how much he had hurt her—he wasn't going anywhere.

If someone was targeting Dorothea, if someone within these walls had meant to harm her, then he would remain exactly where he needed to be: at her side.

Even if she loathed him for it.

He settled back in the chair, silent now, eyes fixed on the flickering fire in the hearth.

Let her rest.

Let her rage.

He would wait.

And he would protect her.

With his life, if necessary.

14

D orothea stirred and slowly opened her eyes, blinking into the dark. Her bedchamber was steeped in shadow, the only light coming from the dying embers in the hearth, casting a faint amber glow along the walls. The sun had long since set and she realized that she must have slept the entire day away.

Oddly, her body no longer felt as heavy or achy. The churning in her stomach had quieted, and her limbs no longer trembled. Whatever had plagued her earlier now seemed to have loosened its grip. She was pleased that rest had helped.

She shifted slightly and turned her head—only to find Dominic seated in the chair beside her bed, his eyes fixed on her. He was leaning forward, hands clasped between his knees, as if he hadn't moved in hours.

His gaze, when it met hers, was strikingly gentle. Steady. Warm in a way that made her breath catch for just a moment. That warmth was what she had once imagined he might offer her freely, if only he let down his guard. For a heartbeat, her anger softened.

But only for a heartbeat.

Because Dominic still intended to cast her aside.

"What are you doing here?" she asked, her voice scratchy from disuse but still sharp.

"I'm here to keep you safe," he said simply.

"From what, exactly?"

He hesitated, then drew a slow breath, his features shadowed in solemnity. "It would appear that your recent misfortunes weren't accidents. Someone may be trying to kill you."

"That's absurd."

"I thought so, too," he said. "Until I began putting the pieces together. The closed damper. The burr under your saddle. The tea. All isolated, they could be explained away. But together?"

He shook his head and pressed on. "It's too much to ignore. And when I went to question the footman who delivered the tea, he was gone. Disappeared."

Dorothea placed a hand over her stomach. "The doctor said it was influenza."

Dominic sat up straighter. "Have you ever heard of Aqua Tofana?"

"No."

"It's a poison. Created in the seventeenth century. A concoction of arsenic, lead, and belladonna. Slow-acting and nearly undetectable. It mimics illness—starting with cold-like symptoms, then escalating to something resembling influenza."

He continued, his voice calm but grim. "The doctor mentioned your pupils were dilated. That's a known effect of belladonna since it was once used in cosmetics to make a woman's eyes appear more alluring."

Dorothea's brows knit together. "And if I'd had more?"

"Four drops," Dominic responded. "That's all it takes. The first causes mild discomfort. The second—influenza-like symptoms. The third brings severe illness. The fourth... is fatal."

A chill crept across her skin despite the warmth of the blankets. "Is there an antidote?"

"There's no guaranteed cure," he admitted. "But vinegar and lemon juice are believed to help combat it if caught early."

Dorothea glanced towards the table beside the bed and saw the glass. "Is that what's in there?"

He nodded. "It is. You should drink it."

"Will I die?"

Dominic met her gaze. "No. Not if I'm right. You've only been given the first two doses. You'll recover."

Still uncertain, she pushed herself upright slowly. Dominic stood as she moved, but she held up a hand. "I do not need your help."

"I know," he said. "But I'm here anyway."

Propping a pillow behind her back, she settled against the wall. "Why would someone want to hurt me?" Her voice had lost its bite—now it was small, uncertain, shaken.

Dominic's jaw tensed. "That's what I intend to find out."

"But the footman is gone, isn't he?"

"Yes," Dominic responded. "But I'll find him. And when I do, he will answer for what he's done to you."

Without another word, Dorothea reached for the glass and took a small sip. The taste was sharp and sour—like drinking vinegar laced with bitterness. She coughed as she set it back down.

"That is vile," she muttered.

"It's meant to be," he said. "It's for your own good."

She stared at the glass, then back at him. "Don't pretend you care what happens to me."

"I do care."

She narrowed her eyes. "That's difficult to believe, considering you're trying to annul our marriage."

Dominic exhaled and returned to the chair beside her, rubbing a hand along his jaw. "That decision wasn't as simple as you believe."

She turned her face away. "If the annulment is granted, I'll be ruined in the eyes of the *ton*. And if it isn't, I'll be trapped in a marriage with a man who doesn't want me."

"I do want you," he said, almost too quickly. "And that's the problem."

Dorothea turned to face him again, her brows raised in disbelief. "Pardon me if I don't follow that logic."

Dominic leaned forward, resting his elbows on his knees. His voice dropped to a murmur. "I care about you, Dorothea. More than I should. More than I dare to admit. But I'm not the man you think I am. I'm not sure I ever was."

She searched his face for the sincerity, confusion, and heartache swirling in her chest. "I thought I knew you. I thought... I was falling for a man who might one day love me in return."

She caught herself, clamping her mouth shut, but the damage had been done.

Silence stretched between them.

Dominic's expression shifted—pain, guilt, longing, all in the flicker of a blink.

"You were," he said softly. "But I lost that man somewhere along the way."

Dorothea didn't speak again. She simply looked at him— truly looked at him—and realized for the first time that the distance between them was not just emotional. It was haunted. Wounded.

And she didn't know if love would be enough to bridge it.

Dominic suddenly pushed back from the chair as if the weight of their conversation had become too much to bear. He strode across the room and came to a halt before the hearth, bracing both hands on the edge of the mantel.

His voice, when it came, was low and raw. "I want the annulment because I do not want you bound to me. Not out of guilt. Not out of duty. I see the light in your eyes, and I fear I will smother it. You deserve a man who will love you freely, openly. A man who hasn't been hollowed out by everything he's seen and done."

"And you couldn't be that man?"

He flinched. "It is better that I not be tied to anyone. It's safer for everyone."

Dorothea watched him, her heart twisting. "Don't you require an heir?" she asked, gently probing.

He turned his face away from her. "As I told you, I don't want children."

She swung her legs over the side of the bed and rose to her feet. With purposeful steps, she walked towards him and came to a stop just a breath away.

"If that is what you truly want," she said, "then I will accept it."

His head turned at last, his eyes meeting hers with a conflicted intensity. "But I must assume that you want children."

"I do," she admitted. "Or... I did." She gave a small shrug. "But dreams can change. They often do."

He exhaled sharply, a sound somewhere between a sigh and a scoff. "I can't ask you to make that kind of sacrifice."

"And if I want to?"

"This annulment," he said, his tone becoming more formal, more distant, "would be the kindest thing I could offer you. I would establish a household for you, ensure you had everything you could want. Your own space. Your own life. Freedom."

Her gaze didn't waver. "Without you?"

He dropped his eyes. "You don't want to be married to me. You think you do, but you don't. The things I've done... the things I've become... they've darkened my soul."

Without hesitation, she reached out and took his hand. To her relief, he didn't pull away. "Then let me help you," she said.

"No one can help me. I'm a lost cause."

Her lips curled slightly. "That happens to be my specialty—lost causes."

He glanced down at their entwined fingers. His voice dropped, more vulnerable than she'd ever heard it. "You want to know what happened... after they dragged me away with the dead."

"I do."

His shoulders stiffened before he began to speak, slowly, deliberately. "I woke up in a shallow grave. There were bodies all around me—my comrades. Friends I'd laughed with. Fought beside. Bled with. The smell..." He closed his eyes, jaw tightening. "It was thick with death. I had to claw my way to the surface."

Dorothea's hand gripped his more tightly. "How awful," she whispered.

He nodded once, almost absently. "It took me days to find a British company. I wandered half-starved and disoriented, unsure if I was even alive or some ghost trapped in a nightmare."

Her chest ached at the image of him, broken and alone, covered in the blood of his friends, staggering through the woods with nothing but sheer will keeping him upright.

"They arranged transport home," he added. "But a part of me... a large part... wished I had never left that grave."

Dorothea stepped closer, gently placing her free hand on his chest. "But you did come home. And that means something."

He looked down at her, pain still etched in every line of his face. But in his eyes, there was something else now, too. It was faint, but it was there, nonetheless. Hope.

She held his gaze. "You are not as lost as you think you are, Dominic." The words hung in the air between them like a fragile thread—tender, steady, and unmistakably sincere.

"I appreciate what you're trying to do, Thea," he said. "Truly, I do. But I can't be the man you want. Not anymore."

He stepped back, and with that single motion, he let go of her hand. The absence of his touch felt sudden, jarring, like a door closing in her face.

But Dorothea didn't wilt under his retreat. Instead, she squared her shoulders. "I'm not ready to give up on you."

Dominic didn't respond at first. Instead, he walked slowly back to the chair near the bed and sank onto it. "I wish you would," he murmured. "Because I gave up a long time ago."

His eyes didn't rise to meet hers this time. He stared into the dying fire, as though the glow in the hearth held something worth remembering—or forgetting.

"You should rest," he added. "Your body's still recovering."

Dorothea remained standing for a moment, her fingers slowly curling into her palm where his had just been. The silence between them was heavy with all the things he couldn't say, and all the things she wasn't ready to stop hoping for.

With a heavy sigh, she turned and returned to the bed. But her gaze lingered on him a moment longer before she slipped beneath the blankets.

He might have given up.

But she hadn't.

Dominic sat in the chair, his gaze fixed on the still figure lying in the bed. The soft, steady rise and fall of Dorothea's chest brought a measure of relief, though it did little to ease the tumult within him. The morning sunlight attempted to pierce through the heavy drapes, but the room remained cloaked in shadows, save for the golden slivers that spilled in around the edges.

Outside, birds chirped with bright indifference, a cruel contrast to the storm still raging inside his mind. His thoughts wandered to the conversation he and Dorothea had shared only hours before—her insistence that he was not beyond saving. She was wrong, of course. She had to be. A woman like her could not possibly understand the rot that lay beneath his skin. She was too kind. Too compassionate. And he was a man well-acquainted with darkness.

She deserved so much more than a broken man grasping at redemption. She needed to be free of him. That was why the annulment had to happen—no matter how much it tore at him.

A soft knock at the door drew his attention. A moment later, it creaked open to reveal Tabitha, cradling a breakfast tray. Her manner was brisk, but her eyes flicked to Dorothea with quiet concern.

"I've brought Lady Warwicke's breakfast," she said in a hushed voice. "I made certain Mrs. Dawson prepared it herself."

"Thank you," Dominic said, standing to make room for her to pass.

Tabitha stepped carefully into the chamber and placed the tray on the nearby table. "How is she faring?"

"She slept through most of the night," Dominic replied, his gaze returning to the bed. "I believe she's regained some strength."

A muffled groan interrupted them.

"I wish you wouldn't speak of me as though I'm not present," Dorothea murmured, her voice rough from sleep but laced with wry amusement. She shifted and opened her eyes, blinking against the low light.

Dominic moved closer to the bed. "How are you feeling?"

"Much better," she answered as she slowly sat up, pushing her tangled hair back from her face. "Though I confess, I'm absolutely famished."

"Then it's fortunate I brought food," Tabitha said with a smile, uncovering the plate.

Dorothea eyed the tray with interest until her gaze settled on the small glass set off to the side. Her face soured. "Must I drink that awful concoction again?"

"It would help," Dominic replied.

She wrinkled her nose. "I'll consider it after I've eaten something tolerable."

He couldn't help but smile. Even with her hair in a wild disarray and the flush of illness still fading from her cheeks, she had never looked lovelier. Perhaps it was the defiance in her eyes, or the strength she didn't even realize she possessed. She was everything he didn't deserve.

Tabitha's voice broke the moment. "Wright asked me to tell you that Mr. Haverleigh is downstairs, my lord. He wishes to speak with you."

Dominic saw Dorothea tense immediately, her hands tightening around the blankets.

"I'll go speak to him," Dominic said, already straightening his coat.

"What do you suppose he wants?" Dorothea asked, her voice tight.

Dominic placed a reassuring hand on her shoulder, his thumb unconsciously brushing against her collarbone. "It doesn't matter. What matters is you. Focus on resting and getting better."

Her eyes searched his face. "I don't want to see him."

"You won't," he promised, his voice firm. "You are safe here —with me. I won't let him or anyone else hurt you again."

She dropped her gaze, but not before he caught the flicker of pain there. A pain he feared he had caused.

He stepped back, his hand falling away. "Tabitha will stay with you until I return."

"You should try to get some rest," Dorothea insisted.

"I'll sleep only when I know the threat to you is gone." He walked towards the door, pausing with his hand on the handle. "Keep the door locked."

"Yes, my lord," Tabitha said with a curtsy.

Dominic nodded once and strode out, his mind already bracing for the confrontation awaiting him. He didn't need to guess why Haverleigh had come. The annulment.

When he entered his study, Mr. Haverleigh was already there, standing rigid in the center of the room with the barely restrained fury of a man who believed himself wronged.

"Good morning," Dominic greeted, tone clipped but polite.

"I'm not here for pleasantries," Haverleigh snapped. "I've come to collect my sister and take her home."

Dominic didn't hesitate. "No."

Haverleigh's brows lifted. "Pardon?"

"I believe I was quite clear," Dominic replied. "Dorothea is not going anywhere. Certainly not with you."

Haverleigh's nostrils flared. "Says the man who seeks to ruin her with an annulment."

"Yes," Dominic admitted. "But if it is granted, she will not return to your house. I will provide her with a household of her own—safe and far removed from your reach."

Haverleigh took a threatening step forward. "You lost the right to care for her the moment you decided to cast her aside. She is my sister, and I will not let you destroy what remains of her dignity," he said. "If you establish a household for Dorothea, she would be considered a kept woman. Is that what you want?"

Dominic remained unmoved. "No, that is not what I want."

"You've ruined her," Haverleigh spat out. "I intend to repair what I can, beginning with taking her home."

"She does not wish to go with you."

His lips twisted in disdain. "Does it matter what she wants?"

Dominic's jaw clenched. "It most certainly does."

There was a smug glint in Haverleigh's eyes now. "I doubt she's agreed to this annulment."

"I am doing what is best for her."

"No, you're doing what is easiest for *you*," Haverleigh sneered. "What is best for her is to come home, where I can see to her future and salvage what reputation she has left."

"So you can beat her again, I suppose?"

Haverleigh's expression faltered, then turned to outrage. "How I discipline my sister is none of your concern."

"Discipline?" Dominic echoed. "Is that what you call it?"

"She married, did she not? Without permission. That sort of disobedience must be corrected."

Dominic took a step forward, his voice a quiet, dangerous promise. "If you ever lay a hand on her again, I will not let the law deal with you. I will."

Haverleigh blanched but held his tongue.

Dominic continued. "Furthermore, she is still my wife. And as such, she will remain here under my protection."

Haverleigh's lip curled in disdain. "You think you're so clever..."

Dominic allowed a dry smile to tug at the corner of his mouth. "I do, actually."

"If the annulment is granted, Dorothea won't be your responsibility anymore. She'll be unprotected. Alone. And you can't always shield her from the consequences of her actions."

Dominic had heard enough. "You may go now," he growled. "You are no longer welcome in my home."

Haverleigh paused, arching a brow. "Interesting choice of words—*your* home. Not *our* home. Not *hers*. Did you ever truly intend to remain married to my sister? Or was this entire farce just another means to ease your guilt?"

"I do not answer to you," Dominic returned, his tone clipped, refusing to be baited.

Haverleigh's eyes flickered with contempt. "Of course not. You're a coward."

Dominic remained composed. "Says the man who raised his hand to his own sister," he shot back. "How very brave of you."

"At least I own what I've done," Haverleigh said with a shrug, shameless. "But you? You sit on your high horse, pretending your hands are clean while you destroy her in a slower, more insidious way."

"I do not abuse Dorothea."

"Not with your fists," Haverleigh sneered, "but what about your silence? Your indifference? Your rejection?" He leaned in slightly, voice dropping to a cruel whisper. "You break her with your words. And you're too much of a coward to admit it."

The accusation landed with precision. Dominic didn't flinch, but the impact was undeniable. He met Haverleigh's gaze with a cold, steady glare, refusing to let him see how deeply the words had struck.

Haverleigh let the silence stretch before brushing past him with a smug expression. "Good day, *my lord,*" he drawled, his mockery thick in the air.

"Before you go," Dominic called out to him, "what of Dorothea's dowry?"

Haverleigh halted, his back to him. "There is no dowry," he said without turning around.

"Strange," Dominic murmured. "Dorothea seems to believe there is."

Haverleigh turned slowly, his expression guarded. "Then she is mistaken. No dowry exists. And even if it did, it wouldn't belong to you."

"That's fair," Dominic acknowledged. "But I'm less concerned about the money and more curious about the conditions tied to it."

A muscle twitched in Haverleigh's jaw—subtle, but telling. "There are no conditions since there is no dowry," he said flatly.

"Did your father leave a will?" Dominic asked, taking a small step forward.

Haverleigh's eyes narrowed, just a flicker, but Dominic saw it. A glimmer of uncertainty, quickly masked by practiced arrogance.

"There was no will," Haverleigh stated. "And if this interrogation is finished—"

"This isn't an interrogation," Dominic interjected. "It's a conversation. I'm merely asking questions."

"Questions you have no right to ask," Haverleigh snapped.

Dominic crossed his arms over his chest. "I find myself curious that a man of your father's station would not leave a will."

"I could not speak for my father, but perhaps he had other things that preoccupied his time."

"Yet Dorothea seems to believe there is a will," Dominic pressed. "She recalls her father revising his will right before they left for the Continent."

Haverleigh scoffed. "My sister does not know what she speaks of," he asserted, turning sharply on his heel.

Dominic let him go this time, not bothering to stop him. There was no need. The man had already revealed more than he intended. Haverleigh was hiding something. But what it was, he couldn't say. At least, not yet.

He would uncover the truth.

Whatever it took.

15

T he late afternoon sun spilled through the tall windows of Dorothea's bedchamber as she turned a page in the book resting on her lap.

Across the room, Tabitha sat in a chair near the hearth, her hands moving with practiced ease as she worked on her embroidery. The quiet click of needle and thread was the only sound in the room, broken only when Tabitha paused, glanced up, and asked gently, "Can I get you anything, my lady?"

Dorothea turned her head and offered a faint smile. "No, thank you. I am quite comfortable."

Tabitha lowered her embroidery to her lap, her expression thoughtful. "Forgive me for saying so, but Lord Warwicke has been particularly attentive to you of late."

"He has."

"I do not believe he is as immune to your charm as he claims," Tabitha continued, a knowing gleam in her eyes.

Dorothea shook her head. "That is not the issue. He's not avoiding affection because he is indifferent, but he believes he is sparing me. He sees this marriage as a trap... for me."

"And what do you believe?"

Dorothea closed her book and laid it aside. "I don't want to lose Dominic," she confessed.

"Then you must continue the fight," Tabitha said with conviction.

A frown tugged at Dorothea's lips. "I've tried, but he remains so resolute. I don't know how to show him that I am better off with him than without him. He is being stubborn to a fault."

Tabitha regarded her closely. "Forgive me if I speak out of turn, but may I ask about your brother? It seems evident that you fear him."

Dorothea nodded. "My brother is not a kind man. He used to strike me. It was always worse when no one was around to intervene. And I cannot go back. I will not live under his roof again."

"I do not believe Lord Warwicke would ever permit such a thing," Tabitha said.

Dorothea looked back to the window. "Sometimes, when he's not thinking, I see a softness in him... something tender flickering behind the walls he's built. But then he remembers himself, and it vanishes like a candle being snuffed out."

"War leaves strange shadows behind," Tabitha murmured. "My husband's last letters were so dark, and his words grew distant, grim. As though hope itself had been bled from him."

"I was there," Dorothea said. "I was never on the battlefield, but I saw the aftermath—the wounded men, the screams in the night, the hollow eyes. I saw what war left behind."

"Then you saw more than most women ever do," Tabitha replied. "Some might say that makes you lucky."

Dorothea gave a humorless laugh. "Lucky?" she repeated. "I lost my father during the war, and now I am losing my husband to it—just in a different way."

"Give Lord Warwicke time," Tabitha urged.

"Time is all I ever give him. Dominic walked into my life as if he had always lived there, like my heart had always been his."

Tabitha's gaze softened with understanding. "You love him."

"I do," Dorothea whispered. "I don't even know why. There is no logic to it. But my heart is quite decided."

Tabitha gave a wistful smile. "The heart seldom listens to reason. I loved my husband from the moment we met. We were young and reckless. He promised he'd make his fortune during the war and come back to us. But he never did."

"I'm so sorry," Dorothea said, her voice thick with empathy.

Tabitha sighed, her expression a mixture of sorrow and resignation. "It's all right. I try to focus on the blessings I still have. I have a good job here, and Tristan is thriving under this roof."

"You've raised a good son."

"I think so," Tabitha replied. "Though I'm rather biased."

Dorothea smiled. "That's the mark of any good mother."

A firm knock interrupted the moment.

Tabitha set aside her needlework and crossed the room. "Who is there?"

"Molly," came the muffled reply from the other side. "Wright asked me to inform Lady Warwicke that Lady Westcott and Lady Bedford have come to call."

Turning towards Dorothea, Tabitha asked, "Do you wish to receive them?"

Dorothea lifted a shoulder. "I suppose. Though I've no idea what they want with me."

Tabitha turned back to the door. "Lady Warwicke will be down in a moment," she informed Molly.

Dorothea rose from the window seat, brushing out the creases in her skirts. "I wonder what they want," she murmured, half to herself.

Tabitha moved to the door and unlocked it, holding it open.

"Lord Warwicke gave strict instructions that I am to accompany you."

Dorothea gave a slight nod. "Then let us not keep our callers waiting."

As they moved through the quiet corridor, Tabitha stole a glance at Dorothea before speaking. "Tristan informed me that Lord Warwicke has hired a tutor for him."

"Yes, I believe that's correct. He mentioned it briefly once."

Tabitha's brows drew together, her voice cautious. "Does he know that I cannot afford such an extravagance?"

"You need not concern yourself," Dorothea replied. "My husband has grown rather fond of Tristan. I believe he sees something of himself in your boy. Perhaps it's the curiosity... or the stubbornness."

Tabitha's lips curled into a small smile, tinged with surprise. "That is awfully generous of him. I shall be sure to thank him personally."

Dorothea smiled back, but before she could respond, they arrived at the drawing room. She crossed the threshold, her gaze immediately falling on the two women awaiting her inside.

They were elegant—almost intimidatingly so. One possessed rich, dark brown hair pinned artfully into a modest chignon, while the other had a cascade of golden curls that caught the afternoon light like spun silk. Both were impeccably dressed, their gowns a clear mark of fashion and refinement. And both were smiling at her—wide, practiced smiles that made Dorothea wonder if she was being evaluated or pitied. Was she merely some new curiosity? A social obligation? Or worse, a charity case?

"Good afternoon," Dorothea said, managing a polite smile of her own.

The brunette stepped forward with graceful confidence. "Thank you for agreeing to meet with us. I am Lady Westcott."

"And I am Lady Bedford," the blonde woman added.

Dorothea clasped her hands together at her waist, unsure whether to feel guarded or grateful. "I'm afraid I'm at a disadvantage since I do not know what occasioned your visit."

Lady Westcott's smile didn't falter. "Our husbands are friends with Lord Warwicke, and we wished to introduce ourselves."

Lady Bedford leaned in slightly, her tone more playful. "Although, my husband insists he is Lord Warwicke's closest friend. He would be most put out if I didn't extend an olive branch on his behalf."

Dorothea gave them an apologetic look. "I must admit, my husband has never spoken of either gentleman."

Lady Westcott did not look concerned. "That doesn't surprise me. My husband says Lord Warwicke keeps to himself. A man of mystery, it seems."

"That he is," Dorothea murmured, gesturing towards the settee. "Would you care to sit for a moment?"

"That would be lovely," Lady Bedford replied, sweeping over to the proffered seat with the grace of someone well-accustomed to drawing rooms and small talk. "We should have come earlier, but we thought it best to give you time to settle in. Newlywed life can be rather consuming, can it not?"

Dorothea took her seat and folded her hands tightly in her lap. "Did you happen to read the Society pages yesterday?"

Lady Westcott and Lady Bedford exchanged a glance, and then Lady Westcott nodded. "We did. Which is precisely why we felt it necessary to come. You see, we ladies must support one another when the gossip columns attempt to reduce us to a headline."

"Aren't you concerned about being caught up in the scandal? About what others might say?" Dorothea asked.

Lady Bedford gave a light, unbothered laugh, waving her hand in front of her. "I have weathered my own share of scandals. I emerged from each one wiser, more resilient, and far less concerned with the opinions of people who hide behind their fans and whisper behind your back."

"You are not alone in this," Lady Westcott remarked. "If there is one thing the *ton* excels at, it is forgetting. The story will fade, replaced by the next bit of juicy gossip."

Dorothea looked between the two women, still unsure what to make of them—but grateful, nonetheless, for the unexpected kindness. Whether it was pity, duty, or genuine outreach, it felt like a lifeline.

And at that moment, she needed one.

Lady Westcott leaned forward, lowering her voice to a whisper. "You should know that my husband intends to vote against the annulment."

"He does?"

Her eyes held kindness as she replied, "Indeed. He said that you are the best thing to happen to Lord Warwicke since he returned from the war. And I daresay he's right."

Before Dorothea could respond, Lady Bedford gave an unladylike scoff and interjected. "As does mine since I told him —in no uncertain terms—that supporting this annulment would be a mistake. A grave one. Honestly, it's sheer madness."

Dorothea's lips parted in astonishment. The honesty, the unexpected solidarity—it was more than she had anticipated from women who were practically strangers.

"I... I don't know what to say," she admitted, her voice thick with emotion. "Thank you. Both of you. Truly."

"You don't have to say anything at all," Lady Westcott assured her. "Just know this—despite what the gossip columns may imply, not everyone in the *ton* is against you. There are some of us who see you clearly, and we are most certainly in your corner."

Dorothea blinked back the sting of sudden emotion. The kindness was unexpected and so genuine that it nearly undid her. She nodded, unable to find the words, but grateful all the same.

Lady Bedford, who had been watching with an amused gleam in her eyes, sat back against the settee and declared, "And if all else fails, we are not above kidnapping Lord Warwicke until he comes to his senses."

Lady Westcott sighed, though there was no true reprimand in her tone. "We discussed this, remember? No one is going to be kidnapped."

"But I've never arranged a kidnapping before," Lady Bedford declared. "I was rather hoping it would be as thrilling as it sounds. Perhaps we could lure him into a carriage under the pretense of a parliamentary emergency."

"Absolutely not," Lady Westcott said with a shake of her head. "I don't believe kidnapping one of the peers of the realm is the best way to show our support."

Dorothea laughed at the exchange, and she found herself sinking a little more comfortably into the settee cushions. For the first time in days, she felt less alone—less like she was fighting an invisible battle no one else could see.

"You two are quite unlike anyone I've ever met," she said, smiling.

Lady Bedford smirked. "That is the highest compliment you could have given us."

"And we fully intend to be the most meddlesome, loyal friends you never asked for," Lady Westcott added with a wink.

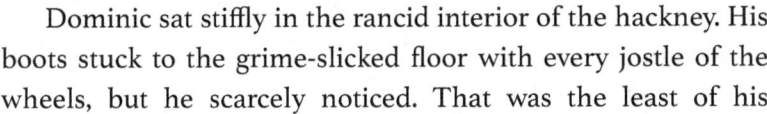

Dominic sat stiffly in the rancid interior of the hackney. His boots stuck to the grime-slicked floor with every jostle of the wheels, but he scarcely noticed. That was the least of his concerns. What he needed now was information and there was only one man in London who might possess it.

The hackney jerked to a halt along a narrow, soot-streaked street on the east side of Town, far from the polished boulevards of Mayfair. Dominic pushed open the creaking door and stepped down onto the uneven pavement. He adjusted the hem of his weathered blue waistcoat and glanced up at the sign swinging on rusted chains above him: *The Black Vulture.*

He handed a few coins to the driver and didn't wait for thanks.

Dominic noted the men idling in the shadows—ragged figures leaning against soot-blackened walls or tucked into the mouths of alleys, eyes glinting with suspicion or malice. They watched him, weighing the cut of his coat and the scuffed quality of his boots. He met their eyes with quiet warning. He was in no mood to be trifled with.

He had come for answers.

Answers about the man who dared infiltrate his household in the guise of a footman. The man who had tried to hurt Dorothea.

The Black Vulture was just as he remembered it. A thatched roof in desperate need of repair. Greasy windows coated with grime. Nothing had changed.

Dominic reached for the handle, but the door swung open before he could touch it. A man stumbled out, his coat askew and his breath reeking of stale ale. He collided with Dominic and gave a bleary scowl.

"Watch where you're goin', Mister," the drunk slurred, before lurching off down the street.

Dominic didn't respond. He stepped inside and was immediately assaulted by the pungent smell of tobacco, sweat, spilled ale, and something acrid he couldn't name. The pub was dimly lit, its rafters low and blackened with age and smoke. Familiar, in the worst possible way.

The tables were crowded with rough men nursing tankards and secrets. Dice clattered. Laughter barked. And in the far corner, half-shrouded in shadow, sat the man he'd come to see.

Blackthorn.

Once a colleague of sorts, now a seller of secrets to the highest bidder. If knowledge was currency, Blackthorn was among the wealthiest men in London.

Dominic wove his way through the hall, skirting spilled drinks and overturned chairs, until two hulking figures rose from a nearby table to block his path.

"I'm here to see Blackthorn," Dominic said without slowing.

The larger of the two crossed his arms. "No one sees Blackthorn unless he says so."

A low voice cut through the noise behind them. "Let him through."

The brutes hesitated, then parted.

Blackthorn hadn't changed much. Average height, lean frame, black hair slicked back from a sharply angled face. But it was his eyes that truly distinguished him—black as pitch and perpetually assessing, as if dissecting a man's thoughts before they were spoken.

He didn't rise, merely gestured to the vacant chair across from him. "I'll admit, I never expected to see Dominic Stevens again. Word was you'd died somewhere on the Continent. Nice scar, by the way."

Dominic sat. "Not dead. Just changed. I left Bow Street and took up a different fight."

Blackthorn's lip curled. "The war? A pointless venture."

Dominic met his gaze. "I disagree."

Blackthorn snapped his fingers towards a passing barmaid. "Well, you look awful. A drink, at least?"

"This isn't a social call," Dominic said, raising his voice loud enough to be heard over all the noise. "I need information."

"Ah, so that's why you've graced me with your presence."

Blackthorn leaned forward, his voice curt. "You disappear for years, no word, and now you come to make use of me?"

Dominic reached into his jacket pocket and withdrew a small velvet pouch. He dropped it onto the table with a dull thud.

Blackthorn's eyes sharpened. He pulled the pouch closer and opened it, the glint of silver catching the low light. "Well," he said, his smile returning, "now you have my attention."

The barmaid returned and set down two tankards. Dominic took a sip and grimaced. "Still serving watered-down ale, I see."

"Have a few and you won't mind so much," Blackthorn replied with a chuckle.

Dominic set the drink down and folded his hands on the table. "Do we have a deal?"

Blackthorn's smile faded. "We do. What is it you need?"

"I'm looking for a man. He posed as a footman in my household. Tall. Dark hair. Passed himself off well enough to get past my staff."

Blackthorn leaned back and surveyed the hall. "That describes half the men in this room. You'll have to do better."

"I know it isn't much. But you've found people with less to go on."

"True," Blackthorn responded. "What's he done to earn your ire?"

Dominic's expression hardened. "He threatened someone under my protection."

Blackthorn raised a brow. "A woman, I presume."

"Yes," he replied. "My wife, in fact."

Blackthorn let out a low chuckle, his voice laced with amused disbelief. "What unlucky woman married you?"

Dominic didn't dignify that with a response.

Blackthorn smirked, but rose to his feet with a languid stretch. "Give me a moment," he said, strolling towards the bar with the ease of a man who had no enemies—or who had already dealt with them.

Dominic watched as Blackthorn leaned in to murmur something to the barman, a wiry man with a thinning hairline and a permanent scowl etched across his face. They spoke in hushed tones, their exchange swift and efficient. At one point, Blackthorn gestured subtly over his shoulder, and the barman nodded in reply.

Finally, Blackthorn returned to the table, resuming his seat with a more serious expression. He leaned forward, his voice lowered.

"Blake—my man behind the counter—mentioned someone who came in here a few nights ago, asking dangerous questions. Tall fellow, dark hair. Spoke of revenge. Matches your description of the impostor."

Dominic's eyes narrowed. "Does he have a name?"

"No name," Blackthorn said, a glint of satisfaction lighting his eyes, "but I can do even better. He's here. Now. Sitting in the corner, drinking like he doesn't have a care in the world."

Dominic turned his head slightly, pretending to scan the room casually. His gaze landed on a shadowed figure at the far table, half-hidden by a wooden beam. The man held a tankard, his posture relaxed, but when their eyes met, recognition flared. It was him. The false footman.

Dominic stiffened, pulse quickening. *Could it truly be this easy?*

He began to rise, but Blackthorn's hand shot out to stop him. "Don't make a mess in my tavern," he warned. "Take it outside if you must."

Dominic gave a single nod. "Understood."

As if sensing danger, the man in the corner abruptly stood. His eyes darted around, then locked on to Dominic again—this time filled with alarm. Without a word, he bolted for the door, nearly knocking over a barmaid in his haste.

Blackthorn sighed. "Oh, splendid. We've got a runner."

Dominic was already moving, pushing through the crowd, ignoring shouted protests and overturned stools as he charged out the door. The cool night air hit his face as he spotted the man careening down the street, shoving past pedestrians and sending crates tumbling in his wake.

Dominic gave chase, his boots pounding against the cobblestones. The man ducked into a side alley, and Dominic followed without hesitation, drawing his pistol as the foul, narrow passage swallowed him whole.

Ahead, the man scrambled up a stack of broken crates, clearly aiming to scale the crumbling wall that marked the end of the alley.

"Stop right there," Dominic barked.

The man hesitated, then froze at the top of the crates, but didn't turn around. "What do you want?" he asked, his voice rough with exertion.

"Answers," Dominic replied, raising his pistol.

Slowly, the man turned, revealing his own weapon—a flintlock, already cocked and aimed directly at Dominic's chest. "I could just as easily kill you as talk," he said.

"Then we're at an impasse," Dominic stated, his grip tightening on the handle of his pistol. "You hurt someone I care about."

A bitter laugh escaped the man's lips. "And you did the same to me."

Dominic frowned. "I don't even know you."

"No, but you knew my sister," the man spat out. "You had her transported for theft."

Dominic's mind quickly scanned years of arrests and cases. "You'll have to be more specific. I've arrested dozens of thieves."

"She was known as the *Mayfair Robber*."

Realization dawned on him. "Yes... I remember her. Clever, bold. I always suspected she had a partner."

"She did," the man growled. "Me. But she never gave me up. Not even when she was caught."

Dominic felt no regret. "Your sister stole thousands of pounds worth of jewelry from some of the wealthiest households in London. She knew the risks. Her sentence was just."

"She didn't deserve to die," he snapped, his voice cracking with raw emotion.

"She wasn't hanged," Dominic remarked. "She was only sentenced to being transported."

"No," the man breathed, his voice trembling with fury barely contained. "She died on the voyage. Fever took her. Starved. Forgotten in the belly of a rotting prison ship while rats gnawed the boards around her."

The words hit Dominic like a blow. He tightened his jaw, his grip steady on the pistol, though a sliver of guilt threaded through his chest. "I didn't know."

"Of course you didn't!" the man snarled, his voice rising with each word. "Why would you? You never cared about her. She was just another name in your ledger. Another criminal to cart away."

Dominic met his gaze without flinching. "That's not true."

The man's lip curled into a bitter sneer. "Isn't it? You claim to care now, but where was your pity then? You never saw her as a person but rather a case to close. But you didn't just ruin her life. You ruined mine."

The man's expression darkened as he continued. "And now," he said, "you're going to learn what that feels like."

Dominic heard it before he saw it—the cold, metallic click of a pistol being cocked behind him. He tensed, then slowly turned his head.

Blackthorn stood at the mouth of the alley, his pistol raised and aimed squarely at him. "Lower the pistol, Stevens. You won't be needing that anymore since dead men can't shoot."

16

Dominic kept his gaze fixed on both men, his tone even. "Why are you doing this?" he asked Blackthorn, lowering the pistol.

Blackthorn's eyes glinted with something far darker than amusement—hatred. "Because I've been waiting for the chance to kill you for years," he said. "And Whitmore here has handed me the perfect excuse."

"What did I ever do to you?" Dominic asked.

Blackthorn's expression twisted. "You took the love of my life," he stated. "You may not have struck the final blow, but you condemned her all the same. So when Whitmore came to me, whispering about revenge for his dead sister, I knew this was my chance to make you pay."

Dominic's brow furrowed. "Whitmore's sister... she was your lover?"

Blackthorn nodded once, his jaw clenched. "Yes. She was everything to me. And you took her from me."

"I had no idea," Dominic said.

Blackthorn's nostrils flared. "Of course you didn't. Because to you, she was just another thief. But to me... she was my future."

"She stole from half the households in Mayfair," Dominic pointed out.

Whitmore scoffed from the side, still holding his weapon steady. "Can we kill him now?"

"Not yet," Blackthorn murmured. "I think it would be far more satisfying to keep him alive long enough to see us kill his precious wife."

Dominic's entire body went rigid. "You will not go anywhere near Dorothea."

"Oh?" Blackthorn sneered. "And what exactly do you plan to do about it? You've no allies here. No army. You're just a man that is cornered and outnumbered."

Dominic's eyes flicked towards Whitmore. "You'd murder a defenseless woman? That's your grand revenge?"

Whitmore didn't flinch. "And you didn't? My sister was left to rot on a floating coffin because of you. What's the difference?"

"She made a choice," Dominic growled. "She knew the risks when she stole what she did. She wasn't some innocent flower caught up in a misunderstanding."

"She stole from people who wouldn't even miss what she took," Whitmore spat. "People with more wealth than sense. You should have let her go."

"The law doesn't work like that."

"The law," Blackthorn drawled, "was always a cudgel in your hand, wasn't it? You used it to crush people like her—like us. And now you want to cry foul because the tables have turned?"

Blackthorn took a step closer as he continued. "I must say, I was surprised when I heard you were given a title. The king must've been scraping the bottom of the barrel."

Dominic tilted his head. "It was for valor and service to the Crown. Something you wouldn't understand."

Blackthorn gave a humorless laugh. "Oh, I understand sacrifice, Dominic. I just never got a medal for mine."

Dominic's grip tightened around the pistol in his hand. "I must say that the most insulting part of all this is that you believe I came here alone."

Blackthorn's confident sneer faltered, the barest flicker of uncertainty flashing through his eyes. "You're bluffing," he said with a glance over his shoulder. "I see no one else."

"I may be many things but a bluffer is not one of them. You each have one chance," Dominic added, raising the pistol until it aligned with Blackthorn's chest, "to lower your weapons and walk away. I won't offer it twice."

Whitmore gave a barking laugh. "And why would we do that?"

"Because," Dominic replied, his tone clipped and deliberate, "if you don't, you'll either end up in Newgate or you'll be dead before you hit the ground."

Whitmore's gaze darted towards Blackthorn. "Can I kill him now?"

Blackthorn gave a shallow nod. "We'll do it together. On three." He raised his pistol higher. "One..."

Dominic tensed, feet braced and finger ready on the trigger.

"Two—"

"Wait!" Blackthorn shouted.

Dominic let out a long breath of relief as Lord Alcott stepped into view, his pistol pressed up against Blackthorn's head.

"You took your time," Dominic said, not lowering his weapon.

Alcott smirked. "I wanted to make sure the constables heard every word of their charming little conspiracy before we stepped in."

"The constables?" Whitmore asked, a tremor creeping into his voice.

"Yes, we've been listening from just beyond the alley," Alcott confirmed. "We heard your confession about conspiring with your sister, your plan to harm Lady Warwicke, and your attempt on Lord Warwicke's life. Very compelling testimony, really."

At that moment, three broad-shouldered men emerged at the far end of the alleyway, their pistols drawn and aimed, their expressions grim.

Dominic moved towards Blackthorn without ceremony, wrenching the pistol from his hand. "You played your hand and you lost."

Alcott stepped closer, eyes still on Whitmore. "It wasn't a very good hand to begin with," he quipped.

Blackthorn's jaw tightened. "You think you're clever, do you?"

"No," Dominic answered, tucking the seized pistol into his coat, "but I was wise enough to know you were never to be trusted."

Whitmore let out a furious growl and suddenly raised his pistol, the barrel trembling in his grasp. "No! You won't win! You can't!"

Dominic turned slowly to face him, his own pistol once again raised. "It's over, Whitmore. There's no need for anyone to die today."

Whitmore's eyes were wild now, darting between Dominic, Alcott, and the constables. "There is," he hissed, desperation etched across his face. "If you die with me!"

Alcott smoothly shifted his aim, the pistol now trained on Whitmore. "If your finger so much as twitches, I will put a hole through you."

Whitmore stood frozen, sweat beading at his brow as the

weight of the moment crashed down upon him. The alley now hung in brittle silence—waiting for someone to flinch.

At last, Whitmore's shoulders sagged and he lowered the weapon fully, letting it dangle at his side. A long, bitter sigh escaped his lips. "I suppose," he muttered, his voice rough with defeat, "I do want to see another sunrise."

Dominic stepped forward, his own pistol still drawn as a precaution. He reached out and relieved Whitmore of his weapon.

"I'm sorry about your sister," Dominic said, sincerity laced through his words. "I never meant for her to die."

Whitmore's eyes flashed with a mixture of grief and fury. "Well, your choices made it happen," he bit out. "You can dress it up with good intentions, but she's still dead."

Dominic knew there was nothing more that he could say.

Two of the constables stepped forward with heavy, purposeful steps. They seized Whitmore and Blackthorn by the arms. Neither man struggled as they were escorted out of the alleyway and into the night beyond.

Dominic turned towards Lord Alcott, knowing what needed to be said. "Thank you," he said. "For saving my life."

Alcott merely smiled. "The way I see it, I still owe you for saving my life a time or two on the battlefield."

Dominic tucked his pistol back into the waistband of his trousers and cast a glance around the narrow alley, its walls slick with grime and its air still thick with damp rot. "Shall we get out of here?"

Alcott chuckled. "I thought you'd never ask."

They stepped out of the alley and onto the cobbled pavement. The misty night wrapped around them, but it felt less oppressive now. The danger had passed. For the moment, all was quiet.

As they walked, Dominic let the silence stretch, each footstep marking a strange, unfamiliar sensation—*peace*. The threat to Dorothea was gone. The men who had plotted against her were in custody. She was safe.

For now.

Was Mr. Haverleigh right, after all? Could Dominic truly protect Dorothea if he went through with the annulment?

Beside him, Alcott broke the silence. "You've gone rather quiet," he observed.

Dominic didn't look at him. "I'm thinking."

"If I had to guess, you are thinking about your wife."

"I am."

Alcott shook his head with exaggerated dismay. "Women. Burdensome creatures, the lot of them. You can't live with them."

Dominic's brow creased, half-amused, half-weary. "I believe the quote you're butchering is by Desiderius Erasmus: '*Women, can't live with them, can't live without them.*'"

Alcott snorted. "No, no. I maintain you can live without them. Happily, in fact. They spend our money, test our patience, and tangle our lives into knots."

He grew silent, retreating to his own thoughts once more. Dorothea wasn't simply a woman. She was his. His wife. His responsibility.

And he was beginning to fear that letting her go might not protect her after all.

It might, in fact, destroy him.

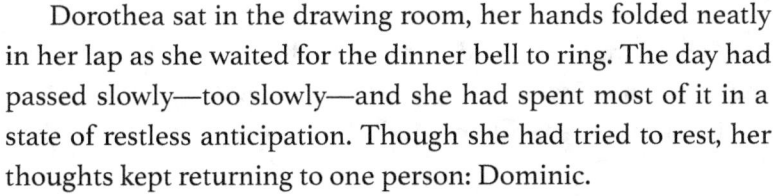

Dorothea sat in the drawing room, her hands folded neatly in her lap as she waited for the dinner bell to ring. The day had passed slowly—too slowly—and she had spent most of it in a state of restless anticipation. Though she had tried to rest, her thoughts kept returning to one person: Dominic.

When they had first met, she hadn't been looking for love. She had long since convinced herself that she didn't need it, that it was a foolish notion meant for others, not for her. But Dominic had come crashing into her world with that intense gaze and wounded soul, and suddenly all of her carefully laid beliefs had begun to unravel. He hadn't asked for her heart, but somehow, he had taken it anyway.

How was it fair to love a man who seemed so determined to push her away?

And yet... she did love him. Fiercely. Unshakably.

Her head turned at the faintest rustle, and her breath caught in her throat. There he stood, leaning casually in the doorway, dressed in his fine clothes and a crooked grin playing at the edges of his mouth. Just the sight of him made her heart swell.

Why did her heart feel so at ease with him? Little by little, without even realizing it, she felt more drawn to him.

"Good evening, Thea," he said.

A soft smile curved her lips. "Good evening, Dominic."

He pushed away from the doorframe and stepped into the room. "You're safe now. I made certain of it."

Her brows lifted. "How?"

"The footman is no longer a threat," he said. "He's in Newgate now. And if justice prevails, he'll be transported soon enough."

"You found him that quickly?"

"I have experience in such matters," he said, lowering himself onto the settee beside her. "I used to work as a Bow Street Runner. I know how to find people who would rather not be found."

"Thank you," she said, her words filled with gratitude. "Did the footman tell you why he tried to kill me?"

Dominic gave a solemn nod. "Do you remember the case I

spoke of before? The one involving a string of thefts across Mayfair?"

"You mean the young woman who posed as a lady and was stealing from townhouses?"

"Yes, precisely," he replied. "She was sentenced to be transported, but she didn't survive the journey. Died aboard the ship before reaching the colonies."

"And the footman?"

"He was her brother," Dominic said, his voice heavy. "He blamed me for her death, but he could not reach me. So he targeted the person he thought would hurt me the most."

She drew in a sharp breath. "Me."

"He believed by taking your life, he would exact his revenge. That somehow your blood would balance the scales."

Her hands trembled slightly at her sides. "How could someone carry so much hate?"

"I ask myself that every day." Dominic's posture shifted, his expression growing more solemn. "I meant it, what I said. I'll always protect you. You'll never need to fear for your safety."

"But I do fear, especially if we're no longer married. If the annulment goes through, what's to stop my brother from taking me back? From controlling me again?"

A shadow passed through his eyes. "I would never allow that."

"But you won't always be there to stop him," she responded.

He ran a hand through his hair, his frustration evident. "Do you even want to be married to me?" he asked suddenly, almost as if he didn't want to hear the answer.

Yes. With her whole, foolish heart.

But she didn't dare overwhelm him with the depth of her feelings. Not yet. "I do," she replied. "I always have."

Dominic turned his face away. "Your life wouldn't be easy if you stayed with me. I'm not... I'm not an easy man. I have darkness in me. I fear you'd grow to resent it. Resent me."

She reached for his hand, gently entwining her fingers with his. "I could never resent you."

He flinched slightly, a wounded look crossing his features. "You say that now, but what about in a few years? When the weight of everything I carry becomes yours as well? I couldn't bear to see you unhappy because of me."

She waited until he met her gaze before speaking. "I wish you could see yourself through my eyes, Dominic. Then you'd understand just how deeply I care for you. You call yourself broken, but I don't see that. And even if you were—truly shattered—I'd help you gather each and every piece. I would never walk away from you."

His throat bobbed as he swallowed, clearly moved. "I don't know if I could do that to you—tie you to a man like me."

"You wouldn't be doing anything *to* me," she said, lifting her hand to cup his cheek. Her thumb brushed across his jagged scar. "You'd be letting me choose you. And I already have."

"Thea..." His voice cracked slightly as he said her name. "I just... I need you to be certain."

"I am certain," she whispered. "Utterly."

He studied her face, as though searching for a crack in her resolve. "How do you know? After everything?"

She smiled. "It is simple," she replied. "I care for you, and I will wait for you. Because, in my heart, I know you are worth it."

Dominic's eyes drifted to her lips. The air between them changed, charged and trembling with what might come next. She could feel it—he wanted to kiss her. But still, she held back. She wouldn't press him. So, she remained still, letting the silence speak what words could not.

And hoped, with all her heart, that one day he would choose her, too.

The chime of the dinner bell rang faintly in the distance, breaking the spell that had come over them.

Dominic cleared his throat, the sound low and rough as he met her eyes. "Shall we adjourn for dinner?"

It was the last thing she wanted. Her hand still rested lightly on his cheek, her heart still caught in the hope that he might finally close the distance between them. But instead, she nodded and slowly lowered her hand.

He rose and extended his hand to help her up. "I find that I am famished," he said, his voice lighter now, as though he hadn't just been inches away from baring his soul.

Dorothea allowed him to lead her from the drawing room, though her thoughts lingered behind. He had been so close to kissing her. She had seen it in the way his gaze dipped to her mouth, felt it in the unspoken hush between them. What was holding him back? Was it some shadow from his past or a fear he had yet to name? What more could she say or do to show him that she wanted him—not just the parts of him he deemed acceptable, but all of him?

As they entered the dining room, Dominic guided her to her chair and pulled it out. She murmured her thanks, and once she was seated, he took the place beside her—close, but not quite close enough.

He turned slightly to meet her gaze. "I had an informative conversation with your brother earlier today."

"Oh? What did he want?"

Dominic reached for his wine glass and took a sip before answering. "He was quite insistent that you possess no dowry."

She furrowed her brow. "That cannot be right. My father assured me that I had a dowry."

"Did he tell you the specifics?"

"Yes. If I didn't marry by my five-and-twentieth birthday, I was to inherit the ten thousand pounds."

Dominic considered her for a moment before murmuring, "Interesting."

"Perhaps my brother misspoke?"

"Possibly, but he also claimed your father left behind no will."

Dorothea frowned. "That's not possible. My father was meticulous. He would never leave something so important unsettled."

"I daresay your brother has not been rather forthright, especially when it has come to you," Dominic shared. "Before I came to retrieve you, your brother had been depositing money that my solicitor had been sending to you."

She pressed her lips together. "Why would he do such a thing?"

"I cannot say."

Before Dorothea could respond, the footmen entered the room and set steaming bowls of soup before them. The scent of leeks and rich broth filled the space, but Dorothea hardly noticed. Her appetite had vanished.

Dominic lifted his spoon and stirred the soup absently. "I'll look into the matter further."

She glanced at him, her voice tight. "How?"

A ghost of a smirk curled his lips. "I have my ways."

Dorothea turned her attention back to her soup, stirring it gently, though her appetite remained elusive. Just as she lifted the spoon to her lips, a flicker of movement in the corridor caught her eyes. She glanced up and saw two curious eyes watching them.

"Tristan," she called out. "What are you doing loitering in the corridor?"

The boy stepped into the dining room, wholly unrepentant, his hands stuffed into the pockets of his trousers. "I'm bored," he announced with a dramatic sigh.

Dorothea arched a brow. "Is it not past your bedtime?"

Tristan shrugged, utterly unconcerned. "Perhaps. But Anna fell asleep in the chair again. Her head was leaning all funny, and I didn't want to wake her." He wandered closer to the table. "What are you eating? It smells delicious."

"Did you not have your supper?" she asked.

"I did," Tristan replied. "But that was hours ago."

Dominic leaned back in his chair and gestured to the one beside him. "Come sit. You can have my soup."

Tristan's eyes widened. "Truly?" Without waiting for further encouragement, he darted to the chair and sat down. "Thank you, my lord," he said before he started devouring the soup.

Dorothea watched the exchange with quiet affection. The way Dominic's expression softened as he regarded the boy stirred something deep within her. He had no obligation to Tristan, and yet here he was—gentle, patient, and instinctively kind.

As Tristan focused on his soup, Dominic turned to her once more. "I was wondering if you might wish to join me for a carriage ride tomorrow."

Her smile came easily. "I would greatly enjoy that."

Before she could say more, Tristan piped up between bites. "Can I come, too?"

Dominic chuckled, a low, genuine sound that warmed Dorothea's heart. "I think it would be best if you stayed behind this time."

Tristan slumped slightly. "That is no fun at all."

"How are your studies going?" Dominic asked.

"Boring," Tristan muttered, scraping his spoon along the bottom of the bowl. "Why do I need a tutor? I already know how to read."

"A tutor teaches much more than just reading," Dominic replied. "There are other subjects—history, arithmetic, science —that are important for a young gentleman to understand."

Tristan gave him a thoughtful look. "Do you think he'll teach me about rockets?"

"You could ask him," Dominic said. "And if he doesn't know enough, I can teach you myself."

Tristan's expression turned unexpectedly solemn. "My father loved rockets." He picked up the bowl and brought it to his lips, slurping the last of the broth just as a voice called from the doorway.

"Tristan!"

All heads turned as Tabitha strode into the room, her expression a mixture of weariness and mild exasperation. "I do apologize," she said to Dominic and Dorothea as she crossed the room. "Tristan should not be interrupting your supper."

"We invited him," Dorothea assured her.

Tabitha offered a grateful nod, though her disapproval remained. "That is generous of you, but he should be in bed and not slurping soup like a common street urchin. Have I taught you nothing, Son?"

Tristan visibly winced. "I was hungry. And Lord Warwicke said I could have his soup."

"Then you should have asked Anna for more food or gone down to the kitchen yourself," Tabitha chided. She placed a hand on his shoulder. "Come along. It's time for bed."

Tristan pushed back his chair, dragging his feet as he rose. "But I'm not even tired."

Tabitha gave him a look. "Why don't we find a book in the library? I can read to you—or better yet, you can read to me."

"Do I have to?" Tristan whined.

"Yes," she replied. "Now, thank Lord and Lady Warwicke for their hospitality."

The boy cast a sheepish glance between them. "Thank you, my lord. My lady."

"Goodnight, Tristan," Dorothea said.

Once the pair had exited the room, the door closing softly behind them, Dominic leaned back in his chair and sighed.

"I used to do the same thing," he said, his voice tinged with amusement. "I'd wait until my nursemaid fell asleep in her chair, then sneak down to the kitchen. I'd eat whatever the cook had left out—cold pies, biscuits, even old scraps of ham. I thought myself terribly clever."

"That does not surprise me in the least," Dorothea said as she set down her spoon. "You've always struck me as the sort of boy who thrived on mischief."

"And what about you?"

Dorothea sat back slightly, folding her hands in her lap. "Oh, I was dreadfully well-behaved. I followed every rule to the letter. I never once dared to creep out of bed after hours, even when I was certain the adults were up to something far more interesting downstairs."

Dominic leaned in just a touch, the candlelight catching in his eyes. "Sometimes it's rather fun to break the rules."

The weight of his words pressed into the space between them, unsaid truths hovering in the air. His gaze—calm, playful, but shadowed with longing—sent her heart stumbling in her chest.

She held his gaze and replied, her voice quieter now, "Perhaps it is."

17

D ominic sat alone in his study as the morning light filtered through the windows. The ledgers before him lay open, numbers neatly inked across the parchment, but he couldn't bring himself to focus. His gaze remained fixed on the page, yet not a single figure registered in his mind.

All he could think about was Dorothea.

Last night in the drawing room, he had come dangerously close to kissing her. The memory still burned at the edges of his thoughts, refusing to fade. Her fingers had brushed his cheek, her eyes held him transfixed, and for one breathless moment, he had nearly surrendered to it all.

But he hadn't. Because he couldn't. Not when everything inside him still warred with what he believed was right.

With a heavy sigh, he pressed a hand over his face. Good gads, it would've been so easy to lean in and take what he wanted—to let himself feel. To silence the world for just a moment and believe he deserved happiness. But Dorothea wasn't just some fleeting comfort. She was kind. Steady. Bright in all the ways he was not. She deserved certainty. And he was nowhere close to having that.

The logical path would be to withdraw the petition for annulment. But could he do that in good conscience? What kind of life would he be offering her? A husband who carried ghosts, who flinched at the idea of joy, who feared he would destroy everything he touched?

Still... these blasted feelings for her refused to loosen their grip. They crept in at unexpected moments, stealing his breath. She made him smile—*genuinely* smile—without even trying. And when she looked at him, it wasn't with pity, but with something dangerously close to belief. No one had believed in him in a very long time.

Botheration.

He leaned back in his chair, exasperated. Was this what falling in love felt like? The endless push and pull? The aching want tangled up in fear? He wouldn't know since he'd never allowed himself the luxury. But if it meant looking forward to seeing her, longing for the sound of her laugh, wondering what she might say next... well, he supposed he might already be halfway there.

A knock on the door interrupted his spiraling thoughts.

Wright stepped into the study. "Mr. Wells has requested a moment of your time, my lord."

Dominic straightened in his chair, grateful for the distraction. "Send him in."

A moment later, Mr. Wells entered the study, a well-worn satchel slung over one shoulder. His ruddy cheeks were flushed from exertion or excitement—possibly both.

"I come bearing good news," the solicitor announced.

"You do?"

Mr. Wells nodded. "Despite Mr. Haverleigh's earlier claim that your wife has no dowry, he has now agreed to grant you five thousand pounds as a gesture of goodwill."

Dominic's suspicion flared. Slowly, he closed the ledger in front of him and leaned back in his chair, arms folding across his chest. "And he offered this freely?"

"I wouldn't go so far as to call it freely," Mr. Wells replied with a wry twist of his lips. "I paid him a visit this morning and informed him that we intended to request a formal inquest into his finances. I believe that suggestion alone was enough to motivate his generosity."

Dominic snorted under his breath. "I see. Blackmail by implication. Clever."

"I prefer to call it... strategic persuasion," Wells said, clearly pleased with himself. He lowered into the chair opposite the desk and set his satchel on the floor with a thud.

"And what exactly are the circumstances that make five thousand pounds a fair offer?" Dominic asked.

Mr. Wells hesitated slightly before replying. "In truth, I'm not certain a judge would grant such an inquest, especially considering the absence of a will."

"How certain are we that no will exists?"

"As I explained before, it wasn't filed in probate court, and Mr. Haverleigh was adamant that his father left none," Wells explained. "At present, the only claim to the contrary is your wife's recollection. And while I believe she speaks the truth, it's not exactly ironclad evidence in the eyes of the court."

Dominic's jaw tightened. He didn't doubt Dorothea's word. Not for a moment. But without a document, her honesty might count for very little in the legal arena. And her brother would no doubt hide the truth if it served his ends.

As if Dominic needed another reason to loathe the man.

"Furthermore," Mr. Wells added, adjusting his spectacles as he withdrew a folded document from his satchel, "if Parliament does grant the annulment, the five thousand pounds will be transferred directly to your wife, per the terms dictated by Mr. Haverleigh himself."

Dominic's fingers drummed against the polished surface of his desk, slow and deliberate. On the surface, it sounded like a concession. Generous, even. But it was too neat. Haverleigh was many things—proud, calculating, vindictive—but generous was not among them. He wouldn't yield five thousand pounds unless something larger was at stake.

Which begged the question: *what was he trying to protect?*

Mr. Wells began to rise, brushing a hand over the front of his waistcoat. "Very well. Shall I send word to Mr. Haverleigh that we are in agreement?"

"No," Dominic said sharply.

Wells paused mid-motion, eyebrows raised in surprise. "No?"

"Not yet," Dominic repeated, his voice firm as he, too, stood.

Mr. Wells gave him a blank look. "My lord, with all due respect, I doubt you will receive a more favorable offer. This is likely the best we can hope for under the current circumstances."

Dominic stepped around the desk. "I'm not concerned with the offer."

"Then what are you concerned with?" Wells asked, clearly baffled.

"That Mr. Haverleigh is too eager to make this go away. I do believe he is hiding something and I intend to find out what it is before we move forward," Dominic replied. "Give me until tomorrow morning to decide on how to proceed."

Mr. Wells adjusted his satchel and gave a respectful nod. "As you wish, my lord."

After the solicitor had taken his leave, the door clicked shut behind him, leaving Dominic alone once more in the quiet study. He barely had time to collect his thoughts before Wright stepped inside.

"The carriage has been brought around to the front, my lord," Wright informed him.

"Very good," Dominic replied. "Has Lady Warwicke been informed?"

"She has, and she is presently waiting in the entry hall."

Dominic moved towards the door. "Then I'd best not keep her waiting."

As he stepped into the entry hall, he came to a full stop, his breath catching ever so slightly at the sight before him. Dorothea stood by the main doors and her pink gown hugged her figure with understated elegance. The top of her head was covered with a straw hat, but two red curls framed her face.

Good gads, he thought, *does she become more beautiful each time I see her?*

She met his gaze, but the frown tugging at her lips quickly dispelled the warmth that had filled his chest. He crossed the room in several strides.

"What's wrong?"

She bit her lower lip. "Do you think this is wise?"

He tilted his head, unsure what she meant. "A carriage ride through Hyde Park?" His mouth quirked into a half-smile. "I daresay we've survived worse."

She didn't return the smile. Instead, her voice dropped. "I'm being serious. What if people stare at us? What if they whisper behind their fans and spread more rumors?"

He stepped closer, his tone softening. "Oh, they'll stare. I have no doubt of that."

A line between her brows appeared, clearly startled by his admission.

"How could they not," he continued, eyes never leaving hers, "when you look so beautiful?"

A faint blush bloomed across her cheeks. "You are too kind."

"I'm not being kind. I'm being truthful," he said, his voice earnest now. "I will never tire of telling you how beautiful you are, Thea. You are—without question—the most beautiful woman I have ever known."

Her eyes dropped to the floor, her voice a whisper. "But I have red hair."

He reached out and captured one of the loose curls between his fingers. "And I happen to adore your red hair," he responded. "As I do *you*."

She lifted her gaze slowly to meet his. "My mother had this same color hair."

"I wish I had met her," Dominic said.

A thoughtful look crossed Dorothea's face. "She would have liked you. I'm sure of that."

He puffed his chest out theatrically. "Well, I am rather easy to like."

She laughed, just as he had intended. "Aren't you being cocky?"

"Come," he said, offering his arm. "Let the gossips whisper all they like. I care not a whit for them. Let us go enjoy being together."

Dorothea accepted his arm. "I rather like the sound of that."

Wright stepped forward to open the main door, and Dominic led Dorothea to the carriage. Once she was situated, he moved to sit next to her, closing the door behind him.

The carriage gave a slight jolt as it lurched into motion, wheels crunching softly over gravel before settling into a rhythmic cadence on the road.

Dominic leaned back into the seat, letting his shoulders relax for the first time that day. The tension he'd carried with him—over Haverleigh, over the petition, over the gnawing uncertainty of what came next—eased in her presence.

He turned his head slightly to look at her. Dorothea sat with her hands folded in her lap, her eyes alight with curiosity as she watched the hustle and bustle on the street, and her lips curved into a soft, unguarded smile. A breeze lifted one of the loose curls that framed her face and sent it dancing across her cheek.

He stared longer than he should have, caught not just by her beauty but by the peace that radiated from her in that moment. *How did she do it?* How did she remain so poised, so hopeful, after all she had endured? Her resilience humbled him.

What was he feeling?

Was it... *contentment?*

The realization struck him, without warning, and yet with an undeniable clarity. He hadn't felt anything like it in years— not since before the war, before the weight of duty had hardened him from the inside out.

And it was all because of Dorothea.

Dorothea sat nestled within the open carriage, her gloved hands resting lightly in her lap as they rolled steadily down the bustling road. The city was alive with movement—hawkers lined the edge of the pavement, waving ribbons, shouting out their wares with exaggerated cheer, while elegant ladies browsed stalls beneath parasols and children darted through the gaps in the crowd. The scent of warm bread wafted through the air, mingling with the faint aroma of coal smoke and horsehair, creating that familiar, chaotic perfume of London.

As she turned her head to glance towards Dominic, she found him already watching her. His expression was unreadable, but his gaze held a warmth that made her pulse skip.

"Is something amiss?" she asked.

He shook his head, the corners of his mouth lifting slightly. "No. I'm merely enjoying your reactions."

Dorothea smiled, turning her gaze outward once more. "I

rather enjoy being outside—watching people, seeing the world in motion. There's so much energy in the streets. So much life."

Dominic gave a short, amused huff. "That is... unusual."

She turned her head, brow lifted. "Unusual?"

"Most people of our class find it chaotic. Tiresome. But you seem to draw strength from it."

"I suppose I do," she admitted. "It reminds me that the world keeps turning, even when one's own has come to a standstill."

As the carriage curved past the crowded shops and turned into the wide, tree-lined lane leading to Hyde Park, Dorothea sat straighter in her seat, her eyes widening with something close to delight. "I haven't been to Hyde Park in years."

Dominic followed her gaze, his voice drier now. "It is a place to be seen. Nothing more."

Dorothea glanced at him. "That's a rather cynical view. It's beautiful here. The trees, the lake... even the bustle of the park itself."

"Not Rotten Row," he muttered, eyeing the long, orderly line of fashionable carriages with clear distaste. "That stretch is nothing but a slow-moving parade. People lining up to observe and to be observed. They pretend to take in the scenery while measuring the worth of every gown and every companion."

Dorothea tilted her head, amused. "If you dislike it so thoroughly, why did you suggest this outing?"

He looked at her then, a devilish smile forming. "Because I wanted to spend time with you. Alone."

She gave a soft laugh, raising a hand to gesture towards the row of carriages ahead of them. "Then I daresay you've miscalculated. We are anything but alone."

Dominic leaned back against the cushions. "We are alone... enough."

She laughed again. "Well then, shall we pass the time by discussing the weather?"

He feigned a shudder. "No, thank you. I'd prefer to discuss anything else."

She regarded him for a long moment before asking, "May I ask you something more serious?"

"You may always ask me anything," he said, his tone suddenly sincere.

She hesitated, then asked quietly, "Do you miss it? Being a soldier?"

The amusement drained from his features, leaving behind something far more solemn. For a moment, he didn't respond, and she wondered if she'd overstepped. But then he spoke, his voice tentative at first.

"There are parts I miss," he admitted. "The camaraderie. The clarity. The rush of releasing a rocket and watching it soar towards its target. For a moment, everything made sense—every choice, every breath."

He paused, his gaze turning distant. "But if I sit in silence too long, I can still hear the echo of it all. The sharp crack of musket fire. The roar of the cannons. And worse still—the screams of the wounded. The dying."

A lump formed in Dorothea's throat. "I'm sorry," she whispered, unsure what words could possibly ease the pain of such memories.

"I fought. I survived. But it's not a chapter I like to revisit," he said quietly. "Though... I'll always carry pride in serving with my unit. Being chosen for the Second Rocket Troop was an honor I never expected."

Dorothea's brows knit with regret. "I should never have brought it up."

"It is all right," Dominic assured her. "Truly, you can ask me anything. I mean that. You may not always like what I say, but I will never lie to you."

That courage—the openness in his voice—made her braver

in return. "Then let me ask one more thing," she said, steadying her breath. "Do you regret marrying me?"

His silence was immediate, but it didn't feel cold—just weighty. Thoughtful.

"At first, yes," he said finally, his voice quiet but certain. "I regretted the circumstances. The rushed decisions. The way it all unfolded."

Her heart clenched.

"But not you," he added firmly. "Never you. And everything since then has changed. I am glad—truly glad—that I married you."

Dorothea turned her face towards the wind, letting the breeze carry away the sting of his initial confession. But his final words—those stayed. Warming her from within like sunlight breaking through clouds.

"I'm relieved to hear that," she murmured.

Dominic shifted slightly in his seat, close enough that his shoulder brushed gently against hers. The contact was unintentional—or at least, it seemed so—but it sent a ripple through her nonetheless.

"Why is it that you seem so surprised by my response?" he asked, eyes searching hers. "You know that I care about you."

Dorothea looked away. "I know you care," she replied. "But that's not the same as staying. Do you still intend to go through with the annulment?"

Dominic winced—just slightly, but enough to answer her question before he opened his mouth. "I haven't decided yet," he admitted, his voice rough with conflict. "It's... complicated."

"Then *un*complicate it," she said, turning towards him, her tone firm.

His brow furrowed. "It's not that simple, Thea. Whatever happens, I'll ensure you're well cared for. You'll have your own household. Your own independence. You won't want for anything."

Dorothea pressed her lips together, hard. *Why couldn't he see?* She didn't want a house of her own. She didn't want security or solitude or financial assurance. She wanted *him*.

He sighed. "I know that's not the answer you were hoping for, but it's the truth."

She arched an eyebrow. "You want the truth?"

"I do."

"Then here it is," she said. "I think you're a coward."

His head snapped back slightly, as though she'd struck him. "I beg your pardon?"

Dorothea squared her shoulders, refusing to look away. "You're afraid, Dominic. Afraid of what this could be. So instead of facing it, you're pushing me away. You keep yourself closed off and convince yourself that you're doing the noble thing."

His jaw clenched. "Thea—"

But she lifted a hand and held it up, silencing him. "Don't," she said. "Don't pretend you're heartless. You're not. You think you're unlovable because of what you've seen. What you've done. But that isn't true."

Her voice softened, but it lost none of its conviction. "You *are* lovable. You just don't believe it yet."

Dominic turned towards her, expression caught between defensiveness and vulnerability, as though the words had cracked something he'd tried so hard to keep sealed.

But before he could speak, a sharp voice called out from beside the carriage.

"Lord Warwicke!"

A tall, heavy-set man on horseback drew near, his riding coat stretched across a barrel-like chest. His face was flushed from the exertion of the ride—or perhaps from self-satisfaction—and his eyes gleamed with too much familiarity as he looked between them.

"And this must be your lovely wife," he said, his gaze lingering too long on Dorothea.

Dominic's entire demeanor shifted in an instant. He grew rigid. "Lord Inglewood," he said tersely. "You may carry on. There's no need to stop and speak with us."

Lord Inglewood ignored the dismissal, reins slack in his gloved hand as his horse shifted beneath him. "Your presence is causing quite the stir," he said with amusement. "I daresay all of Rotten Row is buzzing."

"That was not our intention," Dominic said. "We're simply enjoying a quiet ride."

"During the fashionable hour?" Lord Inglewood's brows rose in mock surprise. "Surely you knew better, Warwicke. This is not the hour for quiet."

Dominic's patience thinned visibly. "What do you want, Inglewood?"

"Only an introduction," he said with exaggerated innocence. "I have not yet had the pleasure of being properly introduced to your bride."

After a long moment, Dominic spoke, his tone clipped. "Lord Inglewood, allow me the honor of introducing you to my wife, Lady Warwicke."

Lord Inglewood tipped his hat with a theatrical flourish. "My lady. You are even lovelier than the whispers suggested. I can see why Warwicke keeps you so well hidden."

Dorothea arched an eyebrow. "My husband does not keep me anywhere, Lord Inglewood."

"Of course not," Lord Inglewood said with a lazy smirk, though there was an edge of sharpness beneath the surface. He adjusted his grip on the reins and turned his gaze back to Dominic with a flicker of expectation. "Now then, have you come to a decision regarding our arrangement?"

Dominic met his gaze. "I have."

The older man leaned forward slightly in his saddle, as if already anticipating agreement. "Well?"

"I will not be supporting your bill," Dominic replied, his tone resolute. "I believe it serves personal interests, not the public good. I cannot, in good conscience, endorse legislation that would enrich a select few at the cost of the nation's stability."

Lord Inglewood's face hardened. The false charm drained away, replaced by something cold and dangerous. "Then I wish you the best of luck securing your annulment in Parliament without the backing of the Tory party," he stated. "I imagine you'll find the path far more difficult than you anticipated."

"I'll take my chances," Dominic replied.

Lord Inglewood narrowed his eyes. "You're either very brave —or very foolish." And then, with a smirk that reeked of cruelty, he glanced at Dorothea. "Perhaps," he drawled, "once you've cast your wife aside, I might have a go with her."

Dorothea's breath caught in her throat. "How dare you—"

But Dominic cut her off, his voice vibrating with fury. "Say something like that again," he growled, "and I promise you, it will be the last mistake you ever make."

Inglewood, to his credit—or perhaps his arrogance—didn't flinch. But a flicker of uncertainty crossed his face. "That's rather bold talk," he said, "from a man so eager to be rid of her."

Dominic's gaze never wavered. "If I were truly eager to be rid of her, I wouldn't be threatening a duel over your disgraceful tongue. She is my wife, Inglewood. And that gives me every right—and obligation—to defend her honor."

Inglewood's lips curled into a sneer. "She is your wife... *for now*," he said, his tone mocking. With a tug on the reins, he wheeled his horse around and rode off, his departure kicking up a trail of dust behind him.

Dorothea looked over at Dominic and said, "That man is vile. Utterly without shame."

Dominic turned to face her. The tension in his jaw began to ease, and some of the fire in his eyes cooled—but not all of it. His expression softened, but there remained a flicker of fierce protectiveness in his voice.

"Never be alone with Lord Inglewood," he said, the command beneath the words unmistakable. "I do not trust him."

Dorothea nodded. "I won't. I promise."

He studied her for a moment, as if trying to gauge whether she truly understood the threat Inglewood posed. Then, ever so gently, he placed a hand over hers where it rested on her lap.

"I would never let him touch you," Dominic assured her, the edge of violence still simmering beneath his calm. "Not while I still draw breath."

"I know," she replied.

And she did. The promise in his words wasn't idle. He meant it, every word, and she should be grateful for such a declaration. But she wanted more. She wanted love, or nothing at all.

18

The moon hung high and bright in the sky, casting a pale silver sheen over the deserted streets. Shadows clung to the edges of buildings like secrets, and Dominic moved among them with practiced ease, his footsteps silent. Each stride brought him closer to Mr. Haverleigh's townhouse and the answers he was determined to uncover.

He hadn't come to ask politely. He already knew Haverleigh would never hand over the truth willingly. There was only one sure way to uncover it: find it himself.

Even if it meant breaking the law to uphold what was right.

Fortunately, he was no stranger to such methods. Years as a Bow Street Runner had trained him well. He knew how to pick locks, move without a sound, and leave a room untouched, as though he had never been there at all.

He reached the edge of Haverleigh's property and slipped through the wrought-iron gate, crouching low as he crossed the gardens. No lamps were lit. The house sat quiet and dark, cloaked in sleep. A check of the lower windows confirmed his hope—the study was unlit, the curtains drawn halfway. He pressed a hand against the frame and smiled to himself when it gave without resistance.

Foolish man didn't even secure his window.

With a quiet push, the pane lifted, and Dominic hoisted himself inside. He landed soundlessly on the carpet, the faint scent of tobacco and stale brandy lingering in the air. The study was exactly as he remembered it—heavy furniture, a cluttered desk, and books lining the walls in regimented order. The moonlight spilled through the window behind him, just bright enough to cast the outlines of the room in silver and gray.

He moved to the large mahogany desk at the center and tried the top drawer. Locked. Not surprising.

Dominic crouched and pulled two slender pins from his inner jacket pocket. He inserted the first into the lock, then the second, his head cocked slightly as he listened. *Click.* The lock gave way.

He tucked the pins away and opened the drawer, careful not to make a sound. Papers rustled as he shifted them aside, sorting quickly through ledgers and correspondence until his fingers caught on something thicker—legal parchment.

Two wills.

One dated ten years prior.

And the second... nearly one year ago.

Dominic's brows furrowed. Two versions. Two very different dates. If the second was valid and properly executed, it should have been submitted to the probate court—*but it hadn't been.*

Which begged the question: *why not?*

He squinted at the text, but the moonlight was too faint to make out the smaller script. He dared not light a candle; any flicker of flame could alert the household. Better to take them both and examine them elsewhere.

Dominic folded the two documents carefully and slid them into the inner pocket of his coat.

He had just closed the drawer when he froze.

Footsteps.

Heavy. Purposeful. Drawing closer.

He scanned the room. There was no furniture large enough to conceal him. Only one option remained. He moved swiftly to the tall, thick drapes near the bookcase and slipped behind them, pressing himself flat against the wall, heart pounding in his ears.

The door creaked open.

"I do not know why you insist on meeting at this godforsaken hour," Haverleigh grumbled, his boots thudding across the floor.

Another voice followed, low and cautious. "I can't risk anyone overhearing our conversation."

Mr. Wells.

Dominic's breath caught.

Mr. Wells? His *solicitor?*

"What do you think I pay my staff for?" Haverleigh snapped. "They know better than to gossip. Now tell me—what is it you want?"

"I'm not certain Lord Warwicke will accept your offer," Wells replied, his voice tight. "He's suspicious. I fear he may act independently."

Haverleigh gave a bitter laugh. "What's he going to do? He knows nothing of the law. And he's certainly not clever enough to suspect you are in my employ."

"I wouldn't underestimate him, sir," Wells murmured.

"No," Haverleigh growled. "You don't underestimate *me*. I want Warwicke pacified. Just get him to accept the five thousand pounds and shut this down."

A pause.

"I understand," Wells said quietly.

"Good," Haverleigh barked. "Now get out. And next time, have the decency to meet at a civilized hour."

Dominic stood utterly still as the men's footsteps receded, the study door clicking shut behind them. Silence returned—thick and absolute.

He remained hidden a moment longer, his mind racing.

Mr. Wells had betrayed him. He had been playing both sides. Feeding information to Haverleigh while pretending loyalty to Dominic.

Fury coursed through his veins.

At last, Dominic slipped from behind the drapes, every movement deliberate. The room was once again shrouded in stillness, but something fundamental had shifted.

He climbed through the window and dropped soundlessly into the gardens. Only when he reached the safety of the street did he allow himself to breathe fully.

The chill of the night did little to soothe him.

He had the wills in his possession now.

But more than that—he had confirmation of the rot festering at the heart of this scheme. And the next time he confronted Mr. Wells, it would not be as his client. It would be as his *enemy*.

Turning the corner, Dominic caught sight of his coach waiting where he had left it. He climbed inside, closed the door behind him, and barely had time to settle before the carriage jerked forward.

His thoughts churned with every turn of the wheels. The two wills pressed like a weight against his chest, the truth nestled in his coat pocket—truth Mr. Haverleigh had gone to great lengths to bury.

When the coach pulled up in front of his townhouse, Dominic didn't bother to wait for the footman. He stepped out quickly, taking the front steps two at a time, urgency driving his every movement.

The front door creaked open beneath his hand, and as he stepped into the entryway, the faint glow of candlelight caught his eyes. He looked up and halted at the sight before him.

Dorothea was descending the staircase, dressed in a white wrapper, her red hair braided and trailing over one shoulder. Her brows drew together. "Where were you?" she asked, her voice edged with worry.

There was no use in lying to her. Not now. "I went to your brother's townhouse."

Her frown deepened. "At this hour?"

"It wasn't to see him," Dominic replied. "I was searching for something. The wills."

Dorothea froze at the base of the stairs, her eyes wide. "You found the second will?"

"I did."

Without hesitation, she hurried to him, her bare feet barely making a sound against the marble floor. "What did it say?"

"I haven't read it yet," he admitted.

She stared at him in disbelief. "Why on earth not?"

He gave a crooked smile, the tension easing just slightly. "At the moment, *you're* the thing stopping me."

A laugh broke from her lips. "Well then, we can rectify that. Shall we adjourn to the kitchen and read the wills over a biscuit or two?"

He gestured gallantly. "Lead the way, my lady."

As they walked down the corridor side by side, he asked, "May I ask what kept you awake?"

She hesitated. "I kept thinking about what Lord Inglewood said to me. The way he looked at me. Spoke to me."

Dominic's jaw tensed. "He can't hurt you."

"I know," she said slowly. "But what is to stop others from doing the same? From thinking that I am... available? Tarnished?"

"You are not tarnished," he said, more sharply than intended.

She paused in the doorway of the kitchen, her expression shadowed. "If the annulment is granted, there will be whispers. And some men will take those whispers as permission. You say you'll protect me, but you can't duel every man who speaks ill of me. You can't guard every room I walk into."

Dominic said nothing at first. Her words rang with truth. He couldn't fight every man who dared utter a cruel word. But he could stop the need for such defense altogether. He could stay.

He could choose her.

The realization settled heavily in his chest. "You're right," he murmured at last. "I can't protect you from everything."

She looked away, a small nod of acknowledgment passing between them. But when his voice came again, it was lower. Steadier.

"But I can protect you by withdrawing the petition for annulment and staying married to you," he said.

———————— ⁓ ————————

Dorothea stared at Dominic, her breath catching in her throat. *Did he truly mean it?* The words he had just spoken were what she had longed to hear—for him to stay, to choose her. And yet... the moment that longing flickered to life, a wave of cold disappointment crashed over her.

He wasn't choosing her out of love.

There had been no such confession. No tender declaration. He was offering to remain married out of protection, out of duty.

Not desire.

Not affection.

Not love.

And she loved him too much to accept that kind of half-hearted vow. To chain him to a life he might one day grow to resent. If she kept him in this marriage—knowing he didn't want it—how long until he looked at her with regret instead of tenderness? That, more than any whispered scandal, was what she feared most.

"Say something," Dominic murmured, his voice hushed but hopeful, as if he sensed the shift in her.

She reached for his hand. "That is very generous of you," she said, "but I couldn't ask that of you."

His brow furrowed. "But I want to."

"Why?" she asked, trying to keep her voice light, though her heart thudded painfully in her chest. *Please,* she thought. *Say it. Say you love me.*

Dominic held her gaze. "Because I can't stand the thought of anything happening to you, Thea. I'd never forgive myself."

Her heart sank.

That was not love.

That was guilt. Concern. Attachment, perhaps—but not the kind that kept a man at a woman's side for a lifetime. A lump rose in her throat, and she blinked rapidly to keep the tears at bay. She wouldn't cry. Not in front of him. Not now.

With a voice that felt far too composed for the storm inside her, she said, "You are kind, Dominic. But I think the annulment would be for the best."

"You do?"

"Yes," she lied. "I'll be fine on my own. And you'll be free to live your life as you see fit."

He stared at her, baffled. "But I thought you wanted to stay married."

"I did," she said, forcing a small smile. "But I've changed my mind."

"I don't understand."

She tightened her grip on his hand. "You're a good man, Dominic. But I won't trap you in a marriage you didn't choose. You deserve more. I do, too."

His brow furrowed deeper. "Why do you think you're trapping me?"

"Because just as you fear I might one day resent you," she said, "I fear the same in return. You may feel content with this arrangement now, but what about in five or ten years? When the silence between us becomes too loud, and duty is no longer enough to keep us tied?"

"I don't believe my feelings would change," he said.

She reached up and brushed a knuckle over his cheek before letting her hand fall back to her side. "I know you mean that. And I believe you're trying to do the honorable thing. But sometimes... the honorable thing is walking away."

"Thea—" he began.

But she raised a hand, stopping him with a soft shake of her head. "Shall we have that biscuit now?"

He paused, his lips parting as if to argue—but then, after a moment, he exhaled and nodded solemnly. "As you wish."

She turned and moved towards the counter, her back to him. Her hands trembled slightly as she reached for the plate of biscuits. Every part of her wanted to turn around, to close the distance between them, to fall into his arms and whisper that she loved him. But she couldn't. Not when she believed he didn't feel the same.

And worst of all—she was beginning to believe he never would.

She placed the plate of biscuits on the table and sat down across from him, folding her hands neatly in her lap to keep them from shaking.

Dominic reached into his coat and withdrew two folded pieces of parchment. He laid them carefully on the table between them.

"One of these wills is dated ten years ago," he said. "The other is much more recent. Just over a year old."

Dorothea picked up the older of the two. Her eyes scanned

the page quickly. "This was my father's original will," she said. "Everything... everything was left to my brother."

Dominic nodded, unfolding the second will and skimming it. His brow creased in concentration before he looked up at her. "But this one," he said, holding the paper between his fingers, "this will names you as the heir. Everything—his estate, his property—it was all left to you."

She blinked in disbelief. "Are you quite certain?"

"I am," he said, sliding the parchment towards her. "It's explicitly stated. Your father intended for you to inherit everything."

Her fingers trembled as she took the document and read it. "And my brother?"

"Left only ten thousand pounds," Dominic replied. "A sizable sum, yes—but nothing compared to the full estate."

She read over the will again, this time more slowly, her eyes scanning every line. There was no mistake.

Almost one hundred thousand pounds.

It was hers.

She was an heiress.

Dorothea leaned back in her chair, stunned. "I can't believe this. He... my father always said he would see me taken care of. I just never thought..." Her voice trailed off, thick with emotion. "Not like this."

Dominic watched her quietly, his expression unreadable.

And though neither of them said it, the truth sat between them, unspoken and weighty: she no longer needed his protection.

And now, the choice to stay or walk away... rested entirely on the heart.

Dorothea gently set the will back down onto the table. "What do we do now?" she asked, her voice threaded with uncertainty.

Dominic leaned back in his chair, his expression thoughtful. "We proceed cautiously," he responded. "This evening, I learned something else—something far more unsettling. Mr. Wells has been working with your brother."

"That's awful. You trusted him."

"I did," he said. "Which is why it stings all the more."

He reached forward, gathering the two wills and carefully folding them before tucking them back into the inner pocket of his jacket. "I'll keep these safe until we've secured a new solicitor. One I can trust."

Dorothea tilted her head. "And how do you intend to find someone trustworthy? If Mr. Wells could be bought—"

"I have friends that I can trust."

A soft smile curved her lips. "Speaking of your friends... Lady Westcott and Lady Bedford called upon me. They were quite the pair."

Dominic gave a wry smile. "I've never been formally introduced to Lady Westcott, but I admire Lady Bedford. She has a fierceness about her that I've always admired."

"Now my interest is piqued."

His lips twitched into a half-grin. "She once dressed as a man and stopped a duel."

"I wish I had seen that. I imagine she made quite the impression."

"She did," he responded with a chuckle.

"You should laugh more," she said. "It suits you."

Dominic looked at her for a long moment, the smile fading into something more thoughtful. "I suppose I haven't felt like laughing in a long while," he admitted. "But when I'm with you... I don't know. Everything feels a little lighter."

"I'm glad."

Leaning forward, Dominic rested his forearms on the table, his eyes never leaving hers. "We need to be smart about this," he said, his tone growing serious once more. "A great deal is at stake now that we've uncovered the truth. Your brother is not going to walk away quietly."

Her expression sobered. "No. I expect nothing less from him."

"You'll need to be strong," he stated. "The next few weeks may be difficult. He'll attempt to discredit you. Intimidate you. Possibly even try to turn the courts against you."

She nodded once, slow and resolute. "I can be strong," she said.

"I know you can," Dominic said. "That's one of the many things I lo..." His voice trailed off.

Dorothea's heart stalled in her chest. Her eyes searched his face. *Was he about to say it?* That he loved her?

But then he cleared his throat, the sound abrupt and awkward, as though trying to chase the words back down before they escaped.

"Admire about you," he finished.

A sharp pang bloomed in her chest, but she forced a smile to her lips. "I see," she replied, doing her best to disguise the sting behind her composed tone. "Thank you."

Dominic rose from his chair, the legs scraping softly against the stone floor. He extended a hand towards her. "It's late," he said. "Shall we retire for the night?"

Dorothea slipped her hand into his. "Yes... I think that's wise."

As they walked quietly through the corridor and up the dimly lit stairs, the house hushed around them, Dominic glanced sideways at her and asked, "Are you happy, Thea?"

"I am," she responded. "Especially now. I feel as though my father is still looking after me, even from beyond the grave."

"I am happy for you. You deserve every good that has happened to you," he said after a moment.

She looked up at him then, her heart aching at the tenderness in his voice. "So do you, Dominic," she whispered. "Even if you don't believe it yet."

He said nothing, but his gaze lingered on hers longer than it should have.

And though no more words were exchanged as they continued up the stairs, something between them had shifted —quietly, irrevocably.

19

———

Dominic sat at the head of the dining table, the half-folded newssheets between his fingers. He kept his eyes trained on the columns of print, feigning interest in the articles, but not a single word registered. His thoughts were tangled, jumbled—a hopeless knot of what-ifs and maybes—and at the center of them all was *her.*

Across from him, Dorothea read the newssheets. Her expression was focused, serene, and utterly lovely. He couldn't stop stealing glances. And with each glance came a gut-deep ache.

He had nearly told her that he loved her the night before.

But the words had stayed trapped in his throat. Because the truth was, he wasn't entirely sure what he felt. Not yet. Or perhaps he was simply afraid to face it.

Now that she was an heiress in her own right, she no longer needed him. She could purchase her own household, hire her own guards, and surround herself with potential suitors. The mere thought made his blood run hot.

What was he to do? Was it selfish to want her now, to keep

her close—not because she needed him, but because he needed her?

From behind her pages, Dorothea glanced up. "Is everything all right?"

"It is," he said quickly. "Why do you ask?"

She gave him a knowing smile. "Because you are reading the newssheets upside down."

He blinked, looked down and cursed under his breath. "So I am," he muttered, folding it neatly and placing it on the table. "I'm afraid I was... woolgathering."

"Anything you wish to share?"

No, his mind screamed. But she deserved more than silence.

Reaching for his fork, he replied, "I was thinking about the state of my estate." It was a lie, but a polite one. And it seemed to suffice.

Before she could respond, Wright entered the room, his expression unusually grim. "I beg your pardon, my lord, but Mr. Haverleigh is in the entry hall. He insists upon speaking with you."

Dominic set down his fork with deliberate care. "Inform Mr. Haverleigh I will join him shortly, once I've finished my breakfast."

Wright nodded and withdrew, but a moment later, a voice like a thunderclap echoed down the corridor. "*Warwicke!*"

Dorothea flinched at the sound. "He sounds furious. Do you think he's discovered the missing wills?"

"I do," Dominic said, standing and adjusting his coat. "But it matters not. I have no intention of returning them."

She rose beside him. "May I come with you?"

Dominic hesitated, studying her face. "Are you certain? You don't need to confront him."

Her eyes sharpened. "He lied to me. Tried to cheat me out of what is rightfully mine. I want to be there when he realizes he's lost."

He offered his hand. "Then we shall face him together."

"Together. I rather like the sound of that," she said, accepting his arm.

As he led her towards the entry hall, a silent sigh lodged in his chest. He had hoped Haverleigh wouldn't discover the missing documents until after the new will had been filed in probate court. But it hardly mattered now. He would face whatever storm came—for her.

In the entryway, Haverleigh stopped pacing and turned at the sound of their steps. His face was mottled with rage.

"*How dare you!*" he roared.

Dominic remained calm. "It would be best if we discussed this in private. Follow me to my study."

Without waiting for a response, he guided Dorothea into the study, and Haverleigh's heavy, angry footsteps trailed after them.

Once inside, Dominic turned. "Now then—what has you so distraught?"

"You know perfectly well what you've done!" Haverleigh growled.

Dominic feigned confusion. "I'm afraid I don't. Would you care to enlighten me?"

"You stole the wills."

"Wills?" Dominic echoed, his tone light. "Plural? So there were two?"

Haverleigh stepped forward until he stood just inches away. "Don't play games with me, Warwicke. I know you have them, and I want them back."

Dominic's gaze didn't flicker. "You're right. I have them. And no, you may not have them back."

"So you admit it."

"I do. And I intend to file the most recent will with the probate court because your father wanted Dorothea to inherit, and I mean to honor that."

Haverleigh's face darkened. "Absolutely not! My father was not of sound mind when he wrote that second will."

In a clear, steady voice, Dorothea replied, "I disagree."

Haverleigh's gaze snapped to her. "Of course you do. You're eager to steal what's mine."

Dorothea stood her ground, lifting her chin. "You are the one who stole from me. Father saw the kind of man you were —*are*—and he did what he could to protect me."

"You know nothing."

"But I do," she replied. "I know that you dismissed my grief, denied me choices, and treated me like a burden. Father knew it, too."

Haverleigh's nostrils flared. He began pacing like a caged animal. "What if I released your dowry to you? Is that enough for you?"

"No, because I will no longer accept scraps from a table that should have been mine," Dorothea replied.

"You would ruin me," he spat. "Leave me with nothing? Have you no decency?"

"Father left you ten thousand pounds," she reminded him, her voice calm. "That is hardly nothing."

Haverleigh's face twisted. "It's not enough."

Dorothea stepped forward, and Dominic instinctively tensed, his hand twitching at his side as if ready to intercept her. But she didn't back down.

"I'm sorry, Matthew," she said. "But I won't apologize for receiving what was meant for me."

With no warning, Haverleigh's hand lashed out, striking her hard across the cheek.

"*Dorothea!*" Dominic roared, surging forward, but he stopped short when Dorothea, without hesitation, drove the heel of her palm into her brother's throat.

Haverleigh staggered back, choking, eyes wide with disbelief as he clutched his neck.

Dorothea stood tall, eyes blazing. "I am not afraid of you anymore," she said firmly. "You have treated me like something beneath you for far too long. It ends here."

Dominic stepped beside her. And for the first time, he didn't see a woman who needed defending. He saw a woman who could defend herself.

After a long, seething moment, Haverleigh drew in a breath through flared nostrils and finally met his sister's gaze. His voice came out low, bitter. "I should have known. Your husband put you up to this, didn't he? He wants your inheritance for himself."

Dorothea didn't so much as blink. "What I do with my money is none of your concern."

Haverleigh gave a sharp tug on the ends of his waistcoat. "You're not clever enough to manage such a large fortune. You'd squander it all on lace and sentiment and foolish causes. Is that what Father would've wanted? His hard-earned estate wasted away on your whims?"

Dorothea held his gaze. "You may go now," she said. "You are no longer welcome in our home."

Haverleigh gave a bitter laugh, his lip curling. "*Your* home? Is that what you're calling it now? Tell me—did your husband suddenly drop his bid for annulment after discovering how much you were worth?"

"That," Dorothea replied, "is none of your concern, either."

Haverleigh's smirk twisted into something uglier. "So typical. He didn't want you when you were nothing. He was ready to cast you aside like rubbish. And now? Now he wants you? And you believe that? Who's deceiving whom?"

Dominic had stood still long enough. His fists clenched at his sides, jaw taut with restraint—but just as he opened his mouth to speak, Dorothea placed a hand on his chest, stilling him. As much as he wanted to hit Haverleigh, to enact revenge for the man daring to touch his wife, he knew that this was Dorothea's fight.

"Dominic is more honorable than you could ever dream of being," she declared.

Haverleigh didn't press her further. Instead, he turned towards the door with the slow, seething dignity of a man who knew he had lost.

"You'll rue the day you treated me this way," he snarled.

"I don't think we will," she responded.

Haverleigh said nothing more. The sound of his booted footsteps echoed as he stormed down the corridor and out of the townhouse, the main door slamming behind him.

Dominic moved to stand in front of Dorothea as he gently lifted his hand to her cheek, now reddened where her brother had struck her. "Are you all right?"

"I am."

His mouth twitched into a crooked smile. "Remind me never to anger you."

Dorothea gave a small laugh. "Thank you," she simply said.

"For what?"

"For giving me the strength to stand up to my brother," she replied. "I've waited so long to do that."

Dominic cupped her cheek more fully now, his thumb brushing lightly against her skin. "That strength has always been inside you," he said. "You didn't need me to find it. You only needed to believe it was there."

Her eyes shimmered with unshed emotion. "I've wanted to hit him for years. And when I finally did... it felt right. Like it was earned."

Dominic chuckled under his breath. "It most certainly was, but I wish I had the opportunity to hit him as well. Heaven knows I wanted to."

"I know, and if Matthew ever comes around again, I give you

leave to," she said. "Now, shall we return to finish our breakfast?"

No.

Everything in him screamed against the suggestion. He didn't want breakfast. He didn't want the dull clatter of cutlery or the polite hum of conversation. He wanted *this*—the quiet intimacy of the study, the warmth of her cheek beneath his palm, the way her eyes looked up at him like he was someone worthy of trust... of *love.*

He wanted to stay here and never let her go. He wanted to kiss her. To tell her that she was everything he had never dared to hope for—that somehow, despite all the darkness in him, she had become the light he gravitated towards.

But he wasn't strong enough.

Not yet.

Not with everything still unraveling inside him.

So, instead of leaning in, instead of speaking the words that trembled on the tip of his tongue, Dominic did the one thing that felt safe.

He let his hand fall from her cheek.

"Come," he said, offering her his arm without meeting her gaze. "Let's finish our meal."

A gentle breeze stirred the hem of Dorothea's skirts as she stood at the edge of the gardens, shading her eyes against the light. Overhead, a vibrant red kite danced and dipped in the wind. Tristan stood a few paces ahead, beaming with pride as he held the string taut, his shoulders squared with youthful confidence.

"Do you want to fly my kite?" he asked, glancing over his shoulder, the excitement in his voice unmistakable.

Dorothea smiled warmly. "No, thank you. I think you're doing a splendid job all on your own."

Just then, the back door opened and Tabitha emerged, brushing her hands down the front of her apron as she made her way across the gardens. "You don't need to entertain Tristan, my lady."

Dorothea turned to her. "I don't mind in the least. It's a beautiful day to be outside, and Tristan's joy is rather contagious."

Tabitha followed her gaze to the boy and nodded, a wistful expression softening her features. "I wish my husband could see him. He would've adored flying a kite with his son."

Dorothea's heart ached at the sorrow beneath her words. "I'm sorry he isn't here," she murmured.

Tabitha gave a faint, resigned sigh. "He was thrilled when he was selected for the rocket troop. His letters were full of pride. He believed he was doing something important."

"May I ask..." Dorothea hesitated. "How long ago did he pass?"

"A little over six months now," Tabitha replied, her voice quiet. "He died helping the Coalition forces on the Continent."

Dorothea's brows lifted. "What troop was he with?"

"The Second Rocket Troop," Tabitha said. "He always spoke of it with such honor. Said it was a small unit of men, but fiercely brave."

Dorothea blinked, her heart suddenly thudding. "That's the same troop Dominic served in. What was your husband's name?"

"John Cooper."

Dorothea's breath caught. She turned to face the woman fully, astonishment plain in her voice. "That's him. That's the man Dominic told me about—the one who saved his life."

Tabitha's brows drew together. "Are you certain?"

"I'm quite certain," Dorothea said. "He carried Dominic

from the battlefield when he was wounded. Your husband made sure he survived. Dominic never forgot him."

She turned urgently, waving a hand. "Come, we must find him at once. He'll want to know."

Tabitha looked hesitant, as if caught between disbelief and longing. "This all feels... impossible."

Before they could reach the house, the back door opened and Dominic stepped outside. "I came to see Tristan's kite flying abilities," he said with a grin.

Tristan beamed over his shoulder. "I am the greatest kite flyer in the world!"

Dominic chuckled. "Is that so? You haven't seen me fly a kite."

Dorothea approached, her hand gently touching his sleeve. "Dominic, I've discovered something. Something remarkable."

His gaze sharpened. "What is it?"

She turned to Tabitha, encouraging her forward. "Tabitha is the widow of John Cooper—the man who saved you."

The laughter faded from Dominic's eyes. His entire expression shifted, sobering into stillness. "Is that... is that true?" he asked, addressing Tabitha directly. "Was your husband truly John Cooper?"

She nodded, her hands clasped tightly. "He died in battle. I was told it was instant, but I never knew how. Just that he served in the Second Rocket Troop."

Dominic's throat bobbed as he swallowed. "He carried me from the battlefield when I was too injured to move. If not for him, I wouldn't be standing here."

"Then he didn't die that day?" Tabitha asked, tears brimming in her eyes.

"No," Dominic said. "He died the next day. There was a rocket—an accidental detonation. I was told he didn't suffer."

A soft sob escaped her lips, and she nodded, her voice shaking. "It's painful... but it's good to know. I've lived in the dark for so long."

Dominic stepped forward, placing a hand over his heart. "Your husband was a hero. My hero. I owe him everything."

"John never did things for praise," Tabitha said, wiping her eyes. "He simply did what he believed was right."

Dominic's voice was thick. "How can I ever repay what he did for me?"

Tabitha glanced back at Tristan, who had resumed his proud stance, gripping the kite string. "You're already doing more than enough for me and my son."

"It's not enough," Dominic insisted. "I want to do more. I'll see that you have your own household, a proper income—"

She shook her head quickly. "That's not necessary."

"It is," he said, with quiet resolve. "You and Tristan deserve stability. Safety."

Tabitha paused, then spoke with a trembling voice. "All I've ever wanted—all *John* ever wanted—was for our son to have a better life than we did."

Dominic nodded, solemn. "Then I'll raise him as if he were my own."

Tears slipped silently down Tabitha's cheeks. "That is awfully kind of you, my lord."

"In truth, I've grown rather fond of him," Dominic admitted with a small smile. "He reminds me of myself when I was his age—stubborn, full of questions, and absolutely certain he's the best at everything."

Dorothea stepped beside him. "What a remarkable turn of events."

"Mum!" Tristan called from across the lawn. "Come watch me!"

Tabitha dabbed her eyes and offered a grateful nod before turning to join her son.

As she walked away, Dorothea felt Dominic's hand brush

against hers—then gently, he took it. Slowly, he lifted it to his lips and whispered, "Thank you."

"I didn't do anything."

"But you did," he said, his thumb grazing her skin. "You've never looked at me like I'm broken."

"That's because you aren't."

His gaze searched hers for a moment, and then he bowed his head slightly, brushing her hand with his lips. "Knowing I can repay John, in some small way... it gives me something I thought I'd lost—a sense of purpose."

She squeezed his fingers. "And you'll do a tremendous job. I have no doubt of it."

"It would be preferable," Dominic said, "if you helped raise Tristan as well."

Dorothea was surprised by the sudden gravity in his tone. "He already has a mother."

"Yes, he does. But I also believe no child can have too many people in their life who love them."

"I suppose you're right."

A pause stretched between them before Dominic said, "Then we shall do so... together. As man and wife."

The last words escaped him almost on a breath—spoken with quiet urgency, as if the very act of saying them risked unraveling something fragile inside him.

Dorothea's smile faltered. "I thought we had discussed this already."

"We did," he admitted, his thumb brushing lightly over her knuckles. "But I was hoping to revisit the conversation."

She studied him, unsure whether to feel hopeful. "Has anything changed since we last spoke?"

Dominic met her gaze, the sincerity in his eyes unmistakable. "Yes. Something has changed. I've come to realize... I don't want to live without you."

She could hear honesty in his words. Longing. But not quite

what she needed to hear. Still, the one thing her heart craved above all remained unsaid.

Love.

She opened her mouth to speak, but just then, the back door opened, and Wright stepped outside.

"Forgive the interruption, my lady," he said with a slight bow. "Lady Sarah and Mrs. Haverleigh have requested a moment of your time."

Dorothea's brows drew together. "They are here? *Now?*"

"Yes, my lady," Wright confirmed.

Dominic turned, his jaw tightening at once. "Send them away."

But Dorothea held up a hand. "Wait."

He looked at her in disbelief. "Why? What could they possibly want from you now?"

She gently withdrew her hand from his. "Arabella has always been cruel to me," she said. "But her mother—Lady Sarah—has never treated me with anything but kindness."

Dominic looked unconvinced, his mouth drawn into a firm line. "Kindness is sometimes just diplomacy in finer clothing."

"Perhaps," Dorothea said. "But I still want to hear what she has to say. If only to understand her reasons for coming."

"If they upset you..." Dominic started.

"I won't let them," she replied, her voice steady. "Not anymore."

Dominic's expression shifted from concern to admiration. "Would you like me to go with you?"

"I need to do this on my own."

He relented after a moment. "Very well. But once they've gone, I'd like to revisit our earlier conversation."

"I can agree to that."

As she stepped through the rear door, a flicker of uncertainty tugged at her thoughts. She didn't know what to anticipate from this unexpected call. But she knew one thing: she would not turn away Lady Sarah, who had always shown her courtesy, even if her daughter had not.

When she entered the drawing room, she saw both ladies were seated on the settee, their backs straight, expressions somber. Arabella's lips were pinched in a pout, while Lady Sarah sat with her gloved hands folded neatly over the silver handle of her cane.

Dorothea cleared her throat lightly to announce her presence. "Good morning," she said, keeping her tone polite.

Arabella scoffed. "What is good about it?"

Lady Sarah reached over and nudged her daughter's arm with a sharp look. "Behave, Child."

Arabella huffed and crossed her arms. "We should never have come here," she muttered, her voice just loud enough to be heard.

Lady Sarah ignored her and lifted her gaze to Dorothea's. "Thank you for agreeing to receive us," she said. "I know this visit is... unexpected."

"I admit, I am curious," Dorothea replied, stepping farther into the room. "To what do I owe this morning call?"

Lady Sarah offered a strained smile. "Arabella has something she wishes to ask of you."

Arabella gave her mother a side-glare but reluctantly leaned forward. "Do you actually plan to take all our money?"

Lady Sarah sighed. "No, no. That's not the question we rehearsed. Do try again, darling."

With a roll of her eyes and a begrudging tone, Arabella finally asked, "Would you allow us to remain in the townhouse... for a short while? At least until we can make other arrangements?"

"Was that so difficult?" Lady Sarah murmured.

Before Dorothea could respond, the door opened and a maid stepped in, balancing a silver tea tray in her hands.

"I hope you don't mind, but I took the liberty of requesting tea," Lady Sarah said. "I thought it might soothe everyone's nerves."

The maid moved briskly, setting the tray down on the carved table between the settee and armchairs.

"Would you care for me to pour, my lady?" the maid asked, turning to Dorothea.

"No, thank you," Dorothea responded. "I shall attend to it myself."

With another curtsy, the maid slipped quietly from the room.

Lady Sarah tapped her fingertips lightly against the top of her cane. "Now... where were we?" she asked, glancing around as if to gather the room's attention. "Ah, yes—Arabella made her request, and we were just about to discuss it over a much-needed cup of tea."

20

D ominic stood outside in the gardens, watching as Tristan ran through the grass with his kite trailing high above. The boy's laughter echoed across the lawn, easing the tension in Dominic's shoulders for the first time in days. There was something profoundly grounding in this moment—the innocence of a child, the steadiness of the wind, and the rare sense of peace that wrapped around him like a balm.

This, he realized, *is what I want.*

He needed to be the kind of man Tristan could look up to— one who could be trusted, who could protect, who could lead. And for the first time in a long while, he felt confident that he could become that man.

But only if Dorothea was beside him.

Because in the silence of the night, and in the noise of the day, she filled his thoughts. Every breath, every step—his world was beginning to revolve around her. He had been so close to telling her how he felt, but they had been interrupted.

The back door creaked open.

"My lord," came Wright's voice. The butler stepped out,

composed but purposeful. "Pardon the intrusion, but Constable Prentice has arrived. He requests a moment of your time."

"Very well," Dominic said. "I'll meet with him in my study."

Wright inclined his head and turned back inside.

Dominic reached out to ruffle Tristan's hair as the boy beamed up at him. "Carry on, Lad."

"Do you want to go riding later?" Tristan asked, his eyes full of hope.

Dominic pretended to consider his reply. "I believe that can be arranged."

Tristan's grin widened. "Do you think Lady Warwicke will come with us?"

"I'll ask her," Dominic said, returning his smile. "Just as soon as her guests have departed."

He gave Tristan a final pat on the shoulder before striding into the house and down the corridor towards his study. When he entered, Constable Prentice was already waiting—a solid man with dark hair, a clean-shaven jaw, and a solemn look on his face.

"Constable," Dominic greeted, "what brings you by today?"

Prentice straightened, folding his hands behind his back. "I came to inform you that Whitmore has been sentenced. He's to be transported."

"And Blackthorn?"

"He avoided being transported, but he'll remain in Newgate for a long while," Prentice replied. "Whitmore confessed to tampering with the damper and placing the burr, but he was firm in denying he had anything to do with poisoning Lady Warwicke."

Dominic frowned. "He is clearly lying."

"I thought so, too," Prentice admitted, "but he seemed... sincere. And with sentencing already passed, he had no reason to lie." He tilted his head slightly. "Do you have any definitive proof your wife was poisoned?"

Dominic leaned against his desk, arms crossed. "I suspect he used a diluted form of Aqua Tofana. It mimics a cold at first, then progresses into influenza-like symptoms. My wife first became ill after taking tea with her sister-in-law. Then again after another visit."

He stopped.

Tea.

Each time, Dorothea had tea with Arabella and Lady Sarah —and each time she'd fallen ill shortly after.

His chest tightened. "She's with them now," he breathed.

Without another word, he spun on his heel and sprinted from the study. He tore down the corridor, rounded the corner, and burst into the drawing room just as Dorothea was reaching for her teacup.

"*Stop!*" he shouted.

Dorothea's hand froze midair. "What is it?" she asked, startled.

He crossed the room in three strides and crouched beside her. "Have you taken a sip yet?"

She shook her head. "No... I haven't. Dominic, what's going on?"

He looked at her, then turned his gaze towards Mrs. Haverleigh, who sat poised, seemingly unconcerned, with her hands neatly folded in her lap.

"I believe your sister-in-law has been poisoning you," he said.

Gasps echoed across the room. Mrs. Haverleigh's eyes widened in mock offense. "I beg your pardon?"

"It makes perfect sense," Dominic said, rising to his full height. "You knew about the second will. You knew what Dorothea stood to gain and what you and your husband stood to lose."

Mrs. Haverleigh scoffed. "I only learned about the second will this morning. Matthew told me himself. I had no knowledge of it before."

"And I'm supposed to believe that?" Dominic asked.

"You are," Mrs. Haverleigh snapped, rising to her feet. "Because it's the truth. And I refuse to stand here and listen to these outrageous accusations."

She made to leave, but Dominic stepped in front of her, blocking her exit. "You're not going anywhere."

"I've done nothing wrong."

Lady Sarah finally spoke, her voice tight with restraint. "Lord Warwicke, unless you have proof, this is slanderous. Accusing someone of poisoning is hardly civilized conduct."

Dominic pointed to the teacup. "Dorothea fell ill after your daughter's first visit. And then again after the second. If I'm right, today would mark the third dose—enough to make the effects unmistakable."

Mrs. Haverleigh raised her brows. "And what kind of poison is administered in three carefully spaced doses?"

"The kind designed to mimic illness," Dominic replied. "Slow. Subtle. But deadly. If I'm mistaken, you won't mind sipping the tea meant for my wife."

Mrs. Haverleigh's eyes narrowed. "This is ridiculous."

"I don't think so," Dominic said. "You stand to gain the most if Dorothea were to die."

Just then, Constable Prentice entered the room. "I must side with Lord Warwicke on this," he said firmly. "If you're so confident the tea is harmless, then taking a sip shouldn't trouble you."

Mrs. Haverleigh turned to him, brow arched. "And who exactly are you?"

"Merely a constable," Prentice said. "But a persuasive one."

Dorothea stood now, beside Dominic, her voice quiet but trembling. "Do you really believe Arabella would do this?"

Dominic didn't look away from Mrs. Haverleigh. "I do."

Mrs. Haverleigh rolled her eyes. "Fine. If it will end this absurdity, I'll drink the tea." She lifted the teacup and raised it to her lips.

"*Wait!*" Lady Sarah's voice cracked through the room, sharp with panic.

Mrs. Haverleigh froze. "What? Why?"

Lady Sarah's face had gone pale, her hands trembling. Her voice was barely audible as she said, "Because... it's poisoned."

A stunned silence fell over the room.

Mrs. Haverleigh stared at her mother, mouth agape. "*You?* You did this?"

With a slow, almost resigned nod, Lady Sarah turned her gaze to her daughter. "It was all for you," she said, her voice composed, but stripped of warmth. "I've known about the second will for some time, and I refused to let you lose everything, Arabella. I couldn't stand by and let you become... me."

Mrs. Haverleigh blinked. "But I wouldn't have, Mother," she said. "Matthew would have seen me taken care of. He promised me—"

Lady Sarah's expression twisted into something bitter. "And my husband promised me the very same. Promises mean little when men lose everything on a roll of dice and a bottle of port. He gambled away our future, our security—*everything.* I was left with debts, shame, and no place in Society."

She paused, her voice trembling as she continued. "I know what it is to be discarded. I would not let that be your fate."

Dorothea spoke up. "But... you were always kind to me," she whispered. "How could you try to kill me?"

Lady Sarah turned towards her, and for the first time, the civility that had always colored her expression was stripped away. "Because love is not always gentle. Sometimes love is desperate. Sometimes, a mother will do anything—even the unforgivable—if she believes it will save her child."

Dorothea took an unsteady step back, and Dominic placed a reassuring hand on the small of her back.

Constable Prentice moved forward then, his boots thudding softly against the carpet. "That's quite enough," he said, his tone clipped. "You can explain the rest at Newgate."

Mrs. Haverleigh shot forward, placing herself between her mother and the constable, her voice rising in a near panic. "No, you can't. She's old and frail. She didn't know what she was doing."

Constable Prentice's eyes remained steady. "Your mother just admitted to poisoning Lady Warwicke. I've little choice in the matter."

Lady Sarah slowly pushed herself to her feet, gripping her cane with a white-knuckled hand. The room seemed to tilt around her as she leveled her gaze at Dominic. "Before I go, I want to know something," she said. "How did you figure it out?"

"Because I've seen Aqua Tofana before," he revealed. "I was acquainted with its symptoms during my time as a Bow Street Runner. Illness that progresses slowly over time but harmless enough to dismiss."

Lady Sarah's lips curved faintly—not in cruelty, but in something that almost resembled relief. "Then I suppose it's for the best that you stopped her from drinking it. I placed two drops in her cup."

Dominic's spine went rigid, the blood draining from his face. "That... would have killed her."

"I know," Lady Sarah said, a trace of grim satisfaction settling in her eyes. "That was the point."

Constable Prentice stepped forward with renewed purpose, his expression hardening. "Come along, Lady Sarah," he ordered, taking her arm. "I haven't got all day."

Without protest, Lady Sarah allowed herself to be led away, her cane tapping rhythmically against the floor as she walked. Mrs. Haverleigh followed behind, her features pale with shock.

When the door finally shut behind them, the silence that remained felt deafening.

And Dominic, glancing at the teacup, realized just how close Dorothea had come to dying at the hands of a woman she had admired.

Dorothea stood frozen, still reeling from the truth that had only just come to light—that someone she had once admired, even trusted, had very nearly succeeded in ending her life. Her hands trembled at her sides. The betrayal ran deeper than any blade ever could.

She turned her head and found Dominic watching her. His gaze was steady, full of compassion, and—could it be?—something softer, something achingly close to love. That look undid her. Without a thought to propriety or to the walls she'd so carefully constructed, Dorothea stepped towards him and wrapped her arms tightly around his waist.

He stiffened for a moment before folding her into his embrace with a quiet exhale. His arms enveloped her completely, strong and sure, and a sob slipped from her throat. In his arms, she felt anchored. Safe. Home. And for the first time in days, she didn't want to run, didn't want to hide—she just wanted to stay right where she was.

Dominic pressed a gentle kiss to the top of her head. "Are you all right?"

Her voice wavered. "No... yes... I don't know. Why does it feel like everyone wants me dead?"

He leaned his cheek against her temple, his breath grazing her ear. "It's over now. I swear it. No one will hurt you again—not while I still draw breath."

She shifted just enough to look up at him. "How can you promise that?"

"Because I would die before I let anyone touch you again," he said, his voice edged with fierce conviction.

Her chest constricted, her heart thudding wildly. That one sentence undid her completely. A tear slid down her cheek, and her lips parted before her mind could stop them. "And that's why I love you—"

The words were out before she could pull them back. Her breath caught.

Dominic went still. "You... love me?"

Panic bubbled up inside her. She could lie and pretend it was a slip of the tongue, but instead, she drew in a shaky breath and nodded. "I do. I've known it for some time."

His jaw clenched, and he looked away, his voice raw. "How can you love me after everything I've done... after everything that's happened?"

Her answer came without hesitation. "I fell in love with you beside a bloodied cot in a makeshift hospital. You were broken and half-mad from pain, but you still held my hand and begged me not to leave. And I haven't. My heart chose you long ago."

He looked down at her, disbelief flickering in his gaze. "But I'm not that man anymore."

"You're right," she said softly. "You're stronger now. You're better."

Dominic's gaze searched hers as if trying to find the lie but there wasn't one. Only truth, plain and bold. "Thea... I don't know what to say, except—"

"You don't have to say anything." She squeezed his hands. "Just know that I want you—all of you. The parts you hide, the burdens you carry, even the nightmares that steal your sleep. You deserve to be loved fully, without condition."

He drew in a breath. "Are you sure? I need you to be sure. I am not an easy man to love."

"I have never been more certain of anything in my life," she replied. "I am not giving up on you—not now, not ever. I love you fiercely, for who you are, not who I want you to be."

Emotion swelled behind his eyes, and he huffed a laugh, almost disbelieving. "Then you should know that I am ardently in love with you."

Hope blossomed in her chest at his words. "You are?"

"I am," he said. "I've tried to tell you—at least a few times—but we kept getting interrupted." He reached up to cradle her cheek. "But make no mistake. You are not just the woman I love. You are the one I trust with everything—my past, my future and every shadow in between. You've seen my worst and stayed."

"Of course I stayed."

His expression darkened slightly. "Then why did you press for the annulment?"

She gave him a rueful smile. "Because I wanted you to stay by choice—not obligation. I wanted to give you the chance to walk away."

"Well, I choose you," he said. "I will choose you again and again, for every day we're given."

He leaned in, eyes falling to her mouth. "May I kiss you?"

"Yes," she breathed. The word left her too fast, too eager.

He chuckled softly, then brushed his lips over hers in a whisper of a kiss. "Just as soft as I imagined," he murmured before kissing her fully.

The kiss was slow and reverent, but there was fire beneath it —years of longing, months of doubt, days of fear all melting into one perfect moment. Dorothea clung to him, her world narrowing to the warmth of his mouth, the strength of his arms, the truth of his love.

When they finally parted, he rested his forehead against hers. "That was even better than I imagined."

She smiled. "I feel the same."

He met her eyes with a new intensity—one that made her breath catch. "I want to take you upstairs and show you how much I love you."

"Why don't you?" she whispered.

He grinned. "Because you deserve a proper courtship. Starting with Vauxhall Gardens tonight."

"I've always wanted to go."

"I had a feeling," he said, brushing his thumb over her cheek. "But truly, I don't care where we go... so long as we go together."

"Together," she echoed. "That sounds... perfect."

Dominic's smile faded into something more thoughtful. "What can I give you to show how much I love you? You have your own fortune—"

"That's yours now," she interrupted gently.

"No," he said firmly. "It belongs to *us*."

Her smile deepened. "Then I already have everything I want."

In a quiet voice, he asked, "What about a little girl?"

She gave him a bemused look. "But I thought you didn't want children."

"I didn't," he said. "Or rather, I was afraid to want them. But... one or two wouldn't be so terrible, assuming they inherit your red hair."

She laughed softly. "Are you sure? Because I don't need children to be happy. Just you."

He stared at her, his expression solemn. "My father was cruel. I've feared becoming him my entire life. But you... you've shown me there's another path. You've made me believe I'm more than my blood. More than my wounds."

"I love you, Dominic."

"And I love you, Thea," he whispered.

A slow, mischievous smile curved her lips. "I know you want to court me properly, but I find myself rather eager to engage in these marital relations I have heard so much about."

He chuckled, low and rough with affection. "Who am I to deny you such a thing, my love?"

Before Dorothea could reply, the door creaked open and Wright stepped in and announced, "Pardon the interruption, my lord, but a Mr.—"

"Send him away!" Dominic shouted. "I plan to spend the rest of the day with my wife. Uninterrupted."

Wright inclined his head. "Very good, my lord," he said before retreating with a bow.

Dorothea gave Dominic a stern look, though she found the whole thing amusing. "That was rather impolite."

He reached out and tucked a loose curl behind her ear, his fingers lingering against her cheek. "Work can wait," he murmured. "But *you*... you, I will never make wait again."

Heat rushed to her face as her smile returned. "I believe we were about to go upstairs."

Instead of replying, Dominic stepped back and—without warning—swept her up into his arms. She let out a small gasp of surprise before wrapping her arms around his neck, laughing breathlessly.

"You will hear no complaints from me," he said, pressing a kiss to her temple as he carried her towards the doorway.

Just as they crossed into the entry hall, a blur of movement caught their attention. Tristan stood in the entryway, proudly clutching an inflated pig bladder like a prized treasure.

"Look what Mrs. Dawson gave me!" Tristan shouted. "I'm going to kick it in the gardens!"

Dominic came to an abrupt halt, still cradling Dorothea in his arms. "That sounds... delightful," he said.

Tristan bounced on his heels with excitement. "Would you like to join me? It's much more fun to kick it with other people."

Dorothea bit the inside of her cheek to stifle a giggle and

looked up at Dominic. "It does sound like an excellent way to spend the afternoon."

"As tempting as that sounds," Dominic said, "Dorothea and I are otherwise engaged at the moment."

Tristan tilted his head, thoroughly unconvinced. "But what's more fun than kicking a pig bladder around?"

Dominic shifted Dorothea higher in his arms and gave the boy a crooked smile. "I can think of a few things," he replied, a teasing note in his voice. "But we will join you later. Much later."

"All right. I'll go see if my mum wants to play instead. She's very good at kicking things," Tristan said.

Without waiting for further comment, he darted off towards the servants' corridor, kicking the inflated bladder ahead of him with a loud squelch.

Dominic shook his head as he turned back to Dorothea. "That boy is going to rule the household by the end of the month."

"He already does. You're just too smitten to notice," she said. "Now, where were we?"

"You mentioned something about carrying you upstairs and distracting you thoroughly."

"Ah, yes," she said, looping her arms more tightly around his neck. "Do carry on."

"With pleasure." He resumed his stride, every step purposeful, as Dorothea's laughter echoed through the halls behind them—a sweet, unguarded sound that filled every corner with the promise of love, of healing, and of a future no longer shadowed by fear.

21

I t was well past midday when Dominic finally emerged from his bedchamber, the heavy door clicking softly behind him. He moved quietly, not wishing to wake Dorothea, who was still asleep in their bed. They had returned late from Vauxhall Gardens the night before, staying up until the earliest blush of dawn to admire the fireworks that painted the sky in bursts of silver and scarlet.

A faint smile tugged at his lips. He had never imagined that marriage could feel like this—like companionship rather than obligation. Dorothea had surprised him at every turn. She was kind, intelligent, unyielding in spirit, and wholly unlike any woman he had ever known. She didn't just hold his affection— she commanded his admiration. And perhaps, if he were brave enough to admit it, she had begun to restore a part of him he thought long dead.

As he descended the staircase, the quiet hush of the household was broken by a sharp knock that echoed across the marble floors of the entry hall. Wright emerged from the corridor and made his way to the door. He pulled it open to reveal Constable Prentice, his face grave.

"Constable Prentice," Dominic greeted as he stepped off the last stair, his boots clicking against the floor.

"My lord," the constable said with a respectful incline of his head. "I was hoping to have a word with you, if you've a moment."

"Certainly," Dominic replied. "We can speak in my study."

He led the constable down the corridor and into the richly paneled study. Once inside, Prentice closed the door with a decisive click.

"I suggest we keep this conversation confidential," Prentice said. "Some matters are best not overheard."

Dominic's interest was piqued. "Is everything quite all right?"

"In a manner of speaking," the constable replied. "Lady Sarah has signed a full confession."

"That is a good thing, is it not?"

"It is, but in doing so, she implicated Mr. Haverleigh." Prentice's voice was grim. "She claims he was the one who supplied her with the poison."

Dominic's heart dropped. "Are you saying he was involved in poisoning Dorothea?"

The constable nodded slowly. "I am afraid so, my lord. Lady Sarah overheard a conversation regarding the second will and confronted Mr. Haverleigh. He threatened her—said he would do to her what he had done to Mr. Poole if she didn't comply."

Dominic's jaw tightened. "I always suspected Poole's death came far too conveniently."

"It did," Prentice agreed. "Mr. Haverleigh acquired the poison from an apothecary in the rookeries and passed it along to Lady Sarah, instructing her to use it on Lady Warwicke."

Dominic's hands clenched into fists. He strode towards the sideboard and poured a measure of brandy into a glass. "Have you arrested him?"

"We have," Prentice confirmed. "He's denying everything, of

course, but Lady Sarah's confession should be sufficient for a conviction."

Dominic took a slow sip as he tried to steady his thoughts. "How am I to tell Dorothea that her own brother orchestrated her murder?"

Prentice didn't respond at once. He seemed to consider his words before saying, "Lady Sarah's age may spare her from being transported, but not the misery of prison. Regardless, it will likely be a death sentence."

"I feel no pity for her. She chose her side."

"As you should. I only mention it as fact."

Dominic let out a quiet breath, then asked, "And Mr. Wells? Have you spoken to him?"

"I have," Prentice replied. "Turns out he's not much more than a pawn. Haverleigh threatened his family to ensure he pushed for the lesser settlement. That's the only reason he acted on his behalf."

Dominic's shoulders relaxed slightly. "That is... oddly reassuring. At least his betrayal had a motive beyond greed."

Prentice adjusted the lapels of his worn brown jacket. "One last thing. If Haverleigh's case goes to trial, Lady Warwicke will likely be called to testify against him. I fear the scandal could be considerable."

"I understand."

"If I can be of any further service, don't hesitate to send for me." With that, Prentice moved to the door and let himself out.

Left alone in the silence, Dominic walked slowly to his desk, the brandy glass still in his hand. He set it down with care, then sank into the chair behind the desk, his thoughts reeling. It was nothing short of a miracle that Dorothea had managed to survive not only her brother's cruelty but his murderous intentions.

Wright stepped into the study and cleared his throat. "Lord Wilton requests a moment of your time, my lord."

Dominic looked up from his desk. Frankly, he could use the interruption—anything to stave off the storm of thoughts swirling in his head since the constable's visit. "Show him in."

Moments later, Wilton entered, his stride deliberate, and his expression unusually solemn. He paused just inside the room, his eyes shadowed with something that felt heavier than mere formality. "I saw you at Vauxhall Gardens last night," he began.

Dominic's brow arched with surprise. "You did? Why didn't you join us?"

Wilton offered a tight smile as he settled into the chair across from the desk. "Because I caught the look on your face when you gazed at your wife. You wore the expression of a man utterly smitten."

Dominic chuckled faintly but didn't deny it.

Wilton leaned back slightly and asked, "May I presume that your absurd talk of pursuing an annulment has been thoroughly discarded?"

"It has," Dominic replied.

"And what changed your mind?"

A slow smile formed on Dominic's lips. "I realized I couldn't live without Dorothea. It was that simple—and that impossible."

Wilton let out a bark of laughter. "Alcott would call you a sentimental fool. He's firmly convinced that love is a weakness."

Dominic shrugged. "Then he's never truly been in love. And frankly, I care very little for Alcott's views on anything involving the heart."

The mirth faded from Wilton's face, replaced by something more somber. "The reason I've come, aside from witnessing your transformation into a lovesick poet, is to inform you that I'm leaving tomorrow."

Dominic straightened. "Leaving?"

Wilton nodded. "I intend to track down the man who married my sister—Mr. Smith, if that is even his real name."

Dominic's brow furrowed. "And how exactly do you plan to find him?"

Wilton sighed and ran a weary hand down his face. "That's the rub. My sister claims he hails from a small village—she gave me the name—but I've my doubts. Now that her dowry has been released, he could be anywhere in England, enjoying the spoils of his deceit."

Dominic didn't hesitate. "Do you want me to accompany you?"

Wilton shook his head. "No. You've been through enough, and your place is here—with your wife. This is something I must do myself."

"How is your sister managing?"

"Olivia is heartbroken. She thought she'd found her future, only to be abandoned like a fool. And truth be told, she is partially to blame. She eloped to Gretna Green with a man she scarcely knew, swept away by romantic nonsense."

Dominic's lips quirked. "Sometimes the heart is a reckless creature."

Wilton gave him a long look, one brow lifting. "Who are you, and what have you done with my pragmatic friend?"

"I'm still here. Just... changed. I'm still adjusting to the whole being-in-love thing."

Wilton stood, brushing an invisible wrinkle from his coat. "Well, wish me luck. I've a feeling I'll need it."

Dominic rose as well. "If I may offer one piece of advice— trust no one. Verify everything, especially the things you think you know to be true."

"That's the plan. I don't know if I'll succeed, but I have to try for her sake."

"Yes... that I understand all too well."

Wilton's eyes held compassion. "I know you do." He turned

and made his way towards the door, his steps slow, as if weighed down by the burden of what lay ahead. Just before reaching it, he paused with his hand resting on the knob. Without looking back, he said, "I'm glad you found love, Dominic. Truly. You, of all people, deserve it."

"As do you, Wilton."

His friend gave a dry, humorless huff. "No. That's not meant for me. I know my duty."

"It only takes one person, Wilton. One unexpected soul to walk into your life and change everything."

Wilton looked over his shoulder then, his face shadowed with wistfulness and something like longing. But he didn't respond. Instead, he gave a faint nod and stepped out into the corridor.

Tristan's face suddenly appeared in the open window, his cheeks flushed with excitement and the inflated pig's bladder clutched proudly in both hands. "Do you want to kick the bladder with me?" he asked, bouncing slightly on his toes.

Dominic found himself smiling. He couldn't bring himself to dampen the boy's enthusiasm. "I'll meet you in the gardens."

Dorothea stood at the window, her hands lightly resting on the sill as her gaze swept over the gardens below. The sunlight bathed the lawn in a warm glow, and there—beneath the swaying branches of the old oak—Dominic and Tristan were gleefully kicking the inflated pig bladder back and forth. Laughter rang through the air, bright and unrestrained.

How could she not love this man? Watching Dominic with the boy, the gentle patience he showed, the ready laughter he so rarely allowed himself, confirmed what she already believed in the quiet recesses of her heart: he would make a wonderful father.

Some would call her foolish for staying. For loving a man who had once sought to cast her aside. But she knew better. She knew the man she'd fallen in love with still lived beneath the shadows of regret and duty. And in moments like this, when his walls dropped, she caught a glimpse of the future she dared to hope for.

A knock interrupted her thoughts, followed quickly by the soft creak of the door. Tabitha stepped in with a tray balanced in her hands.

"Since you missed breakfast, Mrs. Dawson sent this up for you," her lady's maid announced.

"That was kind of her," Dorothea murmured, though her eyes remained fixed on the gardens.

Tabitha crossed the room and set the tray down on the table before drifting to the window to join her. "I do so love hearing Tristan laugh."

"You have a remarkable boy," Dorothea replied.

"I think so, too—when he's not climbing on the furniture or hiding frogs in my shoes," Tabitha teased with a fond smile.

Dorothea turned to her. "Have you given any more thought to what Dominic offered? Your own household—"

But Tabitha raised a hand, stilling her words. "I'm happy here."

"Then... perhaps you might consider being my companion?"

A firmer shake of her head followed. "No, my lady. I'm content as I am. I like my place in this house, close to you and to Tristan."

"But if you had your own home—"

"I'd miss this," Tabitha said simply, motioning to the scene outside. "I want Tristan to grow up surrounded by people who love him. Including Lord Warwicke. He's a fine man."

"That he is," Dorothea agreed.

Tabitha offered a knowing smile. "Our arrangement may not be conventional, but I wouldn't change it."

"Then we shall keep it just as it is," Dorothea said, returning her smile.

Another knock came at the door. Tabitha moved to answer it and a maid entered, dipping into a quick curtsy.

"A Mr. Stevens is here to see Lady Warwicke," she announced. "He says he's Lord Warwicke's uncle."

Dorothea's brow lifted. "Very well. Please show him into the drawing room."

Once the maid departed, Tabitha turned to her with urgency. "We must dress you at once, my lady."

Not long after, Dorothea descended the stairs dressed in a soft green morning gown that brought a touch of color to her cheeks. Her hair had been gathered into a loose chignon, a few wisps escaping to soften her features. She felt oddly nervous but also curious. Dominic had spoken highly of his uncle, with rare affection.

As she entered the drawing room, her eyes fell on a tall, broad-shouldered gentleman whose hair was white at the temples, though streaks of black still lingered. There was something in his bearing, in the quiet strength of his stance, that reminded her strikingly of Dominic.

He turned at her approach and bowed deeply. "My lady," he said with warm formality. "Thank you for meeting with me."

She dipped into a curtsy. "It is my pleasure, sir."

A smile broke across his face, gentle and sincere. "Please. We are family now. You may call me Adam."

"Then you must call me Dorothea," she replied, stepping farther into the room.

Adam studied her for a thoughtful moment, then said with a glint of humor, "So you are the woman who managed to capture my nephew's heart."

Her cheeks flushed. "He captured mine as well."

"I'm pleased to hear it," Adam said. "He was always determined to remain unwed—as if solitude could atone for his past. So you can imagine my delight when I saw the news in the newssheets."

"What news?"

"Ah, you haven't read it yet," he said with a chuckle. "A Mr. Fairchild penned the article. I rarely indulge in the Society pages, but I never miss one of his pieces."

Dorothea smiled faintly. "Mr. Fairchild does have a certain flair."

Adam grinned. "Indeed. And if even half of what he wrote is true, then my nephew is a very fortunate man."

A low, familiar voice echoed from the doorway, dry with humor. "I wouldn't believe everything you read, Uncle."

Dorothea turned and found Dominic leaning casually against the doorframe, arms crossed, the faintest quirk tugging at the corner of his mouth. He looked relaxed—unburdened in a way she rarely saw—and her heart stirred at the sight.

"And you, dear husband," she said with a playful lift of her brow, "are supposed to be charming."

Dominic gave a shrug, but amusement danced in his eyes. "It's possible Mr. Fairchild exaggerated my charms. What's he gone and said this time?"

Adam gestured towards him with a knowing smile. "He claimed the annulment has been officially called off. I do hope that part is accurate."

Pushing off from the frame, Dominic stepped into the room with steady purpose. "It is."

"That is wonderful news. And to commemorate such a momentous occasion, I've brought you a wedding gift."

"You didn't have to—" Dominic began, but his uncle cut him off with a wave of his hand.

"Nonsense. I had to. And besides, this gift was meant for

you long ago." With a subtle flick of his wrist, Adam signaled to a footman waiting just beyond the door. The servant entered bearing a large, cloth-covered frame. As he gently set it down near the settee and withdrew the fabric, a gasp slipped from Dorothea's lips.

The portrait revealed a woman of striking poise and beauty, seated with regal grace. Her dark hair was arranged in soft curls, and a young boy stood at her side, his features solemn— so familiar in their resemblance to the man now standing beside her.

Dominic's expression stilled as he stepped closer. His gaze remained riveted to the painting, his voice quiet with memory. "I remember this. I was six... maybe seven. The painter made me sit still for what felt like an eternity. I hated every minute of it."

Dorothea moved to his side, her hand slipping into his. "She was beautiful," she said gently, studying the woman's serene expression and the elegance in her posture.

"She was," Dominic replied, his voice roughening as moisture welled in his eyes.

Adam stepped forward and rested a firm hand on his nephew's shoulder. "Your mother would've been proud of the man you've become. I know I am."

Dominic swallowed. "Thank you. For this—for everything. I'll treasure it."

Dorothea gave his hand a soft squeeze. "We should hang it over the fireplace in here."

"I would like that," Dominic replied.

Adam's hand lingered for a moment longer before he stepped back with a smile. "Well, I ought to be off. If I don't go now, I'll be stuck behind carriages and won't make it home for hours."

Dorothea turned towards him and asked, "Must you leave so soon? We'd love to have you stay for dinner."

Adam hesitated, then conceded. "Dinner would be lovely, but you must excuse me. I should wash up first," he said before departing from the room.

Dorothea turned back to her husband, only to find Dominic still gazing at the portrait. His expression was thoughtful, quiet —haunted, perhaps, but not broken. Not anymore.

"I wish I had met your mother," Dorothea murmured.

Dominic turned towards her and tucked a loose strand of hair behind her ear, his fingertips lingering against her cheek. "I know my mother would have adored you."

"And why is that?"

He took a step closer, his voice lowering into something almost reverent. "Because you make me happy, my love. More than I ever thought possible... more than I ever believed I deserved."

Dorothea's heart twisted in the most exquisite way. "I'm glad," she whispered. "Because you make me happy, too. In ways I never expected."

Dominic leaned forward and captured her lips in a kiss— slow, sure, and achingly tender. When he pulled back, his voice was roughened by affection. "And, just so you know, I have a rather particular fondness for kissing you."

Dorothea let out a soft laugh, joy bubbling up through her chest. "You'll hear no complaints from me," she said. "You're welcome to indulge in that fondness as often as you wish."

"Those are dangerous words, my love," he teased.

"And yet I regret nothing," she said, slipping her arms around his waist.

For a long moment, they stood there, surrounded by the quiet stillness of the room, and it felt as if a blessing lingered in the air.

As if love itself had finally found room to breathe.

EPILOGUE

Five years later...

D ominic sat in the warm glow of the nursery, cradling his six-month-old daughter against his chest. Elizabeth's soft breathing tickled his collarbone, and her tiny fist clutched a fold of his cravat. He glanced across the room and smiled fondly at the sight of his four-year-old son, John, sprawled in his small bed, one chubby arm dangling over the edge.

Contentment filled Dominic's chest until it nearly overwhelmed him. This simple moment meant more to him than any fortune he could have amassed. His greatest accomplishment was not counted in lands or titles, but in the small, precious lives he had helped create. His family completed him in a way he had once believed impossible.

He was finally at peace, at peace with where he had been, at peace with what he had been through and at peace with where he was headed.

The soft click of the door opening drew his gaze upward. Dorothea stepped into the room wearing a maroon gown that shimmered in the candlelight. Her red hair was swept into an intricate knot atop her head and a delicate headpiece of diamonds nestled amongst the curls.

Their eyes met, and she smiled—a smile just for him. "We are going to be late for the ball if we do not leave now," she said in a hushed voice.

Dominic only tightened his hold on Elizabeth and murmured, "We can afford to be late."

Dorothea laughed under her breath, a sound that still stirred his heart after all these years. "You say that now, but your uncle would be most displeased. This ball is to celebrate your cousin's engagement, after all."

Dominic scowled good-naturedly. "My cousin is worthless."

"Perhaps," Dorothea conceded with a smirk, "but you are still expected to attend."

His gaze dropped back to the sleeping babe in his arms. "I would rather spend the evening holding Elizabeth."

Dorothea arched a stern brow, though her eyes danced with teasing affection. "Lay Elizabeth in her crib and step away, my love."

Reluctantly, Dominic pressed a kiss to the crown of his daughter's head and rose carefully, mindful not to disturb her. Elizabeth stirred, letting out a tiny, sleepy groan of protest as he settled her into the cradle. In the corner of the room, the nurse-maid rose from her chair, her movements gentle and watchful as she moved to tend to the babe should she wake.

Dominic turned and silently gestured for Dorothea to lead the way. Once they stepped into the corridor, he closed the nursery door behind him and pulled Dorothea into his arms.

"Perhaps we should forgo the ball altogether and have our own private celebration instead," he murmured flirtatiously against her ear.

Dorothea gave a mock gasp of outrage and swatted lightly at his chest. "Behave, Husband," she chided, though she made no effort to move away. "We are required to attend. Besides, your friends will be there."

Dominic snorted. "Friends? More like a collection of people I barely tolerate."

"Well, their wives have become some of my dearest friends," she countered, resting her hands against his chest.

He leaned in and stole a lingering kiss. "Very well. We shall attend but you must allow me to steal you away at the first opportunity."

Dorothea shook her head with a resigned smile. "You are incorrigible."

Dominic's grin widened. "It is hardly my fault. It is near impossible to find time alone with you anymore, thanks to our needy children."

"And whose fault is that?"

He dropped one hand to rest gently against her stomach, his thumb brushing slow, tender circles. "I agreed to having one, maybe two children. I never consented to a third," he teased, a mock gravity in his tone.

Dorothea's eyes gleamed. "And yet, as I recall, you had a rather enthusiastic part in creating this third child."

Dominic opened his mouth to reply, but was interrupted by the arrival of Tabitha, bustling down the hall towards them.

"The coach is waiting out front, my lord, my lady," Tabitha announced with a slight curtsy.

Dominic sighed dramatically but released Dorothea, though he kept her hand in his. "This is your last chance," he said, lowering his voice. "We could run off to Scotland instead. A few days of peace and quiet. No balls, no obligations..."

Dorothea arched a knowing brow. "You would miss the children before we crossed the border."

"I would," he admitted without shame.

Tabitha, undeterred by their banter, reached into her apron

pocket. "I nearly forgot. A letter arrived for you, my lord. It is from Tristan."

Dominic accepted the letter with a smile. "How is my ward faring at Eton?"

"He writes that he is enjoying it," Tabitha said. "Although he has a rather unusual request."

Dorothea's eyes narrowed with amusement. "Oh, dear. What now?"

Tabitha tried to keep a straight face. "He wishes to bring a pet back with him after the break."

"A pet to Eton?" he asked. "Do they even allow such a thing?"

"Apparently, Lord Byron kept a bear at Cambridge when dogs were forbidden, and Tristan sees no reason why Eton should be any different," Tabitha replied.

Dominic let out a bark of laughter that echoed down the corridor. "I am not acquiring a bear for Tristan."

Tabitha grinned. "I do believe that is sound judgment, my lord."

Turning towards his wife, Dominic extended his arm with a flourish. "Shall we depart for the ball, my love?"

Dorothea looped her arm through his with a smile. "I think that would be wise."

As they walked slowly down the corridor, Dominic stole a glance at her from the corner of his eye. Her steps were graceful, but he did not miss the slight paleness to her cheeks. Concern crept into his voice as he asked, "How are you faring?"

Dorothea pressed a gloved hand lightly against her stomach. "I have been rather ill with this pregnancy," she admitted. "More so than before. I am hoping the sickness will ease soon."

Dominic frowned, slowing his steps. "Would you prefer to stay home and rest? We can make our excuses."

She shot him an exasperated look. "You are not going to wriggle out of this ball, Dominic."

He shrugged with a mock sigh of defeat. "It was worth a try."

Ahead, Wright stepped forward and pulled open the main door. The cool evening air swept into the house as Dominic carefully assisted Dorothea into the waiting coach. He climbed in after her, settling onto the cushioned seat at her side as the coach lurched forward into motion.

Without hesitation, Dominic reached for her hand, his fingers lacing through the fine silk of her glove. He tilted his head slightly. "Do you hear that?"

"Hear what?"

Dominic leaned closer and whispered, "Exactly."

She laughed, the soft, musical sound filling the small space between them.

"No incessant talking. No crying. No small feet pounding through the corridors," he said with a sigh as he leaned back against the seat. "It's quiet. Blessedly quiet."

For a few long moments, they simply sat there, feeling the gentle sway of the coach, listening to the muted clatter of hooves on the cobbled street.

Then Dorothea said, "I miss the children."

Dominic turned his head towards her, a wry smile tugging at the corner of his mouth. "So do I."

She gave a rueful laugh. "We are hopeless, are we not?"

"I do hope our children will grow up and be close with one another."

"They will," Dorothea replied. "For they will be nothing like Matthew. Quite frankly, I only feel relief that he was transported."

"As do I."

"But I do not wish to talk about him ever again, or his obnoxious wife."

He cast her a curious look. "What would you prefer to talk about?"

"Anything, really," she replied.

Dominic shifted in his seat, angling himself so that he could fully face her. How could he not love this woman? She had changed the very course of his life. He tightened his grip on her hand and said, "Even in my wildest dreams, I could never have imagined being this unbelievably happy. And it is all because of you."

"I feel the same way," she murmured.

Dominic reached up and cupped her cheek in his hand, his thumb brushing a tender path along her skin. "Promise me," he started, "that when we are old and gray, we will still fight for one another. That no matter what life throws our way, we will choose each other—again and again."

"I can promise that," she replied, her hand coming up to cover his where it rested against her cheek.

Leaning closer until their foreheads nearly touched, Dominic whispered, "I cannot wait until our children are older, and we can sit them down and tell them our love story."

"It all started," Dorothea whispered, her breath mingling with his, "when I saw you for the first time—and you stole my heart."

Dominic closed the distance between them and captured her lips with his own in a kiss that was slow, reverent, and full of everything he could not find the words to say.

He didn't know many things with certainty. Life had taught him how quickly everything could change, how easily things could be lost. But he did know, with every beat of his heart, that he had never loved another as fiercely, as wholly, as he loved Dorothea.

She showed him that love can exist in the most imperfect and broken people. And for that, he would be forever grateful.

The End

NEXT BOOK IN SERIES...

She was meant to be his bait, not steal his heart.

Richard Kendall, Marquess of Wilton, is a man on a mission. Determined to find the scoundrel who ruined his sister's life, he tracks the elusive Mr. Smith to a quiet village—only to discover the man has vanished once again. In his place, Richard encounters Miss Theodosia Smith, a vexing young woman who insists she knows nothing of this mysterious relation. Unconvinced, Richard hatches a bold plan: he'll take her to London under the guise of serving as his sister's companion, hoping her presence will lure Mr. Smith out of hiding.

Theodosia finds Lord Wilton to be arrogant, overbearing, and far too handsome for his own good. She has demanding responsibilities managing her deceased father's estate. Yet the chance to see London is too tempting to resist, even if she must endure his constant suspicion. As their uneasy alliance grows, Theodosia glimpses a man weighed down by duty, while Richard discovers a woman far stronger and more capable than he imagined.

But Richard's loyalty to his family leaves little room for trust—or for love. And when long-buried truths come to light, he must decide if protecting his family's reputation is worth the cost of breaking Theodosia's heart. Because this time, it isn't just scandal he risks...it's the only woman who could claim his guarded heart.

ABOUT THE AUTHOR

Laura Beers is an award-winning author. She attended Brigham Young University, earning a Bachelor of Science degree in Construction Management. She can't sing, doesn't dance and loves naps.

Laura lives in Utah with her husband, three kids and her dysfunctional dog. When not writing regency romance, she loves skiing, hiking and drinking Dr Pepper.

You can connect with Laura on Facebook, Instagram or on her site at www.authorlaurabeers.com.

www.ingramcontent.com/pod-product-compliance
Lightning Source LLC
Chambersburg PA
CBHW060858250626
47159CB00008B/2798